1

Jack Cage

Slaves to the Sword

ISBN: 0-692-94998-4

ISBN-13: 978-0-692-94998-6

Twitter/Instagram/Facebook: @jackcagewrites

#MakeBelieveIsReal

# Slaves

## to

## the

## Sword

## By

## Jack Cage

1

The sun was slowly returning to the earth, ending a particularly hot 14th century African day. Amri Sefu and his younger brother, Endesha were hunting small animals for their village. Amri stopped mid-stride to survey the land with a long gaze. "Why did you stop, Amri?" Endesha asked quietly.

"I am looking for tracks while we still have some light in the sky," Amri responded stoically.

"It is getting late in the day and we should return to the village while the sun is still out," Endesha said.

"I know, but Father is depending on us to bring meat back to the village, I do not want to return home empty handed," Amri replied angrily as he gazed across the vast plains.

The heat of the day was fading as the brothers continued to walk the plains. They only carried spears the length of their legs. The cooling of the day turning to evening was pleasing to young Endesha; He found pleasure in the gentle breeze that cooled his dark-brown skin. He looked to the sky and noticed the gentle change in its colors as the sun descended to the edge of the earth. Endesha asked his older brother, "Do you ever notice the sky and all of the colors it makes at this time of day?"

"We do not have time to discuss such things, Desha," Amri barked impatiently. "I need you to look for something we can kill and take home, that is the only thing that concerns me."

The sun was almost down completely, so the brothers had to return to their village. Disgusted with his failure, Amri led his brother to a familiar ridge bordering the land close to their village. "I want to check something here," he told Endesha as he looked closely at what seemed to be a hole in the ground.

Amri took his hand and brushed the ground, gazing curiously at the area of disturbed dirt surrounding the hole. "Give me a spear, I think I found something here for us to take home," he whispered to his brother. Endesha's heart started beating violently as he handed his older brother the larger of the two spears they were carrying. "Get behind me, and if I miss with my spear, kill whatever comes out of this hole with yours," Amri told his brother confidently.

Amri's heartbeat had strengthened as well, but without the anxiety that his younger brother had—Amri felt alive. His vision was focused on the hole. His hand was steady, and same wind his brother felt earlier blew across the tip of Amri's nose. It created a slight itch, but he would not dare scratch his nose. He was prepared to strike.

While on his knees peering into a hole the size of a small infant, Amri gripped the spear his father made for him four years ago on his fourteenth birthday and mightily lunged the spear into the hole. Suddenly, a piercing squeal was heard. The spear shook violently in Amri's arms. Amri yelled to his brother, "Use your spear!"

Endesha thrusted his spear uneasily into the hole. "Again!" Amri yelled loudly. "Strike it again!"

"I am!" Endesha responded as tears of fear begin to release from the edges of his eyes. Endesha was not scared of what was in the hole. He feared letting his older brother down which would ultimately mean the two of them failing their father—that was more frightening to the young boy than any beast could be.

After several strikes from Endesha's spear the two brothers seemed to have subdued the creature in the hole. Amri's spear had pent the creature in place while Endesha's strikes killed the creature.

The brothers noticed their spears grew limp—success was imminent. Endesha retracted his spear out of the hole slowly to ensure their fallen prey would remain impaled on the blade. It was a medium sized warthog, a far better catch than what they initially hoped to find. "Look, Desha, a warthog!" Amri said proudly. "Father will be pleased."

The fallen beast would provide enough meat for the village to eat for a few days. Amri looked up to the darkened sky. "We must hurry back to our village before the smell of blood attracts scavengers. Take the rear legs, and I will hold the front," Amri commanded his brother.

The boys set off for the long walk from the ridge toward the valley of their village. The brothers walked one in front of the other with their catch tied to the spears. Amri walked confidently while thinking about his success while Endesha—tired from the day's events—welcomed the loving gaze from their mother, Furaha and the satisfying pat on the shoulder from their father, Zuberi.

Several minutes into their march home, the boys heard a sound that made the hairs on the back of their necks raise at attention. It was a growl. A growl that was too close and too clear to be a predator that was just passing by.

This growl was the sign of intent to attack. Apparently, the squeals of the warthog and the accompanying smell of blood attracted a male lion. The elder brother, Amri, knew what was about to occur. He quietly told his younger brother to go on to the village, and he would stay with their prized kill.

"I can't leave you," Endesha said quietly.

"You must!" Amri whispered sharply. "I am not going home without this hog."

Amri slowly lowered the warthog to the ground and slid the two spears from the loops of string used to carry their blessing. The familiar breeze that followed the brothers into the evening had abandoned them.

The air seemed still and Amri knew his brother would no longer be able to retreat to the village. Another growl. Amri lowered himself into a defensive crouch, he now knew where the unseen lion was.

Amri thought about the lessons he learned from his father, Zuberi, and he thought about his desire to not let his father down. Lastly, he thought about his younger brother; he loved, Endesha. He knew if he fell to the lion, his brother would not survive the attack. Amri was a tall, young man, standing over six feet tall with large, long muscles and equally large hands. Amri was focused and steady.

"Wait here I'm going to draw it to me," Amri told his brother.

"I will," Endesha replied quietly.

Amri remained crouched and moved away from this brother, gripping his spears tightly in his hands. The silence was deafening. The only thing he could hear were the shallow breaths of his brother behind him.

Amri did not want to move too far away from Endesha, fearing the lion would go for him instead. In an instant, a mighty roar was heard.

The glowing, moonlit eyes of the lion were upon Amri as he advanced instinctively toward the animal, not thinking about his own safety. The beast lunged, striking Amri across the face with its massive claws.

Simultaneously, he fell backward under the lion, dropping a spear so he could force the lion's massive jaws away from his face with one hand and used his other hand to quickly shove the spear into the lion's neck.

The injured lion roared in pain as it rolled off of Amri, determined to strike again. Severely injured, Amri picked up his second spear.

In the moonlight, he could see the first spear still embedded in his neck. Endesha watched the events in horror as his older brother, bleeding and standing erect with his shorter spear in his hands, faced down an almost full-grown male lion.

To Endesha, time seemed to halt for a moment. The beast looked at his brother in what seemed a gaze of mutual respect. Perhaps it was nature's way of acknowledging each other's power, or, maybe, it was a mutual fear. Amri, a young man and a wild beast, both performing a function that would could result in one another's death.

Suddenly, the lion sprinted away and Amri dropped to his knees. "Get help," he uttered to his brother as his bloodied face tried to get the words from his lips.

"Amri!" cried Endesha.

His cry was heard by Coffa, the uncle of the Sefu brothers, and one of the leaders from the village. "Zuberi! That was Endesha!" he screamed to the group of elder men nearby.

"My children!" screamed Furaha, the boys' worried mother.

"Coffa will get them," Zuberi, her husband of twenty years assured her.

He was sitting in their hut, unable to go with the boys on their hunt due to a childhood injury that made walking difficult for him.

Coffa led a group of ten men armed with spears and torches toward the darkened wilderness. They found the warthog, and a few feet farther, a crying and hysterical Endesha holding his brother in his arms. "He saved us. He saved us!" Endesha went on, "Is he going to die Coffa?"

"I don't know, Desha," said Coffa calmly. "Let's get you two home."

Coffa sent six men to go after the lion, fearing it would attack again. The remaining men helped Endesha to his feet, picked up, the severely injured and unconscious Amri, and the surprisingly large kill from earlier that tragic evening. Endesha walked back to their village with his uncle Coffa's arm supporting his weight. He was welcomed by loving tears and kisses from his mother and the sight of his father standing next to her.

Endesha then passed out from exhaustion—his last memory of that terrible day was feeling the slight breeze return to him after fleeing the brothers earlier in the evening.

## 2

The next day, Endesha woke to the sounds of his mother crying. "Mother," he called to her.

"Yes, son," Furaha replied.

"How is Amri?" Endesha asked with a concerned quiver in his voice.

"He is not well" Endesha's father, Zuberi interjected.

"But you two are safe." Zuberi had a concerned look on his face.

The family's hut was filled with people from his village, and Endesha could hear more outside. "Why are there so many people outside, Father?"

"They are here because they heard about what happened to you and your brother," Zuberi replied. "They wanted to see the boy that killed the lion."

*The boy that killed the lion?* Endesha thought to himself.

Endesha wiped his eyes and sat up to see what the elders were doing by Amri's bedside. Standing up, he slowly walked toward what looked like his brother. There were five or six older women surrounding Amri. They were singing songs and rocking themselves side to side as they spoke in an old language Endesha did not understand.

One of the women closest to Amri was his mother. She was crying while she and some of the elder women put oils and large leaves on Amri's severely lacerated body.

Endesha was taken aback by the three, six-inch gashes on Amri's face that stretched from the side of his head and moved diagonally across his face, missing his right eye by millimeters.

The bright-white color of Amri's flesh was a significant contrast to his dark skin. Seeing the result of his older brother's effort to save their lives made Endesha feel sick. He decided to leave the hut and get some fresh air.

Endesha found himself in the midst of several of his fellow villagers and guests from neighboring villages. They were gathered around Coffa, all of them looking toward the ground at the defeated lion. Endesha made his way through the crowd and the people started to cheer.

"Look at this boy" they said. "Him and his brother slayed this lion all by themselves." They cheered.

"No, I did not!" Endesha barked at the crowd. "My brother is the one that killed the lion, I did nothing and now he is dying!" Endesha screamed.

Coffa walked over to Endesha and calmly said, "'Yes, Desha, your brother is hurt, but he is alive and you are too. This is a time for celebration."

"I do not feel like celebrating, Uncle," Endesha said while staring curiously at the carcass of the lion.

The lion was found near where the boys were attacked. It was not too far away due to the severity of the strike that Amri gave the beast with his spear. The lion had bled to death and Coffa's men brought the lion back to the village.

"What of the lion now Coffa?" asked Endesha.

"We will have a wonderful meal and celebrate the gift that the land gave us," Coffa said with a slight smile. "My brother will keep the skins as a reward for Amri, and this day will become legend in our village for years to come."

Some men in the crowd cheered at Coffa's words. Endesha took a moment to look at the beast that frightened him so much several hours before. He looked at the animal's massive claws and sharp teeth, and he wondered how his brother could have defeated such a thing.

He then thought about his own abilities and wondered if he could ever be so courageous. The Sefu boy's father, Zuberi, had been a great hunter in the past, and he would have assisted in searching for the lion if he was not hurt by his brother, Coffa, in a fight during their youth. Endesha wondered if he could live up to his father's standards, his brother's courage, and his uncle's leadership.

These thoughts upset Endesha, and he wanted to clear his head. He escaped to an elevated ledge that overlooked the valley where the two brothers would sit and talk with their father.

Endesha could not help but blame himself for not helping his brother during the attack. *I should be laying there with my brother instead of sitting here,* he thought to himself.

Suddenly, a cool breeze brushed Endesha's face, and he looked to the sky. It was turning gray, which meant a storm was coming. He thought this was fitting because the village elders taught him that the rains represented the land's way of renewing itself, and that was pleasing to the fourteen-year-old boy.

He hoped that it was a good sign and beneficial for his brother's recovery. The voice of the thunder in the distance welcomed the villagers below, and Endesha set off down the hill to check on his wounded, but now conscious, brother.

"How is he?" Endesha asked his mother curiously.

"He is better, Desha—he has been asking for you," Furaha replied.

The elder women were working quickly. They were taking the rain water and mixing it with crushed berries and oils and covering Amri's face and body with the mixture then putting large leaves over the wounds. He groaned as the women put the medicine on his body. They said the initial pain would go away and he would feel better in a few weeks.

Endesha noticed his father was on the other side of their hut observing the ladies' actions and noted his lack of evolvement. "Father, what are they doing to Amri?" he asked curiously.

"They are doing what they were taught to do, Desha. Those women are going to heal your brother with the gift of water the land gave us. The land gives us everything we need to survive, and this rain was what the women were singing for this morning." Zuberi said as he held his young son close to his body. "The land heard the songs they were singing and gave us the water we needed to help heal Amri. The land always provides for us son." A slight tear fell out the corner of his eye.

Endesha had never seen his father show such emotion. He knew his father was very grateful for the gifts the land gave his village.

He thought about the songs that the women were singing along with his mother earlier in the day and was overcome by feelings of gratitude for the

13

gift of the water that would eventually heal his brother. Reassured, Endesha watched as his mother and the elder women finished tending to Amri and went outside into the rain. The women then left the hut, and in the rain, they danced and sang their songs.

All of the villagers that witnessed the event of the previous night were cheering. "This is a sacred day; the land gave us two gifts in a row!" they cheered. Furaha and the elder women sang and danced in the rain like children. Coffa and the older men looked up to the sky and cheered with the visitors.

Endesha stood in front of his hut, also looking up at the sky. He saw all of the guests and his family members singing and dancing, and yet, he could not help but still feel responsible for his brother's condition. Suddenly, the thunder ceased, the rain stopped, and the sky started to clear. The villagers erupted in even more song and dance as the sun returned to the sky.

"Do you see Desha?" Zuberi said as he walked up to his son. "The land provides everything we need."

Endesha fell into his father's arms and they shared an embrace as he cried in his father's arms. Soon, his mother joined her son and her husband in the tender embrace.

All of the emotions and feelings of the last two day's events were released from Endesha's body during his quiet moment with his parents. Suddenly, Endesha was overcome with wonderful feelings of happiness and gratitude along with a very familiar feeling that he had not felt in hours— hunger.

## 3

The air was filled delicious smell of cooked meat, and the entire village celebrated in communion as Coffa and his men prepared the lion and the warthog to feast upon. "Eat well young Endesha," Coffa said proudly as he approached Endesha. "You deserve to have the second portion of the lion after your brother."

Endesha ate ravenously; he had not eaten in over two days, and was grateful for all of the foods the guests brought to the village. The various wild berries and leaves tasted good, and the fresh water collected from the rains earlier was a welcomed treat. Endesha drank heavily; the water was sweet and cool to his tongue. He poured a little water over his face from his drinking container and wiped his face with it—Endesha felt renewed. A villager touched Endesha on the shoulder and told him his mother beckoned him to come.

He returned to his family's hut to find his brother was awake. Their mother had just finished feeding Amri, and she and the elder women cleaned his wounds and reapplied the medicine and leaves to his body.

"There you are. I have been looking for you," Amri said softly to his brother while surveying the room with his eyes and blinking quickly. "How bad is it, Desha?"

"You will be fine in a few weeks," Endesha replied.

"I heard the people cheering for us outside," Amri said, coughing slightly. Furaha proceeded to give him a drink of water.

"No, they were cheering for you, I did nothing to help you," Endesha said softly.

"You would have done the same thing for me, Desha," Amri replied.

"Alright, that is enough talking for you, Amri," Furaha cautioned her son. "You two will have plenty of time to talk later."

Zuberi and Coffa came inside with serious looks on their faces which prompted Furaha to take Endesha out of the hut.

The two elder brothers sat down by Amri's bedside. Zuberi observed his son's wounds and tried to find the words to express the pain it gave him to see his first-born in so much pain. It reminded him of his own struggles with being injured and all of the personal limitations he had to endure during his life. He thought about the fact that it was *he* that should have fought the lion instead of his precious Amri.

Coffa could instinctively feel his older brother's pain; he took his elder brother's hand and placed it on his nephew's hand. Zuberi started to cry; this was something he had never allowed anyone to see—not even his wife. Zuberi continued to hold his son's hand. "It is not time for you to leave us. You will survive this because you have already proven your strength," Zuberi said confidently. "You will heal and you will live to be a mighty warrior. Right now, you must rest and get better. You have greater challenges ahead of you in the future."

He placed his hand on the left side of Amri's face. The other half—covered with leaves—hid the terrible slash wound that would identify Amri for the rest of his life.

A few weeks later, long after the visiting villagers left, life seemed to return to normal.

Endesha's spirits were lifted, and Amri was showing signs of progress.

One day, Coffa wanted to spend some time with his young nephew.

"Desha, gather your spear and twine," he commanded. "We are going on a hunt."

"A hunt?" Endesha asked cautiously.

"Yes, it is time for you to go back into the wilderness."

"I'm not ready to go back, I'm scared."

"There is nothing to be scared of, Desha." Sensing his nephew's anxiety Coffa sat down next to his young nephew. "Desha, you can't live your life scared about what *could* happen to you."

"But, I'm not strong like you and Amri, Coffa."

Coffa smiled and laughed to himself. "Desha, you are and will be stronger than all of us," he said, before continuing in a more serious tone.

"You and I are the younger brothers, and we learn from our older brothers. I learned how to be a man from my brother—your father, and Amri is already teaching you how to be a man." Coffa stood to gather his spear and supplies. "Now, come young warrior, let us venture into the land and see what it provides for us today."

Endesha could see his mother standing behind him in his peripheral; he turned to look at her, and she gave her youngest son a reassuring nod of approval for the day's journey.

Meanwhile, Zuberi was in the back of the village working on Amri's spear—broken from the lion attack. He was highly skilled at creating weapons and in his youth, had been a ruthless warrior, bested only by his younger brother, Coffa.

Endesha looked up to the sky, the sun was almost up to its highest point, and Coffa did not want to hunt at the height of day.

He took a big breath, and thought to himself, *I can do this,* then quickly picked up his supplies and ran to catch up with his uncle as they set off to find food for their village and restore Endesha's confidence.

## 4

The heat of the African wilderness can be brutal. Endesha and his uncle spent the majority of the late morning talking and playing while they looked for animal tracks. As they walked, Coffa noticed an opportunity for a quick lesson. "Desha, look at this plant. It is called Water Root. Take hold of the bottom of the plant, and carefully pull it out of the ground without breaking the roots." The boy complied with his uncle's request and pulled at the base of the long, green, leafy plant. "Now, take hold of the bottom of the roots and gently pull up," Coffa requested with a smile.

Endesha successfully pulled the plant out with the roots intact, then looked up at his uncle and said, "What now?"

Do you see the larger roots toward the bottom of the plant?" Coffa asked.

"Yes."

"Those have water that we can drink. We will get to those last. We will start with the smaller ones first." Coffa placed a couple of the smaller roots in his mouth and began chewing them. "Put these in your mouth and chew the water out. This is how you can survive during the heat of the day," Coffa informed his surprised nephew.

Endesha chewed a few small roots in his mouth and made a face of displeasure. "This taste bitter."

"I did not say it would taste good. It is meant for you to be able to survive out here in the wilderness.

Now for the larger roots, we do not want to waste anything the land gives us, and that is why we save the larger ones for last, Desha."

The flavor of the water the roots held was terrible to the taste. Endesha appreciated the refreshment it provided, even though the initial flavor was shocking. "We are not finished here, place the plant back in the hole it was in." said Coffa.

"Why?" Endesha asked with a surprised look on his face.

"Because the land provided us with a gift, and we owe it to the land to put back what we took from it. The plant's roots will grow again, and we will be able to drink from it in the future."

The lesson was over, and a familiar breeze approached the two hunters. The elder of the two noticed a smell in the air. "There is a kill nearby, we should go see if the land will give us another opportunity," Coffa said confidently.

"Let us go," Endesha said with youthful enthusiasm.

Coffa was able to track down the site of the kill. It was a male gazelle, with a rather large lioness feeding on it. "See, Desha? Life resets itself. The land has a rhythm and a cycle that never changes. If you are knowledgeable in your part of that rhythm and cycle, you can survive here forever. When we go outside of what we are supposed to do, it upsets the cycle and we suffer because of it," Coffa whispered as they hid behind a bush several yards away from the kill site.

"Are we going to kill the lioness, Uncle?" asked Endesha.

"No, we are not, Desha. If we killed that mother lioness her cubs would either die, or become so desperate for food they may attack a person.

Those actions would disrupt the cycle I was just telling you about. We are here to observe—to see if there are any other opportunities for us, as well," Coffa said while surveying the land for potential danger. "Come, let us move on before the winds carry our scent. We do not want another issue with a lion today."

The day went on, and the two warriors were successful on their hunt. Two wild rabbits, and a small wild bird was a great day's worth of hunting, and young Endesha was pleased.

Coffa and Endesha returned to their village and gave their bounty to the elder women to prepare. Endesha, about to run toward his hut, turned to his uncle. "Thank you for taking me to hunt today. I will remember the lessons that you taught me," he said.

"You are welcome Desha, go on, I know you want to see your brother," Coffa said with pride.

Endesha went into his hut and saw a welcoming sight—Amri was sitting upright on his bedding. Zuberi was sitting at his bedside, supporting Amri's back with his shoulder. "Amri, you are looking better," Endesha said happily.

"Yes, I am feeling a little better," he replied, followed by a slight cough.

Amri's scars were starting to darken. The oil and mud wraps were successful in stopping the bleeding and infection, but he was still very weak. Endesha started to tell Amri about his day's activities, but was interrupted by his father.

"Go around to the back, and get your brother's spear." Endesha obliged his father, and returned with his brother's spear.

"I want you to have it," Amri said. Endesha held a hand up, refusing to take the spear.

"But it belongs to you, Amri. Father carved your name on it."

The spear had been broken during the lion attack, but Endesha knew it was his brother's because their father had carved Amri's and his family's name onto the weapon. Zuberi was a skilled carpenter and ensured all of the weapons his sons and fellow villagers had been sacred and meant to protect their holders from harm. Endesha had not yet been gifted one of his father's spears, as he was still too young, but it was then he noticed some of the carvings had been changed. "Father, why did you change Amri's spear?" he asked.

"I changed it because the story of the spear and its owner changed. When I made that spear for your brother, I knew it would keep him safe."

Zuberi assisted Amri in laying back down. "The story of the attack had to be told for future users of the spear. This spear is special, and it will continue to keep its holder safe. We must tell the story of how the mighty lion was killed in the carvings, so people that carry it will know it is unique. Our story and our history are told by the elders, right?" Zuberi asked his son.

"Yes, Father," Endesha replied.

"But what if there are no elders to tell our stories? Our history has to be kept in some other form.

That is why I tell our stories through the things that we hold closest to us: our weapons, our tools, and in my carvings," Zuberi said as he pointed toward a section of their hut with several stone and wood carvings. "Each one of these pieces tells a story—a story about our people. Amri wants you to have the spear so you will not be afraid to go out in the wild." Zuberi took the spear from Endesha and rubbed his fingers along the grooves of his very intricate carvings.

"It does not belong to me! I do not want it!" yelled Endesha as feelings of guilt returned to his young mind.

"Stop acting like a baby!" Amri grunted, then coughed.

"You don't understand, Amri. Everyone thinks you are a hero, and *I* was the reason you were hurt," yelled Endesha.

"Desha! You will not say such things!" Zuberi said sternly. "You are not the reason for your brother's wounds. The lion was meant to attack your brother, and he was meant to survive. That was Amri's battle to fight, no one else could have done what he did at that time, and it is a part of his story." Zuberi pointed the spear in Endesha's direction. "You *cannot* blame yourself for someone else's destiny, Desha."

"Enough of this talk," Furaha finally spoke.

"Desha, come eat. You can discuss this with your father and brother tomorrow." She gave a strong, disapproving glance at her husband.

Endesha woke the next day still feeling responsible for his brother's injuries.

He looked at his newly gifted spear, and now, with the morning light shining, he could see more of his father's detailed handiwork. The spear was the length of his leg with a sharpened stone tip. The top was heavier than the bottom for proper balance—good for throwing and strong lunges. As Endesha looked closer, he noticed the detailed carving of a man, and another of a lion falling with a spear in its neck. On the other side of the spear there was a saying in the language that the people in Endesha's village spoke. It said:

*"The person that holds this spear is protected from evil by the creator of the land that evil travels on."*

Endesha was impressed with his father's skilled work and finally understood the lesson from the night before. "Desha, help me up," said Amri from across the hut. "I want to go outside."

"I will get father and Coffa," Endesha replied. "Are you sure you want to go out?"

"Yes, I am tired of laying here."

With that, Endesha went to get Coffa and Zuberi who arrived shortly after to gently bring Amri to his feet. "Stand here, next to your brother, Desha. Take his arm over your shoulder, and walk him slowly toward the ridge." Zuberi said.

The hut Amri's family shared was on the west side of the village, a few feet from the ridge that looked out over the vast African landscape. Amri welcomed the change in scenery.

The elder women sang songs as the Sefu men walked toward the ridge. They sang of the triumphs of Amri and how the land protected him and healed him. It was a special day, indeed. A day Amri Sefu did not think he would ever see again.

## 5

The fresh air was a welcomed feeling to Amri. He had been kept indoors for a month. During that time, he thought about many things. He kept reliving the events of the lion attack and questioning his actions. *Should I have been more alert?* he wondered. *Why did I not notice it was tracking us?* While sitting under the day's warm sunlight, those thoughts finally escaped him.

Amri had not yet seen the vast scars the lion's attack had left on his body. The four large gashes to his face were now hardening and prevented him from talking normally. Amri reached for his face. "No, don't touch your face. Not yet, Son," Zuberi warned. But Amri did not listen to his father and ran his right hand over the ravaged right side of his face, feeling a slight sting as he touched the slashes through his flesh from the lion's claws. Amri, the confident young warrior, did not yield any emotion.

"Can I have a water pot?" asked Amri.

"I will get it for you," his uncle replied.

Coffa returned moments later with the large pot they used to collect the rainwater they drank. In the day's sunlight, Amri could see the severity of his wounds in his reflection. At that point, he had a very unsettling feeling about his mortality. He now understood how close to death he had been, and was very grateful to be alive.

The rest of the Sefu men: Zuberi, Coffa, and Endesha watched Amri closely to see how he would react to the sight of his ravaged face, but once again, he did not show any outward emotion.

Zuberi told Amri he should have a drink, and he declined. His feelings of sadness turned to anger.

He was angry because he felt he allowed himself the chance to be hurt. He felt his scars were a message from the land, telling him to be more alert, and never let his guard down. He made a vow to himself at that moment. *I will never again let anything hurt me like this.* Rage was swelling within Amri's spirit, and he welcomed the feeling. Thoughts of what he would have done differently in his battle with the lion constantly replayed in Amri's mind once again, just as they had when he was recovering in the hut.

Thoughts of that terrible event, which would give most people nightmares, now proved almost entertaining to Amri. After two additional weeks of rest, Amri felt significantly better. "Coffa!" Amri barked.

"Yes, Nephew?" Coffa replied.

"I want to go back out and hunt," Amri said confidently. At the same time, Zuberi and Coffa both started to laugh joyfully.

"Son, you are in no condition to hunt," Zuberi said.

"You cannot stand on your own yet, Amri, how can you hunt?" Coffa stated while still laughing to himself.

"Then I will work on getting my strength back," Amri professed.

"I will help you too, Amri," Endesha chimed in.

"Fine, in the morning we will begin," Zuberi said.

The next morning, Amri was already awake when his brother Endesha awoke. "How long have you been awake?" Endesha asked while yawning.

"I never went to sleep," Amri confessed. "All I could think about was getting out of this hut and back on my feet."

Later on, that morning, the Sefu men gathered outside of their hut with Amri, once again, surrounded by the elder women.

They rubbed oils and mud on his legs, believing it would help them respond to his body's request to support his muscular frame.

"Coffa, take his arm, and I will take the other. Amri, I need you to take a step with us," said his father encouragingly.

"I will," Amri replied. The three men walked with a slow stride. Amri was frustrated that he could not support his own weight. However, over time, and with the help of his family, his legs began to feel sturdier under his weight. Amri was relieved to walk under his own power once again, but he noticed his body did not move the same as it had in the past.

He still had some less severe wounds on his upper body that prevented his arms from moving freely without pain. Amri winced with pain as he struggled to lift them up above his head. His muscles ached with stinging surges of pain as sweat went into in his healing wounds. Amri winced in pain again during his supervised movements. Furaha watched her eldest son closely as he tried to regain the range of motion in his arms. After observing Amri in such pain and duress, she told Amri, "Enough, you need to rest." This time he did not protest and walked slowly to their hut.

The next day, Amri did not wake up until later in the morning.

Each day, the elder women had tended to Amri's wounds, however, on this day, he did not want their attention. He quickly stood up on his own and walked outside to start working on getting his strength back. The air was brisk on this particular morning, and Amri felt happy for the first time in many days. He took a deep breath, and focused on his task for the day. He thought about his brother and called out for him. "Desha, let's go for a walk," Amri said.

"Not too far away!" Furaha bellowed from a distance.

Endesha quickly gathered himself, and the two brothers set off for a short walk along the perimeter of the village. "You are very brave, Desha," Amri said.

"What do you mean?" Endesha asked.

"You went back out with Coffa not too long after the lion attack." Amri said as he held his arms up over his head, testing his body's strength.

"Coffa and I had a great adventure that day, and he taught me how to live in the wild."

"Oh, he made you eat the Water Root plant?"

"Yes."

"Tasted terrible huh?"

"Horrible." Endesha laughed.

The two brothers enjoyed each other's company, and for a brief moment, Endesha forgot the scars on his brother's face, and Amri forgot the pain he was feeling in his body.

Back at the village, Zuberi and Furaha were observing their children. Furaha asked her husband, "Is Amri going to be okay?"

"Yes, he will be fine. He has the spirit of a warrior."

"He was so close to death. I am amazed he is walking and playing with Endesha again." A tear released its grip from the corner of her eye.

"We are fortunate to have a child with such a strong desire to live. We should not worry so much about him anymore, he is a man now."

"What do you mean?"

"That attack was Amri's transformation, he is no longer a child," Zuberi said as he held the spear that now belonged to Endesha.

"Soon he will want to go back into the wilderness to challenge the land and regain confidence in his abilities."

"Challenge? Do you mean he wants to find a lion to slay?"

"No, if another lion challenged Amri, I would fear for the lion," Zuberi said confidently.

## 6

In a remote portion of a rainy southern forest in England, a band of soldiers stumbled onto a fascinating sight—four maidens standing back to back in a creek with only their long hair covering their nude bodies. One of the soldiers thought he was seeing things in the heavy downpour, but as he gazed harder those thoughts were dashed.

"Keymus! Look at those whores down there in the marsh," the solder said while pointing down the hill at the group of women.

"I see them," he replied to the soldier. Keymus was the first officer of the Carpenter's Army, and he could not resist the opportunity to capture and rape these vulnerable women. "Let's introduce ourselves." He laughed to his group of seven soldiers.

They marched down to the marsh where the women were still standing back to back with their arms behind them. The sun was shining at the same time as it was raining—producing an almost angelic image to the soldiers. After a few moments of gazing at the women, Keymus became tired of waiting. "Why are you just standing there in the wet like this? Surely, you are seeking men like us to take you to our camp?" he declared.

"Not exactly," said one of the maidens softly while looking down into the water.

"What do you mean, whore? You are standing in a marsh nude, surely you are looking for something." Keymus barked at the women.

"Indeed, we do want something," a second maiden replied. "Your lives."

Suddenly, from behind their backs, the women brandished bows with arrows nocked, and fired them into the group of soldiers with deadly accuracy—striking four of them in the face.

"Attack!" Soldiers of the Red Guard burst from the waters of the marsh, and emerged from the adjoining muddy walls of the hill.

"Ambush!" Keymus screamed as he drew his two-handed broad sword.

The maidens scrambled to withdraw as the captain of the Red Guard, Stuart Miles, brandishing his long sword, attacked the remaining enemy soldiers. Stuart could see Keymus in the distance, and quickly moved toward his position. He engaged one of Carpenter's soldiers with a downward strike with his sword. The opposing soldier blocked the strike with his buckler and returned with a crossing strike with his broad sword.

Stuart, a master swordsman, dodged the enemy soldier's crossing strike, countered with a blow to his midsection with his sword's pommel, and a deadly downward slash to the back of the enemy soldier's neck, killing him. Keymus stood behind his remaining two soldiers and commanded them to retreat.

"This is not over, Stuart Miles!" Keymus screamed as he and his wounded soldiers turned to run away.

"Should we go after them, Your Highness?" asked a soldier of the Red Guard.

"No, let them run. Our mission is done here," Stuart said. "Gather our sisters, and let us ride to Harkstead."

Harkstead Castle was the home of the Red Guard and the heart of the Midland Kingdom of Southern England overseen by King Phillip Miles.

The king's Red Guard was unique to the House of Miles in that every soldier was an orphan from different parts of the kingdom.

Soldiers, both men and women, were trained from young children and into adulthood to become the kingdom's most elite fighters. However, until they reached the age of thirty-five years old, they were not allowed to marry. After this coming of age, the king allowed them to live within the kingdom and marry whomever they chose.

The Red Guard was revered throughout the kingdom, and whenever the townspeople saw the red and orange flags of the House of Miles they cheered. Prince Stuart Miles was an orphan, as well. He was adopted by King Phillip as a young child and raised as a Midland prince. However, that meant, with a lack of royal blood, Prince Stuart could never be his father's successor.

As the leader of the orphan army, Stuart was painfully aware that the throne to the Midlands would never be given to him, and as they rode toward Harkstead Castle, he was reminded of this fact. Prince Harold, his younger, royal-blooded brother was waiting for him in the armory. "Did you kill many soldiers today, Brother?" asked Harold.

"You are only eight years old and should not be concerned with such things, young brother," Stuart answered.

"Father is requesting your presence in the main chamber"

"Tell him I will be there after I wash and change," Stuart barked at the young prince.

"I will."

Harold ran across the courtyard of the castle as he gazed at the large horses and workers in the area. The ground was still wet from the rains earlier in the day and Harold intentionally splashed in the puddles of water as he ran through the corridors of the centuries-old castle.

He waved to the guards as he made his way through to the family's private area, and upon reaching his father's quarters, attempted to pull the massive iron door open. One of the guards at the door saw him struggle and moved to help the little boy. "I can do it!" Harold snipped.

He propped both feet on the wall while he pulled the large round handle, and after a moment, it budged just enough for him to squeeze himself through.

King Phillip heard his youngest son yell at the soldier and waited with a smile on his face for his true first-born to greet him.

"Father, Stuart is back!" he exclaimed as he gave his father a hug.

"Very good. Is he well?" Phillip asked.

"Yes. He is well. He said he will come to you after he bathes."

"That is very good, Son." The king smiled.

"Father?"

"Yes, Son?"

"Can I be a soldier in the Red Guard like Stuart?"

King Phillip paused and thought about how he should respond to his son. "Well, maybe you would do better here in the castle."

"The castle is boring. There are no adventures here in the castle," Harold responded.

The king could hear the disappointment in his young son's voice.

"There are many important things to do here at the castle, Son. You are not old enough to know this yet. Rest assured, when your time comes, you will have many adventures to tell your children, just like the ones I tell you in your bed chamber."

King Phillip was aware of Harold's youthful enthusiasm and how talks of him succeeding Stuart for the crown could cause problems within the kingdom. The public did not know that Stuart was not the true heir to the throne, and if that secret were to ever get out, it could damage the stability of the Midlands. Stuart was a young child when King Phillip found him in an abandoned cottage.

His late wife, Queen Jane Miles, cared for Stuart as if he was her own until she died shortly after Harold's third birthday. Phillip loved Stuart dearly, but he was painfully aware he could never give the throne to him.

Before long, Stuart arrived at his father's chamber. "Hello, Father."

"Stuart, my son, how are things in the south?"

"We were able to successfully ambush some of the rebel soldiers that had been attacking the villages, Your Majesty," Stuart reported.

"What of their leader?" Phillip said.

"It was Keymus. He was with several of Carpenter's soldiers." He sat across from his king at the alder wood table and reached for a large cobble of wine.

"His involvement with Carpenter's army is becoming a nuisance to our kingdom," Phillip said with a stern look on his face. "We need to alert the outlying villages to be aware of the potential threat from Keymus and Carpenter's Army."

"Yes, Father."

"His behavior is too unstable. I am afraid if he gains too much power, he will defect from Carpenter's Army and raise a fighting force of his own.

Stuart, you must find Keymus and kill him before he becomes a threat to the Midlands. Order the cavalry to ride to the border villages of the kingdom to ensure their safety.

While they are there, make sure they collect my taxes, and have a rider return to Harkstead with payment and word of any rebel activity." Phillip stood and made his way over to his son. He laid a gentle kiss on his forehead. "You did well, my son." The king's praise was comforting to Stuart; he knew father valued his efforts for the kingdom.

"Thank you, Your Majesty." Stuart rose and kissed his father's hand.

As he departed his father's quarters, he was met by one of his officers in the hallway and Wayne Turner, a top-ranking member of the Midland Cavalry. "What are our orders, Your Highness?" asked Wayne.

"Send one hundred of your cavalry to the border towns to collect taxes and search for any rebels.

If they find any, they are to kill them, and send word back to Harkstead Castle immediately," Stuart commanded.

"Do you want an escort for the rider with the taxes?"

"Yes, prepare your men to ride tonight. We will expect the riders to return throughout the week. The Red Guard will be prepared to support the cavalry if needed."

"Yes, My Lord," Turner replied, and with that. The officers left their captain in the main corridor of the castle.

Stuart pondered on his feelings about not being truly the heir to the throne. *I will never be King of the Midlands*, he thought to himself. *I don't know what my future holds for me here in this kingdom.*

Indeed, his feelings were valid, and he would have liked to approach his father about his concerns, but Stuart dared not. King Phillip's gentle touch extended to his children, and even though his rule was fair, he was never keen on anyone questioning his motives or actions. Family was not excluded from his temper when it came to issues like this.

Stuart bit his tongue once again, and headed to his quarters to eat and rest. Three village maidens lustfully awaited him there, to ensure his comfort.

***

In a small, remote village outside of the Midland's borders, Keymus arrived with his remaining soldiers. Sore from the battle earlier in the day, he yearned for wine and rest.

Thomas the Carpenter, leader of the rebellion, had been waiting for Keymus' report, when the captain entered his cottage without the majority of the soldiers he had left with the day before.

"It looks like you were thrashed today. A quarrel with some Midlanders perhaps?" Carpenter asked as he carved away at the tiny wooden horse resting in the palm of his hand.

"Yes, Your Majesty," Keymus responded.

"Cavalry?"

"No. It was Stuart Miles and a contingent of the Red Guard, Your Majesty." Keymus stared down at the table, too uncomfortable to make eye-contact with his leader.

"And what of the soldiers you had with you?" Carpenter asked.

"They are dead," Keymus replied in an aggravated tone as he drank wine from a large wooden cup. "It was an ambush."

"Oh, an ambush. I see."

"They used females to lure us into the marsh where they were waiting beneath the mud and water."

"Females?"

"Yes, Your Majesty, female soldiers."

"Let's summarize this; you were with some of my best men, and yet, you were beaten by a group of females and some men hiding in the mud?"

"Yes, Your Majesty... but they were not *just* females. Those whores were soldiers, and they were naked, and they—"

"Silence, you fool! You led your men to their deaths because you did not think! Of course, the Red Guard has whores within their ranks.

Phillip Miles has always stooped to such forms of trickery to gain an advantage over his adversaries, and your ignorance is justification of his plan's genius!" Carpenter roared.

Thomas the Carpenter was taller and larger than most of the men that followed him.

His weapon of choice was a two-handed billhook that was almost as long as he was tall, and he could wield it with deadly efficiency. His long black hair with streaks of gray swayed behind him as he walked across the room toward his weapon. "You need rest Keymus, you had a difficult day today. Unfortunately, I no longer need you—you can join your soldiers in death!" He grasped his billhook and in midstride spun around and delivered a deadly strike to Keymus' neck.

The soldiers gasped in horror at the sight they had just witnessed. Keymus' eyes were still open on his now decapitated head. "Let this be a lesson to all of you. Failure is a word I do not understand." He wiped Keymus' blood off of his ax. "Gentlemen, ensure you use better judgment in the future or face the same fate as Lord Keymus of Tawny. Lord Calvin!" Carpenter bellowed.

"Yes, Your Majesty?" Calvin replied.

"Take your soldiers to Hainsbridge, and burn it to the ground."

"We will leave immediately, Your Majesty."

"Very well, I will ride to Remington Castle tonight. Send word of your victory to me by rider. I am hoping for better results this time."

"Yes, Your Majesty. We will not fail you." Calvin replied, and walked out of the cottage.

Carpenter set off to his personal estate, Remington House. He called it a castle, but it was by no means a proper castle. He had taken the property from a wealthy baron who had tried to put up a fight against him and his men.

He was of the opinion that if the Baron of Remington wanted the property so badly, he could remain to fertilize the plants and trees and buried the man and his family alive on the estate grounds. Thomas Carpenter was truly ruthless.

He had been an esteemed member of King Phillip's advisory council, and brother to his late queen. When it was found out he had been stealing taxes throughout the kingdom and using his personal soldiers to threaten the victims into secrecy, the king banished him from Harkstead Castle. Had he not been the queen's brother, his punishment would have been grave. Thomas Carpenter, upon learning his fate, broke free of the king's soldiers, fled the kingdom, and disappeared into hiding.

It had been seven years since that fateful event, and the two men had been bitter rivals ever since. Carpenter's Army, with the promise of power and riches, was growing quickly. King Phillip, aware of his nemesis' increased numbers, was not fretting one bit. He had something the banished man did not—two skilled, highly-trained armies. The question was—would they be enough to stop Thomas Carpenter?

## 7

Later on that night, Lord Calvin and his small army of mercenary lancemen rode quickly to Hainsbridge. The thunder of their horses could only be heard minutes before their arrival. The villagers that were awake had few moments to wake up their loved ones out of their deep slumber. Those that did not awaken in time were consumed by the flames that rained down on them as Calvin's men burned the entire village to ashes. Villagers screamed as they ran out of their homes—their bodies on fire. Calvin's men were waiting with their swords and quickly killed all that breathed.

Calvin did not burn everything. He kept all of the wine and treasures he could find, and, ordinarily, he would have kept a selection of local maidens for himself and his men, but this attack was going to be done properly as his Majesty, the Carpenter, wished. Knowing this, Calvin commanded his soldiers to leave nothing to chance, he ordered them to search every part of the village, and kill every person, in every home. He even slaughtered the village hounds.

By morning light, the town was a smoldering mess. Lord Calvin's men were finishing their task and one soldier reported, "We are done here. Do you want to send a rider to Remington House?"

"Yes. Send the rider, our work is done here. We shall ride on to Tawny to await further instructions," Calvin commanded.

The mercenaries departed, leaving behind one of the most horrific sights in the history of the Midland Kingdom. The stench of burnt flesh permeated the air; the streets of Hainsbridge were laden with the charred corpses of men, women, and children.

Later that morning, the Midland Cavalry arrived in Hainsbridge, horrified by what they saw.

A rider was quickly dispatched to Harkstead Castle to alert King Phillip of what had occurred. Word of the attack traveled quickly through the outer perimeter of the Midland Kingdom. This was what King Phillip had been afraid would happen. The attacks caused fear and instability, and it was only the beginning.

Villagers from the outer perimeter became unwilling to pay the cavalrymen their taxes because they felt King Phillip was not keeping them safe. This was troublesome indeed for the king, and something had to be done soon.

Back at Harkstead Castle, King Phillip was eating his morning meal with Harold and Stuart when a page banged his chamber door.

"Your Majesty!" he yelled.

"Come in," King Phillip replied.

"My King, Hainsbridge was attacked overnight."

"How is that possible? The cavalry was sent there yesterday."

"Yes, Father, but it takes longer for the cavalry to ride to Hainsbridge at night," Stuart responded.

"Your Majesty, the rider said there were no survivors," said the page.

King Phillip motioned one of the servants to take Harold out of the chamber as the page waited on his next order. Once the servant and Harold were out of the room the king lost much of his composure.

"I want the entire kingdom on alert! Carpenter's bloody army is not going to take my kingdom away from me. Assemble the advisory council immediately!" Phillip bellowed his commands.

"Yes, Father!" Stuart stood and swiftly left the room to do his father's bidding.

King Phillip had many thoughts in his mind. He pondered on the stability of the outer reaches of the kingdom.

He also thought about the loss of taxes Hainsbridge afforded him. The villagers on the outer reaches refusing to pay their taxes would be substantial with the addition of the losses from Hainsbridge.

There were many things that King Phillip needed to address, and orders for actions needed to be given. He was in distress and without a wife to ease his tension. This thought turned his distress to anger, and he flung his chalice across the room.

The advisory council arrived in the king's chambers with Stuart entering the room last. "Your Majesty, we are sorry to hear of Hainsbridge," said one of the council members. Phillip nodded his appreciation.

"We need to ensure the safety and stability of the Midland villages," declared Stuart as the group of men looked upon the large map of the kingdom that hung on the wall of the king's chamber.

"Order the cavalry to split, and go to the remaining three cities: Derron in the east, Neally in the southwest, and Aveston to the north," Phillip said.

"Father, the cavalry will be vulnerable to attack if their ranks are split between the cities."

"I am aware of that, Son, but we do not have a choice. If we send the Red Guard to aid the cavalry we may be falling into a trap by leaving Harkstead Castle insufficiently guarded and prime for attacking. Send word to the North and South regions to prepare to receive the cavalry.

I will prepare an announcement and send it today by way of riders to alert the kingdom of the potential dangers, and give our people a chance to arm themselves," King Phillip said.

Many days had passed, and throughout the Midland Kingdom word of the Carpenter's Army and their destruction of Hainsbridge sent waves of fear amongst the villagers. What began as quiet whispers about the king's inability to keep them safe, soon turned to genuine public fear.

King Phillip was not short of ego but was known to be very fair with his people, so he tolerated the reports of public meetings and criticism of his actions. He knew he had to make a statement to his people soon, or he would lose the love, and most importantly to him, the taxes of his people.

Deep inside Harkstead Castle, the brown and silver bearded king paced as he spoke with his advisors. His long red robe with golden accents flowed on the floor softly, and made it seem as if Phillip was walking on air. It was truly a grand form of attire, fitting for a king of his stature. "The Midlanders are growing weary of our leadership," Phillip declared.

"Yes, Your Majesty, but we have not yet heard from the cavalry replied one of his advisors.

"It does not matter!" Phillip snorted with saliva leaving his lips. "I have to respond to the Carpenter's attack with one of my own."

"We can do so, Your Majesty." Stuart asserted as he entered the room wearing a brown jacket with red accent, similar to his father's attire.

"Father, allow me to lead the Red Guard on a mission to attack one of the Carpenter's estates," he said as he poured some wine into a medium-sized chalice.

"Such actions would assuredly lead us into war, my son. We must look at all of the potential outcomes before making such a strike," Phillip responded, then continued to say, "However, we cannot allow what happened to Hainsbridge to go unpunished. We will respond with a show of force of our own." The king looked up to map of his kingdom. "We must strike the Carpenter's army on their grounds."

"Father, I have been informed by some of our scouts that several groups of men rode into Tawny overnight," Stuart reported.

"Then that is where we will avenge the fallen of Hainesbridge." said Phillip with a familiar frown on his face. "We will remove every memory of Thomas the Carpenter's men from the world. Send word to your sisters in Tawny.

Tell them to be swift with their work and report back to Harkstead Castle. Send a battalion of the Red Guard to the border of Aveston to retrieve them in the morning, and ensure their safe passage back to the castle."

"Yes, Your Majesty, I will see to it myself," Stuart responded.

## 8

Tawny, a small village on the outer boarders of Aveston, was the furthest northern village of the Midlands, and well known for its women, wine, and abundance of lancemen mercenaries. Thomas the Carpenter's men, led by Lord Calvin, were still in the village—drunken and overstimulated by the riches of the flesh that Tawny was famous for.

Night had fallen over the village when a scout from the Midland kingdom approached one of the cottages along the tree line. In a crouch, he whistled a series of sounds only a soldier of the Red Guard would know. Immediately, several women stopped what they were doing to confirm they had indeed heard the faint call of their army. When they heard a fellow female warrior's sensual response—disguised as a moan, they responded in kind, and the men they were servicing became greatly excited—unaware their pleasurable muses were in fact Red Guard soldiers now called into action.

The Midland scout replied with another instructional whistle, and again, the same woman responded with her sensual warrior call. The women that could not respond understood the message, and could now hear it clearly throughout the small village.

Lord Calvin was one of the men confidently pleased by the female warrior's sensual bellow, thinking it was of his own doing. However, he was gravely mistaken—that bellow meant that his death, and the death of all of his men, was eminent.

Deep inside a fire-warmed room, Lord Calvin lay with a maiden, exuding drunken confidence after making love.

"I have been with many women, but you are special. You are a dirty whore, and the way you yell is like that of a banshee," he slurred to the maiden, then downed another swig of mead.

"Indeed, my love. I am a *dirty* whore," said the maiden.

"Where are you from? Are you from the north?" Calvin asked.

"No, I am not." She mounted Calvin and presented him with a deep kiss.

"Are you from Aveston?"

"No..." She arched her back in a display of pleasure. Slowly, the maiden ran her fingers through her hair and removed two, small, pointed barbs from her long, flowing, brown hair and drove them violently into Calvin's neck. "I am from Harkstead, and you will die for what you did to my people in Hainsbridge." She whispered into Lord Calvin's ear. Blood gurgled up through the puncture wounds and began filling his throat quickly—he could not talk. He threw the maiden off, and stumbled across the room, his flailing movements sent blood spewing across the room. He attempted to get to his sword but was unsuccessful as his body failed him, and within seconds, he fell to the ground. His naked body laid still, his eyes still showed a look of betrayal. Or maybe it was fear? The Red Guard maiden wondered if it was the same look he saw in the eyes of the villagers of Hainesbridge.

While Lord Calvin was dying in his cottage, he could not understand how the maiden that pleased him so well could kill him with such ease. It did not matter anymore. Throughout that night in Tawny, all of the Carpenter's men were killed.

Some were poisoned, some decapitated, and some, the Red Guard women saw fit to castrate, as well.

It was a legendary attack that was quiet, extremely violent, and cunningly executed, all at the same time. As instructed, the sisters of the Red Guard were collected by Stuart and his men in Aveston the following morning.

Lord Calvin had not known Tawny was a village occupied by the women of the Red Guard. It was essentially a trap within a trap for the enemies of the Midlands. The remaining mercenaries that survived fled the village upon seeing the artistic display of death the Red Guard maidens made when they carved the mark of King Phillip upon the flesh of Lord Calvin. This was not done by chance; it was a message to the Carpenter that war indeed was upon both groups.

When Carpenter received word of Lord Calvin's demise, he ordered an immediate attack on Aveston. The war for the Midlands was about to start, and it would be fifty years before the region would see peace again.

Remington House was a seven-day ride from Tawny, and inside the house, the stench of masculine chemistry wafted throughout; sticking to the displays of false royalty in the way of poorly executed self-portraits of the owner of the estate, Thomas Earl Carpenter. The man was in his library virtually vibrating with anger, making it nearly impossible to carve the finishing touches on his miniature wooden horse.

"How could Calvin *and* his men perish by the hands of those Midland whores?" he bellowed. Carpenter had assembled his small group of associates:

John Hammish, Royce Pennington, and Seth Murray to discuss strategy—and none were eager to speak. They remembered all too well Keymus' death by his blade two weeks earlier.

"Does anyone want to share a reason why Tawny, a wretched, filthy village full of the most desperate lancemen mercenaries, would be filled with Red Guard whores?" Thomas screamed as he threw the dagger in his hand across the room, narrowly missing Hammish's head.

"*At least* poor Keymus put up *some* form of fight against Phillip's whore warriors! I am growing weary of him and his bloody tricks!" said Carpenter.

He paced from one point of the room to the next while his advisors stood at the table, awkwardly waiting for permission to sit down.

Finally, noticing the group, he bellowed, "And *why* are you all just standing there?" They promptly sat down awkwardly and kept their silence. Carpenter was starting to sweat visibly; his skin was flush, and his heart was beating as if he was running a race while standing still. His anger made it hard for him to maintain his thoughts. He remembered saying Keymus' name moments earlier. "Oh, you poor children. You thought I was going to kill you like I did Keymus?" he said, referring to them as children as a slight to show his dominance over them.

He considered himself to be like a father, as well as king to them; demanding they title him "Sire" and "Your Majesty," even though none of his blood was royal.

"No, Sire. We were merely waiting for you to calm down," said Pennington, summoning all the courage he could at the moment.

"I brought you here to discuss Phillip's Red Guard whores and revenge for Calvin," said Carpenter.

"Well, Sire, we do not have much information on the specifics of King Phillip's most elite army," said Murray.

"What we do know is that they are a part of a specialized fighting force comprised of orphans from throughout the Midland Kingdom," said Pennington.

"They appear to be highly trained given the two instances we have engaged with them," said Hammish.

"I don't care how well trained they are, they fight a coward's fight with their whores doing all of the work. I want to explore the true might of Phillip's cavalry, and maybe then we will see if he sends his Red Guard whores to rescue his men," said Carpenter, before taking a large gulp of wine from his tarnished cup.

"Sire, are you suggesting we attack the Midlands?" asked Murray.

"Indeed. I shall take Aveston and make it my own." As a dribble of wine ran down the corner of his mouth.

"For years we have been watching Phillip go about with his wretched orphan army, acting as if he has complete authority over every living thing! But now we have the chance to exercise our will on his bloody Midland Kingdom. We will soon cleanse the land of the stench of King Phillip Miles and his precious Prince Stuart.

His band of crimson orphans will be no match for my army," said Carpenter as he looked through a cloudy window overlooking the manor grounds. "Prepare the army. We will march to Tawny and stage there."

"Yes, my Lord we will make the arrangements immediately," said Pennington.

Over the next few days, the Carpenter's Army grew to battle strength—two hundred soldiers in all.

Some of the ranks were made of men that either owed the Carpenter money or were prisoner soldiers of villages he conquered in the past and forced them to fight for him or perish. The remaining ranks were made up of lancemen mercenaries, some of whom escaped the Red Guard slaughter back in Tawny.

King Phillip was alerted to the growing swell of soldiers staging on the outskirts of Tawny. He understood that he was going to be fighting for Aveston. What he did not know was how fiercely the Carpenter's Army would fight or what to do if Aveston fell to the Carpenter's swords.

## 9

His eyes were blurred, and his hearing was muted. The Midland soldier was fighting not only for his freedom, but his life, as well. He was only down for a moment, but knew he only had seconds to recover from the concussive blow to the head from the Carpenter soldier wielding a flanged mace. His body armor minimalized the damage from strike moments before, but his body couldn't handle another. The Midland soldier rose to his feet, and quickly raised his shield just in time to block the next downward blow from his enemy.

His own flanged mace was a heavy weapon in his left hand. The handle was of solid oak, and tipped with a steel orb that, when used properly, could kill or severely injure its intended target. The Midland soldier countered the enemy's strike with one of his own, aiming for his shoulder.

The Carpenter soldier screamed in pain as the war hammer found its way into his flesh through the chink in his armor where the shoulder plate and breastplates meet.

Sensing the advantage, the Midlander screamed as he rammed his weapon down sharply into his enemy's now semi-detached shoulder, driving the opposing soldier to the ground. He screamed aloud as he sensed the imminent death of his opponent coming.

Standing over the Carpenter's soldier, he pinned the mace to the ground with his shield and simultaneously dislodged his war hammer from the shoulder.

He followed with a deadly blow to the Carpenter soldier's neck between his bascinet and breastplate, killing him instantly.

Straddled over his fresh kill, between several heaving breaths, he roared like a beast. He looked up, ready for another opponent nearby, but there wasn't. Exhausted, his body requested more air for his battle-fatigued lungs. With his immediate safety confirmed, he breathed in mightily. A blinding amount of sweat ran into his eyes as he tried to look into the distance—assessing the current status of the Midland Army.

He saw a friend a few feet away, and time seemed to stand still for a moment. He was yelling toward his direction, "Archers!" he hears suddenly as his ears cleared. The Midland soldier quickly rose to his feet, and turned as he lifted his shield to cover his face. However, he was not quick enough, and before he could raise his sturdy shield, a perfectly crafted arrow—hand carved by Thomas the Carpenter himself—flew into his helmet, piercing his eye. What seemed a victory for this Midland soldier was fleeting, as it only took moments for his own life to end shortly after.

The violent sounds of men screaming in pain echoed throughout the valley. More than four hundred men waged war on this day. Two hundred of the Carpenter's best and most expensive soldiers fought tirelessly against as many members of King Phillip's Midland Army. The incessant clanging of shields, swords, and the corresponding grunts and groans filled the land.

The Carpenter's Army continued their strong push through Tawny only to be met, as the day faded to night, by the small contingent of Red Guard Calvary who had made their stand at the border of Aveston.

Far behind the battlegrounds, Carpenter was bathing in satisfaction as he watched his men advance forward on the battlefield. His expansive, but costly fighting force was slowly pushing the Red Guard and Midland Armies back toward Aveston.

"Archers, fire again!" he yelled. Fifty archers fired into the Midland ranks causing men to run and scatter or fall to their death.

The Carpenter was not one for strategy; he was only focusing on taking Aveston with a massive amount of brute force.

He urged his commanders to have the soldiers push toward the Southeast. His commanders tried to inform him that he would suffer more losses if he continued to fight at the current pace. "I don't care about the losses! I want Aveston burnt to ashes. That is the only thing that matters!" Carpenter bellowed. "I will see my victory to the end. King Phillip's armies cannot stop our advances toward Aveston!"

*** 

The sun surrendered its hold of the horizon, and night fell upon the battlefield. King Phillip's forces were severely weakened. They had to retreat and regroup on the outskirts of Aveston to make their final stand. A rider was inbound to the city of Aveston with a message for Stuart Miles.

"Your Highness, I bring word from the battlefield," he said.

"Go ahead," Stuart responded.

"The Carpenter's army is pushing toward the Aveston border. The cavalry is holding them back for the moment."

"We have to ready the villagers. They need to know the battle is coming to Aveston," said Earl Baker, a Midland Cavalry Commander, and a trusted advisor to King Phillip and Stuart.

"Indeed. We shall hold a meeting in the town plaza immediately," Stuart said while looking out of the window and into the distance. This was the first major battle Stuart had to oversee. He knew if he lost Aveston to the Carpenter he would lose some of his father's respect, and that meant more to him than the lives lost protecting not only the city but his father's reverence for him as well.

Shortly thereafter, the town plaza was filled with Avestonians awaiting Stuart Miles' words. "Let me be first to tell you, we are in a dire place today. A few miles from here the Carpenter's Army is fighting our soldiers and pushing toward Aveston.

However, I can promise you—as your prince and on behalf of your King, Phillip Miles—we will fight the Carpenter's soldiers to the death to protect Aveston. We ask all women and children ride immediately to Harkstead Castle where you will be safe. The remaining men will be needed to fortify the outer walls of Aveston, we need men that can handle a bow, tend to the tar making, and swordsmen," Stuart said, while looking throughout the crowd for any visible signs of fear. "I sense some of you are afraid, and you should be. The men we will be fighting will tend little mercy on you, and you should not allow them any mercy in return," Stuart said.

Suddenly, a rider rode into the crowd. "The cavalry is returning to Aveston. The Carpenter's Army has broken our ranks, and the Red Guard Cavalry are retreating to the safety of these walls!" exclaimed the rider.

"Raise the portcullis, and archers to the ramparts. Take your places!" Stuart commanded.

Sounds of galloping horses could be heard, and over in the distance, the light from the Red Guard Cavalry's torches could be seen.

They were riding quickly, though several cavalrymen were clearly holding on with their last bits of strength. "Ready archers!" Stuart commanded. "We don't know if the Carpenter's soldiers are giving chase."

The wounded cavalrymen returned to the safety of Aveston's gates. "Lower and fortify the portcullis!" a voice yelled. Several of the mightiest Avestonians began turning the enormous gears that unwound the chains needed to bring the huge steel gate back down.

When it finally touched the ground, its weight was felt by the thump it created under the feet of the people closest to it. Large wooden doors were slid into place, barred with iron, and the outer gate was now secure.

The remaining eighty-eight cavalrymen were safe—at least for now. Stuart was assessing their ranks and demanded a report. "What was the status of the battle prior to you returning to Aveston?"

"We tried to hold them off, but their advances were too much for our ranks, Your Highness.

We have reduced their numbers to around half of their original fighting force, but we could not hold our position. I gave the order to retreat so we could regroup here, said the Red Guard Cavalry Commander. "I am sorry we failed you."

He looked toward the ground sullenly. Eighty-eight cavalrymen were left; some too injured to fight, and another estimated fifty Avestonian fighters available to defend the outer wall.

"Dispatch a rider for Harkstead. Give word that we will be holding our position at the outer wall, and if we fail, send more cavalry and infantry to the south to protect Harkstead," Stuart commanded.

The sound of riders could be heard in the distance. It was the remaining fighting force of Carpenter's army, along with the Carpenter, himself. Yet, they did not advance. Carpenter, sensing the weariness of his men, decided to make camp for the night just beyond the range of the Avestonian arrows. Prince Stuart Miles was standing on atop the twelve-foot-tall Avestonian wall seething with anger, yet fearful at the same time.

The temperature was dropping quickly as the night went on, and the familiar mist could be seen emanating from his nose upon every breath he took. It was easy to see he was breathing hard. Thoughts of strategy clouded his mind.

No Red Guard trickery was going to help him with this particular fight. He knew he had to rest but he was hesitant. The remaining Red Guard Cavalry had to be tended to and a status report was warranted.

"Lord Baker!" Stuart called.

"Yes, My Lord," the commander responded as he walked quickly toward his prince.

"What of our soldiers?"

"Your Highness, the wounded are being tended to, and the rest are being fed."

"We need to inventory our weapons and prepare to fortify the wall.

The Avestonian men will tend to the tar, and we will prepare to make our stand behind the wall," Stuart said confidently.

"Your Highness, what is your plan if Carpenter breaches the wall?" Baker asked with fleeting confidence.

"We will take as many heavy items as we can find and fortify the wall—we may even set it on fire with the tar. Whatever it takes to keep them from breaching the wall is what we will do."

***

Meanwhile, back at Harkstead Castle, King Phillip had just been informed of the news regarding Aveston. "What? They are just outside of the border wall?" he bellowed.

"Yes, Your Highness," replied the messenger.

"I cannot believe we are losing to Thomas Carpenter and his army of paid minions." Phillip walked quickly into his chamber where he had already called together his advisory council.

"What is your will, Sire?" asked one of his council members. King Phillip showed the same look on his face that his adopted son had earlier in the evening. Thoughts of losing his son and his village sent his mind racing.

King Phillip knew he could not send reinforcements to Aveston because that would leave Harkstead vulnerable to attack. He also contemplated sending the Red Guard Infantry to aid Stuart, but their numbers were not as large as the cavalry and would be a last resort if the battle became dire.

Young Harold was awakened by his father's bellowing voice and made his way the kings chambers to see what was upsetting him.

However, he did not enter—he hid around the bend in the hallway, just close enough so he could listen to the group of official-sounding men inside. "Suggestions?" Phillip said stoically.

"What of Stuart, Sire?" said one of the council members.

"I am afraid he will have to fight this battle without me. I have to trust my years of training him has prepared him to lead his men into battle," he said while sitting on his throne.

"If we lose Aveston, Sire, Carpenter may go after Derron in the East or head south toward Neally," said another council member.

"Indeed, those are all possibilities, and we must ensure their safety. Send riders to Derron and Neally immediately with orders to fortify their perimeters," Phillip ordered. He turned to one of his advisors and bade him to follow as he rushed his way out of the chamber, speaking softly, "Have word sent to my son in Aveston to return to Harkstead if the Carpenter breaches those walls."

***

The night sky was clear, but it was cold in Aveston as the Carpenter stood next to a tree urinating.

As he voided, he was almost dancing to himself—pleased and amused by the day's fighting. His hips were rotating in a circular motion as he laughed out loud.

His lancemen commander saw his actions and hastily interrupted, "Sire, the men are resting, and we are waiting on your orders for the morning's fight."

"Orders? I have no orders. My only order is to take the city. They will have fortified their gate by now, and are probably counting on gathering all of the muscle and hands they can find. We will not advance on their gate, that's too easy. We will, in fact, make them come to us."

"Forgive me, Sire, but how are we going to make them do that?" said another commander.

"Dear child, I do not want Aveston in order to claim it as my own. The city itself holds no value to me. There are far more valuable places within King Phillip's Midland Kingdom." The Carpenter sat beside the fire, took a drink of mead, and smiled as his commanders—cavalry, infantry and lancemen alike—looked bemused. "Children, we will burn Aveston down from out here. Have the archers prepare their longbows for a fire assault on Aveston in the morning. Before the sun rises, we will have riders arrive with more supplies," said the Carpenter as he drank more mead.

"Sire, you knew we would break the ranks of King Phillip?" asked one of his commanders.

"No. I knew we would either be dead at this point, or we would be here. Either way, I wanted to have resources in case we needed them." said Carpenter.

"Besides, if I were to perish on the battlefield their orders were to find me and to take my body away. I would never give those Midlanders the opportunity to desecrate my body."

"So, when the morning light shines on the Aveston wall, we will make fire rain down on the Midlanders as if the sun was punishing them for their insolence!" exclaimed one of the Carpenters commanders. The grouped laughed heartily as the cool night continued on.

\*\*\*

Atop the barbican of the Aveston gate, Stuart Miles was troubled by the next morning's looming battle. "Your Highness, are you well?" asked Earl Baker.

"No, Commander Baker, I am not," Stuart replied.

"What is troubling you, My Prince?"

Stuart took a moment, then responded, "I've been reviewing the day's fight in my head, and I feel like we are missing something." He continued, "Carpenter pushed most of his soldiers through our cavalry ranks and took many casualties."

The Midland Prince leaned on the Aveston battlement overlooking the clearing below that would become the battlefield in the morning, staring at the Carpenter's camp in the distance. *Why would he risk so many soldiers to get to this point?* Stuart thought to himself.

"Commander Baker, see to it that all available men are atop the battlements with bow and arrow. We will try to use our archers to strike them from a distance.

The Avestonian archers will be used to strike the Carpenter's men as they advance on the gate. I have a feeling we are in for a long fight at the first light of day—a long fight, indeed," said Stuart softly.

## 10

The morning's light was an uneasy sight in Stuart Miles' mind. If Carpenter could see all of the activity going on behind Aveston's walls, he might think they were afraid of him. This was an extreme contrast to Carpenter's camp. His cavalry, infantry, and archers were already lining up and getting prepared for the morning's fight. The Carpenter was still asleep. The Avestonian Midlanders were busy preparing their armaments and gathering available fighters. Soldiers from the previous day's battle that were too injured to fight rode back to Harkstead Castle under the safety of the night's darkness. The Red Guard Cavalry were not going to receive any additional men this morning. A rider from Harkstead presented word from King Phillip Miles to his already nervous son, Stuart. "Your Highness, I bring word from your father," said the rider.

"Go ahead," Stuart responded.

"His Majesty says he cannot risk any further men to Aveston due to the losses that have already occurred. He needs his remaining soldiers in the Midland villages for their fortification."

"Then we are on our own."

Long after the sun had crested the horizon, the Carpenter was awakened by the rhythmic beating of his soldiers' swords on their shields. He rose, donned his battle armor, and addressed his men before initiating the attack on the Aveston gate.

"Children, bear witness to the day at hand. Today is the day we take Aveston. We will not claim it as our own. We will not search every space that we can for valuables.

We will not take any of the Avestonian women for ourselves, nor will we take any prisoners today." He smiled joyfully.

"Today is the day we do what we were made for—what we are destined to do. Today we will drown those bloody Midlanders in a rain storm of fire from the sky." He paced side to side as he spoke to his army. "To victory!" yelled the Carpenter.

"To Victory!" said his army in return.

"Ready the archers!" the Carpenter commanded.

\*\*\*

Back at the Aveston gate, Stuart Miles and his small army—standing ready on top of the battlements—could see the Carpenter's men. They heard the rival army's war cry, which led to a sense of concern amongst the Midland fighters. Prince Stuart could feel the tension in his men. He went to the center of the barbican and looked toward the Carpenter's fighters before he turned to speak to his men. "Today we either defend this place, *or* die trying to. The fear you feel is genuine, and it is a good thing. It is something that should be respected. Use it to fuel your will to fight. Use your fear and your emotions to give you the strength to fight," he said confidently as he paced the barbican.

"Think of your families that were forced to leave their homes. Think of those we have already lost. We cannot let their deaths be in vain. Let us strive to end the villainy of Thomas the Carpenter right here, right now, today!" Stuart bellowed triumphantly.

The Midland fighters made a raucous cheer as their prince gave them the increase in confidence he sensed they needed.

***

The Carpenter heard the Midlanders cheer, and without hesitation commenced the day's fight with a simple statement to his archers, "Make your flaming arrows feel like the sun itself is crashing down upon them!"

Carpenter's soldiers were lined in formation and his archers—with sights set above the battlements—released their arrows toward Aveston.

There was a problem though; the arrows were not clearing the Avestonian wall. The archers were too far back. Carpenter took small satisfaction in seeing several Avestonian infantry struck and set on fire with the initial targeting shot.

"Oh dear, someone was hurt. My heart will shed many tears for them," he said sarcastically before bellowing, "Advance fifty paces and fire again!" His soldiers responded and started the advance.

***

Back at the Aveston wall, there was much confusion. Men were screaming as their flesh burned off of their bodies. The Avestonian fighters were visibly disturbed. Prince Stuart could see his fighting force was not prepared for the battle they were about to encounter.

Hundreds of fiery arrows rained down on Aveston that dreadful morning. The Carpenter ordered his archers to advance within a few yards of the Avestonian arrows reach. His arrows were not meant to kill the men on top of the battlements; they were meant to destroy the city from the inside out.

Carpenter was sitting joyously under the shade of a tree with his trusty carving knife, whittling a small crown. He stood and bellowed, "Pressure! We must push them to fight us on open land.

They will eventually tire of trying to save their beloved city from our flaming arrows and raise their portcullis. That is when we will strike with all of our might."

***

Indeed, his flaming arrows were causing much damage within Aveston. Several portions of the small city were on fire, and Prince Stuart could see that they were expending too much energy trying to save the city. He knew he had to do something. He had to devise a plan.

*Should I command a retreat, and let Aveston fall into the hands of the Carpenter?* he thought to himself. *Or should we bring the fight to him, which is probably what he would prefer?*

Stuart knew he could not waste any more time trying to save the portions of Aveston that were not on fire.

It would only be a matter of time before the Carpenter's arrows would find their way toward the un-scorched areas. "Men! To arms, we will bring the fight to them! Clear the path to the barbican and assemble. We will rush the Carpenter's army once the portcullis has cleared the tallest man's head," Stuart commanded, the Avestionian's large, ornately carved war horn under his arm.

As the heavy portcullis raised, Prince Stuart gazed down from the top of the Avestonian battlements as dozens of Midland cavalrymen prepared to lead a large group of Avestonian men into battle. The more the portcullis rose, the louder their war cries became.

As the portcullis cleared the tallest riders head, the Red Guard and Midland Cavalrymen raised their weapons and charged the battlefield. The Carpenter had the outcome he had desired.

"May God grant us favor on this day," Stuart prayed quietly to himself.

"We will need a miracle in order to be victorious today."

\*\*\*

Carpenter heard a thunderous noise as the Aveston gate raised and dozens of horsemen poured through the city walls as if it were bleeding riders. Their swords were raised and their battle cries could be heard all the way to the back of the Carpenter's Army ranks. "Dear Lord, they *actually* think they can succeed today?" he said to one of his commanders.

As the Red Guard and Midland riders approached, he could see the hope in their eyes and it incensed him. Insulted by their bravery, the Carpenter, without thinking, made to run fervently toward the fight, but was restrained by his commanders. His face was red as fresh berries as he bellowed to his soldiers, "Let their bones crack from the weight of our steel and their blood soak the land beneath us!"

\*\*\*

They rode into the midst of Carpenter's Army, and the sounds of metal crashing against metal rang in all of their ears. The chaos was immeasurable as weapons swung, and in such close quarters, didn't always strike the enemy, but anyone near blade or bludgeoner.

Many horsemen were thrown from their mounts—one of them being an Avestonian warrior by the name of Fitzgerald.

Extracting his unscathed leg from under his massacred stallion, the warrior quickly rose and re-set the hilt of his falchion in his palm. It was a beautifully crafted single-edged sword, and he was a lethal expert in wielding it.

Fitzgerald was prepared as a Carpenter soldier attempted to strike him with a downward thrust. He easily dodged the strike and countered by ramming his boot into the soldier's knee.

As the Carpenter's soldier knelt in pain, Fitzgerald swung his mighty falchion across the back of the enemy soldier's neck and killed him instantly. He quickly raised his sword to block another strike from an enemy soldier, reached for his stiletto dagger, and fought with both hands. They exchanged violent blows, neither man giving any ground as both of them were wearing light-duty battle armor. The two were evenly matched, and their energy was leaving them with every missed and blocked strike. Fitzgerald was growing weary of the swordplay and knew he had to make his move soon.

He took a step back to wait for the Carpenter's soldier to make a reaching strike with his two-handed broad sword. When he did, Fitzgerald charged and rammed him with his shoulder, knocking the enemy to the ground.

He dropped his falchion, leaped onto the soldier's chest and drove his stiletto into the eyehole of the helmet with both hands. Captain Fitzgerald was one of few skilled Avestonian warriors and the Carpenter's soldiers killed many riders from the first wave.

Once the riders left the gates, the Avestonian infantry stormed onto the battlefield. An over-confident Thomas Carpenter commanded his army, "Advance on the Aveston wall. Dispatch the remaining Red Guard Cavalry, and march on toward their foot-soldiers!"

Suddenly, a horn sounded, one Fitzgerald recognized well. He killed another enemy soldier and used the body to cover him as a torrent of Avestonian arrows darkened the sky.

The Avestonian infantrymen, recognized the sound as well, stopped running toward the battle, knelt to the ground, and raised their shields. The Carpenter's soldiers were completely exposed as they ignorantly sprinted into the Avestonian's aerial trap.

Dozens of arrows lodged in the mouths, necks, and every unprotected part of the Carpenter's soldier's bodies as they made for the slowly descending portcullis. The resulting losses were immense.

This flawless execution of death was done on the orders of Prince Stuart, the leader of the Red Guard. He lacked his father's leadership ability, yet he excelled in military strategy—something his father had not allowed him to prove in previous battles. "Archers, fire again!" the prince commanded. More of the Carpenter's soldiers went down under the barrage of Avestonian arrows.

\*\*\*

The Carpenter was rife with anger; his sweaty face was red with fury as he took notice of the severity of the losses from the Aveston Midlander's counter attack.

He quickly commanded his archers to aim at the Aveston gate's archers hoping to suppress their onslaught. "Advance forward and kill those archers!" Carpenter commanded.

The arrows loosed from his archer's fingertips just as the Avestonian horn sounded again. This sound had the Avestonian warriors running toward the frontline, trampling the bodies of the enemy soldiers killed from the first arrow onslaught. Within moments, the Avestonian infantry was making progress.

They hacked at the legs of Carpenter's Cavalry war horses—dismounting the riders and killing many of the first ranks.

Prince Stuart was proud of his warriors, and from his perch on top of the Aveston battlement, he could clearly see he had received the miracle he was praying for.

They were close to advancing on his archers when Carpenter started to contemplate retreating, and it wasn't long before he shouted, "Regroup! Withdraw the archers and stop their advance right bloody now!" Ordered the Carpenter. His commanders obliged, and bellowed to the over matched and under protected archers to fall back as the remaining members of the Carpenter's Cavalry advanced forward to meet the inspired Aveston infantry at the newly created front line.

*** 

"Your plan is working, Your Highness," said Earl Baker.

"That seems to be the case Commander Baker. Yet, I am not fully content in believing our success is imminent. We must push the Carpenter back to the point of retreat, or, if we are lucky, we kill him first." Stuart was surveying the battlefield several yards in front of him.

"Shall we sound the horn again to signal a final push, Your Highness?" Baker asked.

"No, Commander Baker, we shall let our fighters press on at the pace the battle provides us. We do not have anyone left to send into the fray, and only a small amount of men to protect the city from behind the walls."

Indeed, the Midlanders of Aveston were stretched thin. Their primary fighting force was already overextended on the frontlines.

The face of Thomas the Carpenter, once brimming with joy, was now showing signs of uncertainty and anger. His self-financed cavalry had suffered heavy losses, and his commanders were seeking his advisement. "Sire, the Midlanders are pushing our army back toward our position, what is your desire?" asked one of his bravest commanders, Scott Donovan.

Carpenter stood still, stoic, and silent. He could not believe his plan failed. Maybe it was his ego that led him to lose most of his fighting force to the Avestonian aerial assault earlier.

"Sire, we must retreat!" said Commander Donovan. Still confounded, Carpenter was standing within several feet of the advancing Avestonian fighters before he came to and yelled, "Fall back on your positions, and regroup at Tawny!"

Captain Fitzgerald, the Avestonian swordsman, looked out on the devastation on the battlefield, and sensed the impending retreat. "Hold your position! Do not advance!" he bellowed. His soldiers complied, and the short-handed band of fighters, priests, and farmers rejoiced with happiness as the last of the Carpenter's Army retreated toward Tawny.

Back at the Aveston gate, the men cheered in celebration of the successful defense of the city they loved. Stuart looked to the sky and tearfully said, "Thank you for my miracle."

# 11

For a gazelle that is trying to survive in the hot African brush, life is a constant struggle. Every day you are trying to survive, trying not to be eaten, or separated from your family. Survival is not only a priority for the gazelle but also a priority for the Sefu tribe. No one understood this principal more than Amri Sefu, now twenty years old, and fully recovered from his injuries. He, along with several of his fastest running kinsmen, flanked the swift running gazelle as it darted toward the nearby watering hole. The creature did not dare run through the water because it, along with the Sefu men, knew death lurked under the cloudy, dark water.

The animal attempted to cut to the right, away from the water which was what the Sefu men were counting on. "Here it comes!" said Amri as he pointed in the direction of the animals next few strides. "Amu, throw your spear now!"

As predicted, the gazelle cut toward the right just as Amu released his spear, striking the beast in its flank. The gazelle stumbled, but the hit was not enough to bring the large male down. The rest of the Sefu hunters released their spears as the animal tried to recover from the initial strike. Several spears hit the beast, but it was still trying to flee. Amri ran toward the wounded animal and slit its throat with the small, handmade stone knife his father had made for him. The Sefu warriors quickly killed the bleeding beast while on the lookout for jealous and opportunistic hunters.

Amu Sefu whispered to one of his kinsmen, "Did you see how Amri dove onto that beast?"

"Fear has no place in his spirit. That is why he is called the 'Killer of Death—Black Lion,'" the Sefu warrior replied.

Indeed, fear had not been a part of Amri Sefu's spirit since the lion attack two years prior.

Since that traumatizing event, Amri had lived his life in a way that puzzled most of the people around him. His train of thought was cautious, but did not factor in any doubt or sense of danger.

Perhaps, in his mind, he was already dead. Maybe he felt the lion that had scarred his face and body for life had taken his earthly life and left him as a living spirit. Many members of his tribe believed this was the reason for Amri's new identity. He did not embrace his "Black Lion" nickname.

As his men quickly secured the gazelle and headed back to the village with their large kill, Amri's only focus was getting home. His posture was defensive, and even though he was the leader of his ten-man hunting group, he brought up the rear. He watched the land intently, never wanting to give up any ground for a surprise attack. Hoping, wishing—almost praying, the spirit of his nemesis, or maybe the son of his nemesis, would come for revenge against him. That was not going to happen today.

The Sefu warriors made it back home safely, and the familiar face of Amri's uncle, Coffa, greeted the men upon their return. "Welcome home. It looks like our warriors were successful today!" He smiled and touched each of the men on their shoulders.

"Yes, Chief!" the men responded as they walked by.

"Nephew, your men did well today. You should be proud."

"We got what the land allowed us to have, Uncle," Amri said with a miniscule grin painfully cracking his scarred face.

"You are making my new role as Chief easier by assisting in providing for us, Amri, and we thank you."

He looked over his shoulder at his sister-in-law, Furaha. She was standing in front of her hut waiting for her legendary warrior son to return home.

"Hello, Mother," Amri said as he walked up to her.

"Hello my son," Furaha responded as she kissed his scarred right cheek.

The three-and-a-half slashes across the right side of his face spanned six inches, and the rest of the scars on Amri's body were camouflaged by his darkened skin tone.

"Son, how are you?" asked Zuberi.

"I am well, Father," Amri responded.

"Have some water, and food with me."

"I will, Father, in a moment. I just want to sit here for a while."

Amri sat with his legs crossed, and his back to the wall as he faced toward the opening of his hut. He slowed his breathing, closed his eyes, and stepped outside of his spirit body—returning to the person *he* believed he was. He could hear children playing, and knew whom each one of the laughs belonged to. He also heard conversations outside and around him. He could smell his mother and father next to him and the food being prepared for them by his mother. Suddenly, he sensed he was being observed and watched closely. His first instinct was to revert back into his spirit self, and Amri quickly opened his eyes without taking a breath.

It was a little girl standing outside of his hut, curiously gazing at the man she was told was "The Killer of Death."

Dinner was hearty and well-needed for a man of Amri's size. Standing at six feet eight inches tall, he had developed into the mythical interpretation of what a human body could be.

His extremely muscular body was not only admired by the men, but by the younger women of the village, as well. His father often marveled at the gift of a man he and his wife created, and his pride far exceeded his fear for his son's future. Furaha had a deeper understanding of her child; she sensed her son's detachment from humanity, and lovingly nurtured the portions of his personality that he only revealed to her, and his immediate family.

"Where is Endesha?" Amri asked.

"He is at the ridge. You know how much he loves tracking now," Furaha said with a smile and a raised eyebrow.

"He should be back soon, it is getting late, and he will be hungry," Zuberi said while inspecting the small knife Amri used to kill the gazelle earlier.

Moments later, Endesha arrived home. His mother welcomed him with a kiss to the forehead, and said, "Hello my son."

"Greetings Mother, Father," said Endesha. His father tilted his head down slightly to acknowledge his son's greeting. "Hi Amri."

"Hello, brother." Amri quickly rose to his feet to hug his younger, shorter brother. "You are growing quickly little brother." Amri punched Endesha playfully in the shoulder.

Endesha smiled confidently at his family as the sting of his brother's strike radiated down his left arm. "Are you ready to eat?" Furaha asked.

"Yes Mother, thank you," he replied, trying not to rub his shoulder.

"What did you learn today at the ridge?" Zuberi asked.

"I was tracking some small animals, and I saw some Ema hunters across the watering hole looking for food along our borders.

"The Ema were that close to our border?" Zuberi asked.

"It was only a couple members of the Ema tribe, but they were right along the water's edge," Endesha responded.

"They are getting too close to our borders lately," Furaha said.

"They are not having much success with their hunting which is why they venture close to the watering hole," Zuberi said.

"Did you talk to the chief about what you saw?" Furaha asked.

"Yes, I did. He said he was aware of the Ema's activities," Endesha responded.

"Be careful brother, if the Ema tribe become desperate they may encroach on our territory and you must be prepared to defend yourself," Amri said with concern showing on his face.

Later that evening, fellow tribeswoman came to the Sefu family's hut to inform them that Chief Coffa was requesting his brother and nephew's presence at the elder's meeting.

Amri quickly rose to his feet from a short rest and assisted his father in getting to his. Ordinarily, Endesha would not be allowed to attend, but Zuberi motioned for Endesha to come with him.

The sun was long down, and darkness filled the sky as Zuberi and his sons joined their tribesmen. There was a large fire burning, and all of the Sefu leadership was in attendance. Coffa was presiding over the meeting—looking very serious in posture and facial expression. "Brothers, we are in a good place today. The land has given us much to be grateful for, and we should be appreciative for that. We are very fortunate to have Amri with us. He has helped us, yet again, with providing for our tribe. However, such good fortune has not been extended to the Ema tribe in the same way it has been extended to us. I have received many reports of recent sightings of Ema hunters near our borders. Sightings that have occurred as recently as today."

Coffa glanced at Endesha sitting in the background. "Let us not forget," he continued, "the Ema are considered our allies, and we should not think of them as the enemy. But we should not allow ourselves to be blind to the strife they may be enduring. If they become desperate they will start to hunt on our land and take food away from Sefu mouths. We must make sure that does not happen." He finished confidently.

"It seems like you are suggesting war is coming, Chief," said a tribesman.

"No. I am suggesting war *could* come if we do not help the Ema. Instead of waiting for their situation to become dire we should extend an offer of assistance. This would prevent them from crossing our borders which would absolutely lead into war," Coffa said.

"What do you require of us, Brother?" asked Zuberi.

"I am asking for a sacrifice from my people. I am asking all of you to prepare an offering of food for the Ema. We will travel to their village and deliver it in good faith."

"Why should we give what we have, when we have little to offer in the first place?" questioned another tribesman.

"The land has been good to us the last few years, and we have enjoyed many nights with full stomachs and happy children. My fear, is if we do not try to help the Ema, they will try to take by force the *little* you speak of. We will prepare an offering of food, we will leave for the Ema village in the morning to deliver it," Coffa commanded.

After the tribal meeting, Amri sat outside of his hut to think as he looked to the brightly shining moon. It was beautiful, and lit the sky sufficiently enough to see the same details as he could during the day. He felt uneasy with his uncle's plan for the following day, and knew he would not be able to sleep.

Endesha, curious as to why his brother was not resting before their trip north to the Ema village, sought out Amri to enquire. "You should rest, Brother."

"No. Not now," replied Amri.

"What are you thinking about?"

"I am not sure about what will happen tomorrow." Amri did not turn to look at his younger brother. "It seems too easy. I do not believe the Ema are going to turn their backs on thoughts of taking our land just because we gave them some food and supplies.

We have spent our entire lives learning the land of our people, and now, we are going to willingly give what our land has provided to a people who do not appreciate it—a people we do not know.

"When you feed an animal, it will always come back for more food. If you do not have any food for it, the animal may choose to attack." Amri turned to his younger brother, looked him in the eyes, and said, "I will be sitting here—looking into the night—waiting for the Ema to run out of food."

"We do not know what Coffa is going to say to the Ema chief."

"The Ema territory is dryer than ours. The animals are more bountiful here, and that is why they are scouting at the northern edge of the watering hole. If things are this bad during the wet months, imagine how desperate they will be during the dry months." Amri stood and raised his arms above his head to stretch his long body. His joints popped in protest.

Endesha thought about his brother's words, then turned to him, and said, "I guess we have some work ahead of us then brother."

Amri nodded his head in agreement, and the two Sefu brothers went indoors to rest before the trip to the Ema village in the morning.

There was an absence of sunlight the next morning as the men of the Sefu tribe prepared to travel to the north. They had filled several cloth bundles with food that ranged from dried berries and wild nuts to dried and fire smoked meats.

This was the type of sacrifice Chief Coffa commanded the Sefu leadership to make in hope that the Ema tribe would not encroach on their land anymore.

The trip to the Ema village would take the entire day. The group of men had to climb the northern mountains that surrounded their tribe's valley of land.

While it was not too high, the path was not an easy one. Amri Sefu was pleased with the change of scenery, but was visibly dissatisfied with his chief's hopeful generosity.

"Are you alright?" asked a fellow tribesman.

"Yes. Just thinking," Amri replied. He was looking at the land around him as he walked.

"My nephew does not believe in sharing the food that he has helped us acquire," Coffa said with a smile, adjusting the heavy ceremonial robe and headdress he had donned for the formal trip. The group of men shared a laugh as the terrain turned more laborious.

Hours passed, and Amri's disposition had not changed. Coffa took notice "What is on your mind, Nephew?"

Amri did not want to question the chief's actions in front of his men, so he walked a step slower to fall behind the others, and walk in stride with his uncle. "I am concerned about this trip, Uncle. Do you believe this offering will prevent the Ema from coming south to hunt near our lands?"

Coffa took his nephews words into his ears and looked toward the sky briefly. He then remembered Amri as a young boy, and forgot about his immense size and the scars on his face.

He wanted to give his nephew the same hope he thought every child should have, but Amri was not a child—not anymore. His youthful innocence was taken away from him two years ago, at the age of eighteen, by a hungry lion. Amri deserved to hear the truth from the uncle he loved and respected.

"Amri, the offering is the only thing we can do to prevent a war between our two tribes.

I am hoping to convince them to work with the Kuno tribe to the west by the big water for more bountiful lands."

"Kuno tribe?" Amri asked.

"Yes, the Kuno tribe. They are a strange group of people you have not met before," Coffa explained as he surveyed the mountainside for a place the group could take a break. "The Kuno's land is next to the big water—the largest watering hole in the land. There is so much water, you cannot see the end of it."

"Do the Kuno and Ema tribes get along?"

"At one point in history, yes, but eventually the two tribes fought, and have been enemies for many years." Coffa sat down on the ground. The Ema land was full of life, and it was providing for their people very well. The Kuno had many meats from the big water, but they did not have water to drink freely like the Ema did." The rest of the Sefu men sat nearby to listen to their conversation.

"So, they fought over water?" Amri asked.

"Yes. Without water, all will perish. There is a waterfall nearby, we should go there and drink before the sun breaks through the clouds," said Coffa. The group of men stood and headed up the path.

79

As the Sefu men descended down the mountain toward Ema territory, Amri was visibly on edge. His eyes were constantly scanning the foreign surroundings, looking for the slightest threat.

"Keep your peace, Nephew," Coffa whispered.

"That is not possible right now, Uncle. When Endesha and I were little, you told us not to feed the animals because they would always come back for more, and if we did not have any food for them, they may turn on us," said Amri.

"That is the truth. It is something all young people should learn about—how the land provides for us and how that balance can be affected by our actions," Coffa explained as he stepped down the hillside slowly.

"I can't help but feel like the Ema are the animal that will turn on us once we run out of food," Amri replied boldly. A few of the Sefu men snickered with hushed laughter at Amri's bold tone with the Sefu chief.

Coffa immediately stopped walking, looked up to Amri's scarred face, and said, "Nephew, remember my position, and do not lose your respect for me the same way your tongue is losing faith in my decisions." Amri was almost a foot and a half taller than his uncle. He weighed over 50 pounds more than him as well. However, he loved and respected his uncle, and was remorseful for any disrespect he may have shown his uncle in front of his men.

"My apologies, Uncle," Amri said quietly.

"You must trust your instincts, Amri. I share some of your concerns, but this is the only way to avoid war—so we must try to help the Ema."

He placed his hand on Amri's shoulder for balance as they walked down the hillside.

The sun was slowly descending into the afternoon sky as the Sefu men approached the Ema village.

Their children were visible from the distance, and their stature was significantly smaller than the Sefu tribe that lived just a few miles to the south.

Amri could see the Ema children had not been eating as well as the children in his village. His attention was quickly diverted to the group of men approaching.

"Greetings, Chief Coffa," said Kahina, one of Ema elders. "Follow me to Chief Ameqran's hut. You and your men can rest there." He smiled and walked with the Sefu men.

Now, closer to the village, Amri could easily see how thin the Ema people were, and they could not help but notice Amri's physical size, and the scars on his face and body. There were very few children, and the ones he saw stared and pointed in amazement. Amri did not show any expression on his face as he walked behind the Sefu contingent.

He did not understand the dialect the Ema people were speaking very well. It was a mixture of the language the Sefu spoke with some words that he, along with a few of the younger men, did not fully understand.

The Sefu men were led to Chief Ameqran's dwelling. It was made from wood and grasses that were tied with strands of animal hair or some vine-like material.

Chief Ameqran was a svelte older man with wrinkled black skin. He had a full head of coarse gray hair, His neck was adorned with lion's fangs and ornate stones. The two groups sat, and as they did, Amri never broke his stare from Chief Ameqran.

The two leaders began to talk, and Amri decided to take inventory of what he'd seen as they entered the village. *Six men outside, maybe twenty within the immediate area, no real threats seen. There were many children outside but no women visible—no women,* Amri thought to himself. The lack of women was a point of concern for him.

He was not going to second guess his uncle again—especially while he was conducting diplomatic activities—so he kept his concerns to himself.

As the conversation went on and pleasantries were shared, Coffa turned to the Ema leader, and said, "Chief Ameqran we brought an offering of food for you and your people."

"We thank you for your generosity, but I do not understand why you traveled so far to bring us this offering."

"We have been seeing your hunters near our watering hole, and figured the only reason your men would travel so far south is because hunting in your territory was not productive." Coffa smiled kindly, and continued, "Is that not the case?"

"I'm sorry, my friend, that is not the case."

The Sefu contingent looked puzzled—all except for Amri. He could only understand the last sentence of the conversation, and started to have a very unsettled feeling in his spirit. Amri was looked to his uncle, and waited for his response to the Ema chief's statement. Coffa remained pleasant, and stately yet slightly unsettled by the chief's words.

Wisely, Coffa switched back to the Sefu dialect, so Amri and the others could understand as he questioned Ameqran. "May I ask why your men were near the boarders of our territory if they were not hunting?" Coffa asked sincerely.

"For many years the Sefu tribe has controlled the watering hole and the entire southern valley.

We have stood by and watched your people thrive under your leadership, and now, even more so because of him," Ameqran said, and pointed to Amri. "That man there is the key to your tribe's livelihood." Amri stared at the Ema chief with fierce intensity.

"I do not understand," Coffa replied.

"Chief Coffa, no other tribe would dare attack the Sefu people because they fear the *Black Lion. He* is the reason why you felt so comfortable in sharing your food. You know he will aid you in finding more." Ameqran looked directly at Amri, returning his stare.

The tension in the room was tangible. Kahina, along with another Ema tribesman, sat on the opposite side of the hut and looked visibly nervous. Amri was now starting to question his remorse for going against his uncle's decision. Coffa, now concerned, wanted to get to the point of Ameqran's words. "Fortunately for us, Amri is a Sefu man, and his reputation does proceed him. However, we are not interested in warring with other tribes, nor do we aspire to expand our territory."

Chief Ameqran nodded his head, and replied, "The Ema *are* interested in expanding our territory."

"You what? I do not understand."

Ameqran went on to say, "We have interest in expanding our territory, and we know we cannot be successful in doing that with your *Black Lion* protecting your people." The Sefu men looked at each other, and though Amri could not understand all of their conversation, he knew his instincts had been correct.

"Imagine how surprised we were to see you brought your special protector right to us. You will not leave this place today, Chief Coffa." His guards nervously produced their spears. "You are surrounded, and there is no escape," Ameqran warned.

Coffa was surprised by his friend's betrayal. He immediately thought about his nephew's statements on the way to the Ema village, and before he could replay the conversation in his mind, Amri calmly said, "Us being surrounded does not mean *you* are safe."

"Did you not hear me? You are surrounded, and there is no way for you to get out of this village alive," Ameqran said with an emboldened tone.

"I do not see it that way," Amri said as he pieced together the words the Ema chief was saying. "The way I see it, *you* are the one that is trapped. *You* are trapped in here *with* me." In a flash, Amri took his spear and slashed the ankle of the nearest Ema guard.

As the guard quickly dropped to one knee, Amri drove the spear up into his neck. He turned toward his left shoulder, and, as he did, he spun the spear in the palm of his hand to an underhand position and threw it across the room, striking Kahina in the chest. The force of Amri's spear penetrated the Ema elder's chest and lodged him against the wall of the hut. Coffa tossed a sharpened stone blade to Amri, and in one swift movement, the Sefu warrior picked up the urine moistened tribal chief, turned him around, and held the blade to his neck.

The Ema guards were outside waiting with spears in hand, they could see the blood seeping from the base of the hut, but they were not sure if it was Ema or Sefu blood.

A brave Ema man pondered the notion of going inside blindly, but reason, and a firm arm grab with a head shake "no" from his fellow tribesman kept him waiting for the slightest sign of Sefu flesh.

Suddenly, the Ema men heard a familiar voice; it was their leader, but his voice was trembling, and it sounded like he was in danger.

"Move away from the opening!" Ameqran commanded. There was a gurgle in his voice, and he was in obvious distress. "We are coming out. Put down your spears!"

Moments later, the Ema's chief emerged from the hut with Amri's left arm around his neck. When his men saw their chief, some of them screamed in horror. Even as warriors, seeing their chief's innards dangling from his body was too much savagery to witness. Amri turned toward the Ema men, his back to the south—his Sefu tribesmen behind him, and when he spoke, his voice echoed across the northern land. "We came to you in peace, and you tried to kill us! For what? Our land? We trusted you, we even brought you food we could not afford to give, yet this is how you repay us?" Amri bellowed in vicious anger.

Amri knew they were outnumbered, and that they had to retreat quickly before the Emu tribe got over their shock, and remembered their courage. He noticed the sky—it would be dark soon—they would use this to their advantage. He looked at his uncle and countrymen and glanced at the southern mountains behind them. They understood and nodded their agreement to him. "Your chief does not want our food, so he must not need his stomach

85

anymore!" Amri yelled. Violently, Amri cut into the Ema chief and retrieved his stomach.

With what little life he had left, Chief Ameqran screamed in horror as the massive Sefu warrior lived up to *The Killer of Death* mystique.

Amri threw the eviscerated chief toward his countrymen, and the entire Sefu contingent took off for the southern mountains behind them. All of the Sefu warriors ran—except one—Amri Sefu. He stood in front of the Ema men, slowly walking backward, expecting them to follow. None did.

Nor did any member of the Ema tribe attempt to pick up their spears—they were not going to challenge the Sefu warrior.

Amri turned slowly before bolting into the darkness toward his village on the other side of the southern mountains.

## 12

The moonlight was particularly bright during the trek back to the Sefu village. This was very useful for the Sefu contingent on their escape into the mountain pass that divided the Ema and Sefu lands. Chief Coffa and his men gathered at the waterfall for a chance to regroup and gather themselves. The men drank their fill and sat in the moonlight in silence. They worried for Amri. His sacrifice for their escape left them sullen but thankful. He had not yet rejoined them, and they wondered his fate. They were not sure if they were being chased, and remaining idle made them nervous. They still had a significant march back to their village ahead of them.

"Chief Coffa, should we continue down the mountain?" asked one of the Sefu men.

"No… not yet," he said hesitantly.

"Do you think Amri is on his way here?" asked another.

"I don't know what to think of my nephew at the moment." His reply was quiet and reserved. "It is best we wait a moment and gather our breath before we depart from this place." Coffa sat in silence as his tribesmen chatted quietly around him.

"Did you see what Amri did to the Ema chief?" was whispered, and followed by, "What about the two men he killed inside the hut?"

The men had so many questions, and Chief Coffa had no answers. He had no understanding as to why his plan was a failure.

He also had no idea why the man he considered a friend, Chief Ameqran, would betray him.

He replayed the day's events many times in his head, and the only thing he could recall was the sheer violent nature of the little boy he watched being birthed twenty years ago. The speed, power, and bravery that Amri showed made Coffa, a man twenty-three years his senior, question his role as the Sefu chief.

Coffa was still in heavy thought when they suddenly heard a noise close by. The men immediately moved into a defensive crouch with their faces and chests hovering inches over the ground. Using the shadows from the moonlight as camouflage, invisible to anyone searching for them in the darkness. The sound of a bird was heard—a distinctive sound. One that only a man from the southern valley would know. It was Amri. Coffa whistled back at him and the Sefu men rose from the shadows.

There were many hugs and jubilation from his tribesmen, and he was glad to see they were okay. Parched and out of breath, he used both hands to drink deeply from the waterfall, and told his friends he had run up the mountain without stopping. He was hoping to catch up with them at some point because, even the bright moon, he could not navigate his way down the mountainside.

"How are you, Nephew?" Coffa asked as he placed his hand on Amri's shoulder.

"I am fine, Uncle," Amri responded as he took in large breaths of air.

"I am sorry, Amri, I should have listened more closely to you. I honestly felt Ameqran would welcome our offering. I never knew that he wanted Sefu land," he said.

"Your instincts are your best defense against attack, Amri, and that is something I taught you many years ago. I forgot my own lesson and took us into a trap. This will not sit well with the village elders."

"We cannot focus on that now, Chief. War is coming from behind us, and we have to get back to the village to warn our people and prepare. We do not have much time," Amri warned.

"Agreed. We should be on our way. Let's go brothers, we do not have much time!" Coffa commanded.

The Sefu men continued down the mountainside in the moonlit darkness. Coffa skillfully guided the group with a renewed sense of purpose, and was determined to get back to the village to prepare for the upcoming battle with the Ema tribe.

Amri's mind was already preparing for the fight that would be soon upon the Sefu people. He was mentally strategizing how he would take on the Ema, and he knew they did not have much time.

Hours later, the Sefu contingent made it back to their village. The villagers knew something was wrong when they saw their chief return without the ceremonial garb he had left with. Furaha was the first to greet the men. "What happened? You look frightened brother," she said before scanning the group of men to find her eldest son. She finally saw him walking toward her with a serious look on his face and blood that was not his on his body.

"Hello, Mother." He greeted her kindly, then made his way to a water to rinse his body off.

"Gather the elders. We bring important news," Coffa commanded. He then walked over to Zuberi and said quietly, "We need to speak. Now."

Zuberi did not understand why his brother's tone was so tense, but he gathered his wife and the trio went to a secluded area of the village to converse before the meeting with the elders. When they found Coffa, he was pacing back and forth with nervous energy.

He looked at his brother with tears welling in his eyes and summoned as much courage as he could, then said, "The child you had twenty years ago died the night the lion attacked."

Zuberi was puzzled by his brother's words. "What are you talking about, Coffa?"

Coffa stopped pacing, looked directly into Furaha's eyes, and said, "The things people say about Amri are true." He then looked Zuberi in the eyes and said, "Amri is a monster, a beast without a master." Coffa was visibly shaking as he went on to say, "Amri is evil with a conscience."

"What are you saying brother?" Zuberi asked.

"Your son has traded places with the lion that attacked him, he is now the lion. The people are correct in calling him the *Black Lion*. I witnessed it myself in the Ema village" Coffa went on to recant the events from earlier in the day. "Your son showed so much bravery in getting us out of a terrible trap—a trap that he warned me about, and I did not listen to him," Coffa said softly.

Furaha reached for his hands and held them close to her heart. Coffa looked into her eyes. "Amri's savagery saved us from certain death today. I have never seen someone so skilled at killing before. He saved us today. I must go prepare for the meeting with the elders, but I wanted to let you know what happened first.

My intention is not to scare you, but you deserve to know who Amri is now." Coffa let go of Furaha's hands and quickly walked away.

Zuberi watched his brother hurry away as Furaha stared at the ground, both lost in thought. After a moment of silence, Zuberi finally spoke, "I remember how big a baby he was—so strong from the start. I knew he would grow to be something special one day." Furaha took her husband's hand, and waited for him to continue.

"He was so different, even as a child. Always aware of his environment, and mindful of people; he invited competition and relished opportunities to exert his will on others. And always ready to prove himself. It made him an excellent student for Coffa and me." He sighed and turned his face to the sky—Furaha joined him in looking.

"I remember his desire for independence and his loving nature," she replied. "I still see that loving nature from time to time, but I believe he has lost much of his humanity. I knew he would be a warrior, but I never thought I would hear him described as a monster." The two parents looked at each other, and Zuberi could see the sadness in her eyes. "War is coming?" she asked.

"Yes. Unfortunately, we are headed toward a difficult period of time. There will be many deaths, and we must prepare to fight." He held his wife in the moonlight for what could possibly be the last time.

The land has lost its calmness as the once familiar winds returned to the Sefu village only to blow upwards and sideways.

The fire at the center of the Sefu village was cracking violently in the late evening darkness; the flames flickered as if they were dancing rhythmically.

The village elders gathered around the crackling fire to discuss what occurred at the Ema village. There were many muffled conversations of what happened, and the energy of the Sefu people could be felt easily—above all, was a sense of uncertainty. Amri sat in the back and picked slowly at the bowl of food resting on his lap.

Chief Coffa came out of his hut looking more like himself, and sat down to deliver the most important speech his people would ever hear him say. "Sisters and brothers, tonight I come to you with a heavy heart. We left earlier today to deliver a gift to our friends, the Ema, to prevent a war we now know could not be prevented," Coffa said with great presence.

"Chief Ameqran informed us that they want our land, and the only thing keeping them from attacking us over the last few years was Amri. We made it easy for him to eliminate that threat by bringing Amri right to him." Coffa made eye contact with each of the Sefu elders. They shifted uncomfortably, but said nothing.

"I ignored my nephew's warnings and believed I knew what was best for our people—I was wrong. Our attempt to aid our neighboring tribe ended with Amri having to kill two of the Ema's best warriors, and Chief Ameqran, himself," said Coffa as the elders started talking softly with each other.

"Chief Coffa, does this mean we are at war with the Ema?" asked one of the Sefu elders.

"Yes. They will come quickly to avenge the death of their chief. We must be ready to fight, and prepare our women and children to travel west toward Kuno land." Coffa commanded.

"The Kuno cannot be trusted either," said Zuberi.

"I know, Brother, but this is our only hope right now. Amri will go with the women and children to protect them from any Ema attacks from the north," said Coffa.

"I will not lead my people away from our home. My place is here fighting the Ema with my fellow Sefu warriors!" Amri bellowed.

One of the eldest members of the Sefu tribe, and former Sefu Chief, Chipo said, "Son, Chief Coffa is correct. You must go with the women and the young to protect them. Without them our future is unsure, and with you protecting them, our future has a chance to endure."

Amri could not process what he was hearing. He knew he wanted to fight alongside his uncle and father. His heart was beating violently, and he had no way to release the anger swelling in his spirit. He put his hands on his head, trying not to scream and show his tribesmen his desire to disobey their leader.

Furaha could see that her warrior child was in distress, and made her way to where Amri was sitting. When he saw her coming toward him, he quickly rose to his feet and walked into the darkness. His mother did not follow, instead, she allowed her legendary son to wrestle with the lion that was trapped inside his soul.

*I do not understand why I cannot help my countrymen protect our village!* Amri thought to himself as he walked in the darkness. "I am not a leader, I am a warrior!" Amri bellowed out loud.

"Yes. You *are* a leader!" a voice said in the darkness.

Without turning his head to look back, or break his stride in the darkness Amri replied, "Endesha, you do not understand what I am feeling right now."

"Yes I do, Brother. You think it is your job to protect everyone, and if you don't you are failing us." Endesha walked five paces behind his agitated brother. "But you are wrong, Amri. We need you to help us go to the Kuno land!" Endesha boldly took a stand against his more powerful brother. "I need you to help us go to the Kuno land, brother!" Endesha said without any quiver in his voice, and for the first time, in a strong tone that reminded Amri of their father.

Amri stopped walking, and turned to face his brother's silhouette in the African moonlight. "I know you want to fight, but this time we need you to be a leader. Coffa has taught you what is needed to lead over the last few years, and it is your time now," Endesha said with a look of desperation on his face.

Amri thought about what his young brother said. He knew his concerns were valid. Endesha was one of few people that he respected and would listen to. Amri thought some more, and said, "If I cannot fight then I will contribute by helping to develop a strategy for our war against the Ema."

The two brothers returned to the village and Amri fell asleep within moments of laying down—a sleep so deep he would not wake easily.

## 13

The sky was clear and the moon shone brighter than it ever had before. Every member of the Sefu tribe was asleep with the exception of a handful of men watching for activity from the north. Zuberi Sefu and his family were well into their night's slumber, but Amri was not sleeping easily. He was grunting softly to himself, his body twitched, and he was sweating profusely. Amri's mind was racing within his dreams. His thoughts were clouded by images that he could not determine were present day or a part of his future.

Within his dream, Amri's spirit seemed to be in an alternate world. Amri was still angry and looking for a fight. He was looking for the source of his anger, his nemesis.

He crouched and took in his surroundings. He slowly raised his head upward to look in front of him and saw nothing. The landscape was gray, barren and dry. Gray dust covered his dark skin but started to slide off of his body as the wind started to pick up. But this was not the familiar wind from his village. It quickly became violent, swirling and blowing so hard Amri's vision was useless.

As Amri's dream continued, he saw visions of men with whips and chains. He heard barely audible words followed by a sharp pain in his back.

No one within the Sefu family's hut noticed Amri's body tense sharply at the pain he believed he was feeling. He started sweating more now and frowned even as he slumbered.

He continued walking slowly through the gray ash. The ground was soft, and made his footing unsteady.

Amri tried to figure out where he was, and searched for anything that could help him determine his location. It was useless, he was lost.

His mind was still angry, still wanting to aid in protecting his village.

Crippling screams shot through his mind. Women screaming, children in tears, and loud crashes of metal clanging together so loudly Amri fell to his knees again.

"What is this place?" Amri screamed as he pressed his hands over his ears. Mentally drained, he fell to his knees and placed his hands down into the gray ash in front of him. As he breathed in large breaths of ash filled air, he felt something under his hands.

He could not see what it was, but it was cold and hard—he rose to his feet, and gripped in his hands was the spear his father had made him.

Amri continued to walk through the wasteland. He wanted another chance to battle the lion that severely scarred his body. He wanted to prove to himself that defeating the lion was not a matter of chance, when he heard the sound he had waited two years to hear—a lion's growl. The voice of his nemesis came again, louder and clearer this time.

Pleased with finding his true nemesis Amri started to smile as he slept.

His skin was dry now and his heartbeat quickened and was stronger than before. Even as he slumbered Amri Sefu was ready to fight.

He began to search for his enemy. The grip on his spear tightened as he walked in a defensive crouch through the blinding gray winds. Amri heard another loud growl as if the animal was the size of an elephant.

He started running toward where he thought it came from. Excited, he yelled into the dusty void, "Come on! Show yourself!"

Amri desperately wanted to confront the demon that had been haunting him for two years. Suddenly, the wind stopped. The ash in the air settled, the sky cleared, and he heard another massive growl behind him.

Amri slowly turned to gaze upon the horror that had been troubling his spirit for so long. This was not the beast he had struck down. It was a lion demon with fangs that shined like bright stars, glowing blood-red eyes, and a body made of rolling black smoke in constant motion. Free of fear, Amri walked toward the violently smoking beast. "Finally, you are here!"

The lion walked toward him and roared loudly in response. Displaying its bright diamond-like fangs as its mouth stretched open.

Amri did not flinch. He did not breathe, nor blink. He was focused on one thing. Retribution.

He circled the lion looking for the opportunity to strike. The smoky outline of the lion tracked Amri's movements and turned with him as he walked in a circle. It emitted a low growl, a warning. Amri violently slapped his chest with alternating hands. "What are you waiting for?" he screamed. "Fight me!"

"Why do you seek a battle with me?" The lion's voice was deep and ominous.

"I killed you before, and I will do it again."

"No, you are wrong. *I* killed *you* that day."

"I struck you down with my spear. I saw my brothers bring you back to our village."

"Did you eat my flesh?"

"Yes!"

"Then you know how we became one. I gave you my mark that day. I gave you your power that day."

"You gave me nothing!" Amri bellowed.

The lion gave a mighty roar, and said, "I gave you what you were destined to have!"

"No. You took my humanity, my feelings, my love for people—I feel nothing! Because of you, I don't even know who I am anymore!"

"I gave you inner strength beyond what any person could have. I gave you extraordinary courage. You believe you lost your ability to feel, but it is only because you are not afraid of anything. I gave you these things so you could prepare."

"Prepare for what?"

"Your destiny," said the lion. "You are going to lead your people to a far land."

"To the Kuno land?" Amri asked.

"No. Even farther." The lion sat on its hind legs and continued, "You will travel to a faraway land—farther than your mind can imagine. Your destiny is rooted deep in a land that you are not meant to be in; a land you are not welcome, nor wanted in."

Suddenly, the sounds of men shouting, and water crashing against a cloudy object filled Amri's mind. He shook his head and tried to refocus on the still-smoking lion in front of him. He knew the lion would not attack him, and, at that moment, Amri surrendered his anger, and asked, "What will happen to my family?"

"You will protect the one's closest to you. All the rest will perish"

Amri stood silently and thought about the lion's words. "Who are you?"

"*I* send the winds that cool your body at night. *I* make the sky rain when you are thirsty. *I am everything.*"

"You say you are everything, but I only see a lion in front of me."

"No, Amri. You see yourself. I am the reflection of your purest form. The smoke you see is from the wars and fires you and your men will make. The light you see reflected in my fangs represents the riches your enemies will seek in the new land. You will lead men against these enemies."

"And your eyes?" Amri questioned.

"My eyes are the blood you shed from your enemies. So much blood— more than you could ever imagine—all by your hands. Your hands!"

A small river of blood began to flow through the gray ground. It moved around and past the lion, toward Amri's feet.

"Your hands!" the lion repeated.

Blood continued to flow, rising to cover his ankles and calves. "Your destiny lies within the blood of your fallen enemies!"

The lion disappeared in a torrent of blood that crashed into Amri, knocking him off of his feet and pushing him backwards.

Suddenly, Amri was back on his hands and knees. Completely dry and covered in gray ash. He heard a voice in the distance calling his name "Amri," and again, "Amri."

He stood, and began to run toward the voice, choking on the gray ash as he breathed. He coughed violently, but kept on running, desperately needing to find who was calling his name…

"Amri." Furaha touched him gently on the face, his eyes shot open, and he took in a mighty breath of shock and surprise.

"Mother!" Amri said loudly. His large chest moved up and down as his lungs begged for more air.

"Yes, my child. Are you well?"

"Yes, Mother. I am fine. Just a bad dream."

The cool wisp of morning air that made its way into the hut was refreshing to Amri after the lack of good rest he had overnight. He rose to his feet and stretched his strangely sore muscles to the point his joints protested, yet again, with pops and snaps. Amri felt physically tired after his overnight battle from within. He could not recall the details of it, but he knew he had to accept his assignment to lead the women and children to the Kuno land. Before that journey began, Amri wanted to help Chief Coffa plan his strategy against the Ema.

"Brothers, we must prepare for the Ema to attack at any moment," Coffa said with confidence. "We don't know when, but expect them to come from the north, over the mountain pass, and down into the valley to our land."

"Do you know how many warriors the Ema will send into battle?" asked one of the Sefu leaders.

"No. But I do know we have the advantage of knowing their path to our land." Coffa looked toward the mountain ridge to the north.

"That is where we will strike them," Amri interjected.

"Yes Amri, what do you recommend we do?" Coffa asked while recalling the mistake he made earlier in of not heeding Amri's intuition.

"We will fight the Ema on the mountain path. That is the first place they would have to go in order to get to our land," said Amri. "But we will not waste time waiting for them to come. We will make the first move. We will use what the land gives us to protect ourselves from the Ema."

"What do you mean?" Zuberi asked.

"We will take our animal kills and place them along the mountain pass that leads to our village. This will make the large birds fly over the pathway. We will watch the sky as they circle around the kills, and when they are disturbed, our scouts will see them scatter," Amri said with a new commanding presence. "We will stage our men along the path during the day, and retreat to a better location at the bottom of the mountain pass during the evening and into the night. The animals should prevent some of the Ema warriors from passing unnoticed before we attack the remaining fighters as they descend from the mountain."

"That will only give us a few moments before they descend into our territory, and we have to be prepared for a large fight.

We cannot afford for them to make it to our village," Chief Coffa warned. "We have to meet them in battle before they get to the watering hole. If we cannot stop them there, they may have a chance to attack the village, and we cannot allow that to happen"

Despite their planning and preparation, the Sefu warriors saw no hint of the Ema tribe throughout the day. This made them nervous, so when night arrived, the members of the Sefu tribe were on full alert. No one was truly sleeping except for the youngest of Sefu children. The rest were either preparing for the journey northeast to the Kuno tribe territory, or looking to the north for any sign of Ema warriors crossing the mountain pass, the low lands, the watering hole, or the outskirts of the Sefu village.

The moon was amazingly bright as the evening sky became clear. Absent of the dimming qualities that the clouds from earlier had provided, the unfiltered moonlight casted a supernatural glow on the land. Amri Sefu sat on the ground and gazed up to the stars. "What are you thinking about, Brother?" Endesha asked.

"The attack is going to happen tonight, Desha," Amri replied.

"How do you know?"

"Because that is what I would do."

"What are you going to do now?"

"I am going to go talk to the chief, and I want you to get Mother and Father. We leave for the Kuno land now. Go now!" Amri commanded.

Endesha ran quickly toward the center of the village shouting, "Amri says we have to leave for the Kuno land tonight!"

Amri followed Endesha at a calmer pace, and found Chief Coffa. "Uncle, we have to prepare for the Ema to attack tonight."

"Is that what you think is going to happen?" asked Coffa.

"Yes. We have to leave for the Kuno land now."

"Then leave now and protect your family."

"Yes, Uncle."

The two men shared a long embrace, and as Coffa made to let go he whispered softly into his nephew's ear, "You are destined to be a great leader one day my strong *Black Lion*."

Within minutes, all of the Sefu women and children awake and ready to start the long walk to the Kuno land. The journey to the northeastern seaside would take them two days.

At least the bright moonlight would make the trek across the land easier and safer for the Sefu contingent this night.

## 14

Walking in the darkness had never been a problem for Amri, even after his infamous lion attack. Endesha had not yet become completely comfortable with the moonlit darkness. Endesha and his family are in the back of the contingent headed towards the Kuno land.

"Do you ever think about the lion when you walk at night?" He asked as he assisted his ailed father.

"No, Desha. To be honest, I used to wish the lion would return so I could have the chance to fight it again." Amri said while looking over his shoulder at the darkened land that led back to their village.

"What do you think you would do to the lion, Amri? What would be different?" Zuberi asked.

"I don't know, Father."

"Nothing would be different, my child," said Furaha. "That beast gave you a gift, Amri."

"Agreed. Your mother is correct, Son. You have the lion's spirit inside you, and you must embrace it. It will probably save your life in the future," said Zuberi.

Back at the mountain pass north of the Sefu village, a scout hiding within the bushes saw a large group of men heading south from the Ema territory.

"Oh no," he said to himself, and took off running down the mountain pass toward the group of warriors stationed at the bottom. "They are coming," he whispered loudly. "We must tell the others!"

"Go, Brother, hurry!" said one of the warriors.

The scout sprinted to the Sefu village, and yelled, "The Ema are coming!"

Chief Coffa closed his eyes, and took a deep breath. With the elderly and the young gone with Amri as their protector, it was up to him and his warriors to defend their village and send the Ema back to their land.

"What is your command, Chief?" asked one of the warriors.

"We will do as we planned, and not allow them to come to our village.

We will fight them as they come down the mountain pass. That will give us the advantage," Coffa said confidently. "We will be victorious!"

The Sefu warriors took their long spears, handmade stone knives, and other weapons to the mountain pass, ready to fight the Ema as they descended.

Within minutes, the Ema warriors were climbing the mountain and making their way along the path that separated the two tribe's lands. The Ema had sent a formidable army to fight the Sefu people. Fueled by rage, the Ema sought revenge for their disemboweled Chief Ameqran, and control of the Sefu territory.

The Ema warriors did not care that Amri Sefu and the rest of the Sefu men were on the other side of the mountain pass, they only wanted to avenge their fallen leader. One of the Ema leaders was asked, "Do you think we can take them by surprise?"

"No. I expect them to be waiting for us at the bottom of the mountain," said Kenje the brother of Kahina, one of the Ema elders that was violently killed by Amri when the Sefu men escaped the ambush a day prior. "We will have to fight our way down to their village. Many of our men will die soon, but we have the numbers to defeat the Sefu if we fight without fear of their "*Black Lion*." The large contingent of sixty-five thin and tall Ema warriors snaked their way past the waterfall.

"Should we wait for them to strike, Chief Coffa? Or should we go up and meet them on the higher ground?" asked one of the Sefu warriors.

"No. We will remain here at the bottom, Brother," Coffa commanded. "We have the advantage of being on land we are familiar with."

He was crouched low in the stringy brush lining the hillside when he caught sight of the first of the Ema warriors heading down to flat land. "Wait..." he whispered to his warriors as more Ema descended from the higher ground. The warriors waited, tensed and ready, and when twenty-five Ema warriors were visible, Chief Coffa gave the order, "Attack!"

Screaming could be heard from the mountainside all the way to the Sefu village as waves of brown-skinned warriors clashed at the bottom of the valley. The Ema men could not all go down mountain path at the same time and were forced to descend down a bottleneck into the hoard of prepared Sefu warriors.

The Ema, propelled by anger, had to either win the fight at the bottom of the valley or die avenging the death of their leader.

Close-quarter fighting was not a Sefu warrior's skill. His swift speed and adeptness with a long spear made him better suited for hunting.

However, these gifts did not serve them when fighting another human. The Ema were better equipped for this type of fighting.

The strikes from their shortened spears and bone daggers made quick work of the less-gifted Sefu fighting force.

Chief Coffa's warriors were outnumbered and inept. Unfortunately, the greatest Sefu warrior that had ever lived was now miles away leading his people to safety. It had been a wise decision, after all.

It was late in the afternoon as blood spattered out of the Sefu warrior's mouth. A screaming Ema warrior mounted the dazed enemy's torso and violently drove his spear into the Sefu fighter's eye. Chief Coffa saw the horrifying display, came up behind the Ema soldier and ended his celebratory yell by slashing his throat with a stone knife. "Go back toward the village!" Coffa yelled as he gazed upon dozens of his fallen tribesmen at the base of the mountain pass.

The Sefu warriors could not hold back the Ema fighters whose size and formidable fighting ability was far beyond that of their foes.

Chief Coffa knew there was a chance they would be overtaken at the mountain pass, so he had kept the rest of his fighting force back in the village.

As the Sefu men retreated south, more of the Ema men were able to come down from the mountain in pursuit. They did not immediately follow the Sefu men toward the south.

The recently injured Ema leader Kenje said, "We shall regroup here quickly. Kill any wounded Sefu men that you find, and we will continue to the Sefu village immediately." Kenje's larger fighting force had proven they were more skilled in combat than their enemies; he had fifty-two soldiers left to lead into the heart of the Sefu village.

Chief Coffa's heart was beating violently as he sat in desperation back in the village. Despite the position he held within the Sefu tribe, he could not mask the fear he felt, or muster the strength to rally his people. He was not afraid to die—he was afraid of failing his people. He looked at his battered warriors and his remaining fighting force of forty fighters, and decided he would have to find courage and share one final thought with them.

"Brothers, we are here because we love our families, and we love one another," he said. "I am sorry I brought this war upon us; I am sorry I brought this pain onto our families. We cannot let the Ema take our village, Brothers. We must defend our land just like Amri would if he was with us. We will fight them with spear and heart, and we will die as warriors not cowards!"

The Sefu tribesmen yelled loudly in support, and within minutes the Ema soldiers were running toward the northern portion of the village. "Throw your spears!" Coffa ordered.

Several long spears were thrown at the advancing Ema fighters; many were hit in stride as they hurtled their way toward the Sefu village.

Several Ema warriors were impaled, but that did not stop them from advancing. "Attack!" ordered Kenje as they dodged the flying Sefu spears. "Burn down everything in sight!"

The battle for the Sefu village was neither graceful, nor was it very efficient. Men's heads were bludgeoned with stones from fire pits, arms were severed by wildly swung stone knives and spears, and, in the end, the Sefu tribe, including their leader, Chief Coffa, could not defeat Kenje and his larger fighting force. All were lost, just as the lion spirit predicted in Amri's dream.

***

Far in the northwestern distance, the remaining members of the Sefu tribe were resting for the evening. Amri was feeling unsettled, and Endesha could tell his brother's spirit was not at peace. "Are you alright, Brother?" Endesha asked.

"No, Desha, I am troubled."

"What troubles you my child?" Furaha asked.

Amri looked down at the ground and said, "They are all gone mother. I had a dream last night, and in it, the spirit of the lion I killed told me all of our people would be lost, and I had to lead us to the Kuno land."

"Is that the reason why you wanted to leave so quickly today?" Zuberi asked.

"Yes Father, I knew we had to leave when we did, or we would perish as well." Amri looked up to the night sky. He wanted to cry and mourn the loss of his tribesmen, but emotion was absent from his body. All he could do was look to the many visible stars, and think about his fallen uncle.

Coffa was not just his chief, he was his family and teacher, and Amri looked up to him as much as he did his father. This was not going to be a peaceful night as the remaining Sefu people wept and mourned the loss of their fallen sons and fathers. The winds were still, yet again, on this cool starlit night.

The next morning the Sefu contingent continued their trek towards the Kuno land. The elder members of the Sefu tribe had slowed the pace, but

Amri was eager to finish the two-day journey as quickly as possible because they did not have enough food for everyone.

Early in the days travel, Zuberi, pained and stiff from the previous day, reluctantly continued the journey on his older son's back. "How ironic is it that you once used to carry Amri in your arms, and now he carries you, old man?" Faraha said jokingly.

"We are lucky to have had such a strong child to help us make this journey across the lands," Zuberi said with a smile, while tapping his son's broad shoulders.

"Ask Chief Chipo how long has it been since he was last on Kuno soil," Amri requested one of the tribesmen.

Shortly thereafter, a response made it back to Amri from the front of the group. "Chief Chipo says he has not been there since he was a young man, over thirty years ago," said the tribesmen.

"I hope we will be better received than we were with the Ema," said Endesha as the group laughed softly.

The setting sun signaled the end to another day as the Sefu people continued to travel toward the North African coastline and the Kuno village.

Amri, Endesha, and some of the older Sefu boys returned from a hunting trip in time to see the sun hide behind the newly discovered horizon. "We have been traveling for a long time," said one of the Sefu children.

"Yes. I believe it took less time to get to the Kuno land many years ago because I was so much younger then," said Chief Chipo.

"We are close to the Kuno land. I can tell," Amri said.

"Oh? How do you know, my son?"

"The ground is different here than it was yesterday." Amri grabbed a handful of the sandy earth.

"Indeed. The ground in the Kuno village is white as the clouds, and there is water as far as the eye can see." A group started to sit around him.

Chief Chipo knew he had their attention, and while their dinner was being prepared, he decided to have Amri assist in the storytelling. "Amri, what else have you noticed about this land?"

The young warrior looked to the sky, and replied, "There is a different smell to this place—sweet, like fruit. I think I can smell the water, too."

"I remember the way the water smells in the Kuno land, and what I remember even more is the wonderful meats that the Kuno people eat.

It is not tough like the meat we eat in our village. It is like you are eating the softest of clouds," said Chief Chipo.

"I don't want to rest anymore. Let us continue walking so we can get some of that food *now*!" Endesha exclaimed as he stood and began walking away from the group.

The Sefu people enjoyed their moment of fellowship, and dined as they continued to listen to Chief Chipo's stories.

Amri was not a participating with the group. Instead, he was walking with Endesha and talking about their dreams. "Do you desire to fight *all* of the time?" asked Endesha as they walked in the moonlit darkness.

"I do not desire to fight all of the time, but I feel the *most* alive when I am taking *other's* lives," Amri replied.

"You do not feel alive right now?"

"No. I feel like this is just a break between the battles I have yet to face in my future." Amri raised his arms over his head to stretch, and his joints popped and snapped in protest.

The next morning, the Sefu tribe started out on the last leg of their journey toward the Kuno land, and by mid-day, they could see the large sand dunes in the far distance. The children ran ahead of them with youthful excitement.

The land was indeed as white as clouds, and the softness of the sand was a welcomed treat for sore Sefu feet. After crossing the sand dunes, gasps could be heard from the front of the group, and as Amri and his family caught up with the rest, they saw why everyone had stopped walking. In front of them was a vast valley of blue water. It looked like the sky was on the ground, but it was moving with a crashing rhythm that never changed, just repeated every few moments.

The wind returned, and its cooling touch was refreshing to Amri and Endesha. Amri exhaled as much as he could before filling his lungs with the largest breath he could take.

As he inhaled, he gorged himself on the sweet smells of this new land, and it was intoxicating to him. The old and young played and sang songs in the water. They were very thankful for making it to the Kuno land unharmed and healthy as the land once again provided for them.

## 15

The Sefu people had successfully made it to the Kuno land. Eventually, everyone became tired from playing and singing in the water, and as they walked away from the water, they noticed there were no other people along the seaside. "Does any of this look familiar to you, Chief Chipo?" asked one of the younger tribesmen.

Looking equally puzzled Chief Chipo replied, "I don't know, my child, but we will continue north and should reach the Kuno village soon.

"All right then, let us head north as Chief Chipo says," Amri commanded. His pleasant distraction by the sea was brought to an end once he was reminded they had yet to find the Kuno village. The sun was quickly retreating to the bottom of the flattened water line, so they had little time before it would set.

As the Sefu travelers regrouped and headed up the coastline, they noticed smoke in the distance. They made their way toward it, and as they did, they began seeing decorative markings on the trees that lined the beach. Chief Chipo immediately recognized the carvings and said, "We are here."

As the Sefu people walked closer to the Kuno village, Elder Chief Chipo called for Zuberi and Amri to escort him, and the other village elders to lead the group to greet the Kuno Chief.

They were greeted by some Kuno warriors. Chief Chipo asked one of them to bend down, and he whispered into the young Kuno man's ear.

He nodded in agreement, and gave the elder chief a welcoming hug and a smile. The Kuno men led the Sefu people into their village where they were greeted with music and smiles from the Kuno people.

Eventually, they were led to the center of the Kuno village and were given food and drink. Just as Chief Chipo told, the Kuno tribe's food was like nothing the Sefu people have ever tasted before. The tribe prepared various grilled and salted fish, and odd-looking shelled fish that was not well received, but clearly the favorite of the Kuno people. This feast was unlike anything that Endesha had ever tasted.

The sweetness of the smoked fish—along with the fresh and dried fruits—provided a semi-permanent smile on Endesha's young face. Zuberi and Furaha took much delight in watching their youngest son enjoy the meal he had dreamed so much of during their travels to the Kuno village. As the Sefu clan ate and fellowshipped with the Kuno people, Amri was not yet willing to drop his guard. He had a better feeling here than he had in the Ema village, but could not forget what happened there. He did not want to have that experience repeated, so he ate slowly, and remained cautious.

Amri noticed the Kuno people did not look like the members of the Sefu tribe. They were tall, and their skin was a lighter shade of brown. Unlike his people's short, coarse hair, the Kuno's hair was long, and appeared soft; some of them even had hair that was white like the sand.

When their feast was almost over, the Kuno people had their musicians play and they sang their traditional songs for the Sefu people. Unfortunately, the only person who knew what they were saying was Chief Chipo.

The music suddenly stopped and the Kuno people knelt down to their knees, and the Sefu people did the same. Of course, Amri did not want to comply, but a swift blow to the back of his head by Zuberi forced him to acquiesce his father's demands.

The Kuno's leader, Chief Olamide came out of his hut wearing a skirt made of twisted leaves and vines with intricately braided grasses that hung down toward the bottom of his thighs. His head was wrapped with an elaborate crown made of the same braided leaves and grasses, and his face and body were painted with bright colors. To his left was his daughter, Nsia, and to his right was his first in command Chike. Chief Olamide started to speak, but Amri could not understand what he said, so he focused his attention on the chief's daughter.

Nsia was different than any woman Amri had ever seen. She was tall with long, flowing, black hair. Her skin was golden-brown, and her body was very pleasing to Amri. He was snapped from his gaze by a nudge to his arm from his brother. Endesha could tell his older brother was smitten, and whispered to Amri, "I know what you are looking at."

Amri quipped back, "Shut up, boy."

Furaha interjected quietly, "Boys, the chief is talking."

Both Sefu brothers silenced themselves as the Kuno chief finished his speech. When he stopped talking, Chief Chipo stood up to formally greet Chief Olamide.

The two leaders hugged, and Chief Chipo kissed the Kuno chief's hand in reverence, then addressed his own people. "Brothers and Sisters, Chief Olamide has welcomed the Sefu people into his village to join the Kuno as members of their tribe.

I have accepted his offer on behalf of the Sefu people, and told him we are grateful for his kindness and hospitality," he said, and proudly continued. "We will sleep here tonight, and, tomorrow, the Kuno will help us build our own huts within the village. Here, we can grow with the Kuno, learn their language, and be a part of their family as one people." The Sefu people cheered with renewed hope.

Over the next couple of days, the younger members of the Sefu tribe worked with the Kuno craftsmen to build their huts. Each round hut would be large enough to fit one family, and some were even large enough for two.

The materials to build the huts were easily found within the Kuno village. Large leaves and vines held securely with twine made from the local trees provided a well-made and secure shelter. Amri enjoyed being taught how to use his hands for something other than hunting. He welcomed the opportunity to use the creativity he had been suppressing over the last two years, and even wondered if he would eventually share his father's love and skill with carving.

One day, while working on the Sefu huts, Amri noticed Nsia walking by him with a large group of children around her. She remembered him from the welcome ceremony a few days before and smiled at him casually. Amri did not return the favor; instead, he stared at her, and did not take his gaze off of her as she walked by. His gaze was uncomfortably broken by a small handful of sand thrown by Endesha. Amri emitted a slight growl as he barked, "Why did you do that Desha?"

"You should introduce yourself to her, Amri."

"Fool. We don't speak their language remember?"

"You could ask Chief Chipo to introduce you."

"I don't need anything from him." Amri did not want to discuss it further, so he regained his train of thought and continued his work.

Amri was truly smitten with Nsia and made a point of always knowing where she was. He did not ask anyone, and did not have to look very hard to find her. He would catch glimpses of her out of the corner of his eye and would be relieved to see her again moments later. It was almost as if she *wanted* him to know where she was and made sure Amri was in her line of sight.

Days later, while Amri was sitting alone on the beach looking at the slowly setting sun, Nsia approached him from behind. He knew it was Nsia because of her familiar scent and smiled to himself as she neared. He turned to look at her and noticed she was wearing a long skirt made of braided grasses with seashells tied at the ends. Nsia slowly lowered herself to her knees beside Amri. In her hands, she held a small cluster of different fruits; she offered them to Amri, who graciously ate some, then smiled awkwardly and tilted his head in gratitude for the sweet tasting gift. Nsia smiled back, and slowly raised her a hand to touch his scarred face.

He recoiled slightly as her fingers met his skin, yet she did not retract her hand. It was as steady as Amri's hands in a battle. He surrendered to Nsia's touch and allowed her to explore his scars. As she traced the lines across his face and bottom lip, she noticed there were more on his chest and shoulders, and ran her right hand down along them as well.

Amri did not know why she was doing this and was uncomfortable with this intimacy he would never have allowed in the past. Nsia slowly reached down into the cluster of fruit in her hand and produced a small clamshell with a blend of oils and herbs inside. She presented it to Amri's nose so he could smell it, and he nodded his approval.

She dipped her fingers into the mixture, rubbed it between her hands, and proceeded to apply it to his scars. Nsia's movements were measured and slow. Her touch reminded Amri of his mother's delicate hands.

A part of him loved the attention Nsia was giving him, and part of him did not understand what was happening. Amri felt undeserving of such compassion from a complete stranger. Nsia's obvious bravery and sympathy for his wounds was a surprise for the greatest of Sefu warriors.

When Nsia was finished with Amri's wounds she walked gracefully to the water and rinsed her hands. She then turned around and walked towards him, and as she approached Amri he could not help but notice her ample breasts and the long flowing hair that barely covered them. She silently returned to her initial position and picked up her items while leaving Amri with a slight smile escaping the side of her mouth.

Amri was smitten and pleased with his beachfront visitor, but the feeling that he did not deserve such attention remained. In the back of his mind, he wondered if she would treat him as nicely if she knew what he had done in the past.

Amri was pondering it all when he heard Endesha calling for him, "Amri!"

"I'm over here!"

"There you are! Mother wants us to come home. Chief Olamide says rain is coming tonight." The two brothers jogged back to their hut in Kuno village.

As a heavy rainstorm rolled in along the coastline, a Sefu tribesman came to Amri's hut with a message from Chief Olamide. "The Kuno chief has requested you sit with him and Elder Chief Chipo. You must go now to Chief Chipo and escort him to the Kuno chief's hut."

Lightening flashed, followed soon after by thunder that shook the sandy ground below. Amri set off for Chief Chipo's hut. Upon gathering the old man, Amri could not move him fast enough to prevent them from being completely soaked by the now pouring rain, so he decided to carry the former Sefu chief on his back as he jogged through the village to the Kuno leader's hut.

"This way Amri," said Chief Chipo as he directed him with his staff through the village. Once they made it to the Kuno chief's hut, Amri very gently lowered the elder from his back, and helped him inside before the storm released its fury. Chief Olamide's first in command, Chike, received the Sefu elder and escorted him to the back of the hut.

Nsia was also present, and as Amri ducked to enter the Kuno hut, she offered to escort him to her father, and they sat down facing each other. Amri was seated to the right of his elder chief, and Nsia, to the left of her father. She offered the group some fruit and dried meats as Chief Olamide marveled at the size of the legendary Sefu warrior.

"So, tell me Amri, how do you like it here in our village?" asked Chief Olamide.

Amri looked at the Kuno chief, knowing only that he had heard his name spoken. Chief Chipo gestured for Amri to lean into him, and whispered the translation to him. "He wants to know if you like it here." Amri had a very uncomfortable feeling come over him. He did not know how to respond.

119

More importantly, he did not know how to compose his thoughts with the Kuno chief's beautiful daughter sitting directly across from him.

"Tell him I am grateful for letting us become a part of his tribe," he finally muttered as his confidence escaped from every pore.

Chief Chipo translated what Amri said precisely, and the Kuno chief replied, "Stories of how you mastered the lion traveled all across the land. Many of our people believe you are not real—more like a spirit that lives with us instead of a man of flesh and bone. How does that make you feel?"

Amri knew Nsia could hear the conversation between Chief Chipo and Chief Olamide. He knew she would learn his true self, and he hoped she would not think less of him. For the first time Amri cared about what someone other than a member of his family thought about him. Chief Olamide was waiting for a response from Amri, and he knew he could not hide who he was from Nsia, so Amri decided to be himself. "I am many things to many people. I am a man, and I bleed like my brothers. The only difference is I make others bleed before I do," Amri said as his confidence rushed back into his body like Kuno fruit going into Endesha's mouth.

Nsia could not help but smile after Chief Chipo translated Amri's last statement.

She knew he was a mighty warrior and had overheard the story of how the massive Sefu warrior killed a lion. When she had seen him sitting on the beach, she could not contain her curiosity, and had to get a closer look at the man called the *"Black Lion."* Nsia thought a man of Amri's size would enjoy some fruit, so she took some with her as a peace offering. The young Kuno woman knew Amri was dangerous, and made sure her movements were slow and inoffensive.

When she saw his scars, she wanted to touch them, but saw his hesitation. Yet, he allowed her to touch them which made Nsia happy. Her intent was not to entice Amri, but she could not help feeling special when he was around her.

She tried to maintain her grace as she left him that day on the beach, but Nsia could not hold back the slight smile that showed how he warmed her heart.

Amri was becoming tired of the Kuno chief's small talk. His highest-ranking officer, Chike, appeared to be equally unimpressed with the stories and adulation of Amri Sefu and his legendary temper. During the conversation between the two chiefs, both Chike and Amri locked and held glares with each other. Neither man wanted to suspend their stare—Amri welcomed the challenge, and Chike wanted to show his strength. As the two tribal leaders continued their conversation, a literal battle was commencing between the two chief's warriors. Chike's glare was imposing, and his commitment to beating Amri in this challenge was both juvenile and impressive at the same time—he even stopped blinking.

Amri took a darker approach, and channeled all of his fury to boring into Chike's hazel eyes. Time slowed to a standstill—as did his breathing, and he, just like his rival, did not blink. Amri started to daydream about ways he could kill Chike.

In his open-eyed blindness, Amri could see himself performing a slow-motion attack on Chike. It literally made Amri happy as he imagined what he would do to the Kuno warrior.

Nsia noticed the masculine eye-jousting between the two men. She was hoping to break Amri's stare but she knew by the way his face looked, she could not.

Suddenly, the two tribal elders burst into laughter; Chief Olamide pat Chike on his shoulder and broke his stare at Amri.

Chike looked at his chief, smiled, and laughed softly at the joke that he had not heard. After Chike finished acknowledging Chief Olamide, he glanced over at Amri, and to his surprise, he had not broken his stare. In fact, it seemed more menacing, and, for a brief moment, Chike's heartbeat spiked as if he was running at full speed.

Proud of his victory, Amri broke his stare and turned his eyes toward Nsia, sitting on her knees across from him. Unfortunately, he had not altered his gaze and had to shake his head to return to his normal non-combative state. He did not want look at Nsia with rage in his eyes. He already knew she would not be capable of upsetting him in that way. In fact, Amri had already started to feel she might be the only person who could make him happy on the inside. Smitten again, a slight grin escaped from the corner of his scarred right cheek.

The evening rains had long subsided when it was finally time to end the meeting between Chief Chipo and Kuno Chief Olamide. The two leaders walked toward the entrance of the hut. As Amri ducked underneath the doorway to leave, he glanced back at Nsia, and gave Chike a bone-crunching handshake.

Neither man had given an inch of ground to the other which pleased both warriors greatly.

After escorting Chief Chipo back to his hut, Amri returned home to his curious mother. "So, did you get a chance to see *that* girl?"

"Yes, Mother. She was there," Amri replied.

"She probably looked good too, yes?" Endesha teased while smiling at his father.

Amri did not respond. Instead, he sat down, and his mother gave him some food to eat.

"Leave me alone, Desha," Amri said sternly. "Besides, we do not speak the same language, so it is impossible to communicate with her."

"When has anything ever stopped you from accomplishing your goals?" asked Furaha.

Sensing his eldest son's temper warming, Zuberi wisely said, "Enough. The two of you need to let the man eat his dinner."

Furaha smiled and walked over to Amri, kissed him on his forehead, and sat down next to her husband. Endesha left the hut to go walk near the Kuno beach.

Amri finished his dinner and noticed his parents were asleep. Endesha had not yet returned from his walk, which meant he had a brief moment to gather his thoughts and review the events he experienced earlier in the evening. He immediately thought about the way Nsia had looked. Amri could not get over her long, flowing, black curly hair.

It was unlike his mother's hair, which was very short and coarse in texture. Amri thought it reminded him of the ocean waves he was slowly becoming accustomed to seeing.

The future seemed bright to Amri as he began to feel the Kuno village might be a place he could consider home. There were many things that made it better than their lost Sefu village: there was more food to eat which meant less hunting; the materials for building huts were stronger, and the Kuno beach was a welcomed difference as well. The only thing Amri did not like was the potential contender for Nsia's heart—Chike.

It was late, and Amri felt weary from too many thoughts. His mind requested rest, he complied, and laid down for the evening to sleep.

## 16

After several months of living in the Kuno village, the members of the Sefu tribe had become more accustomed to their new surroundings. Endesha became an avid swimmer, Zuberi was working with Chief Chipo on tribal relation topics, and Amri was aggressively learning the Kuno language. His teacher, Nsia, was not only patient, but also enjoyed the time spent teaching the massive Sefu warrior her language. Unfortunately, Furaha was becoming ill. She had developed a slight cough that would not go away, and more often was in considerable pain, but she did not let her children know.

The sun was shining brightly, and the wind was blowing briskly when Endesha came into the hut and said, "Nsia is looking for you Amri."

"Did she tell you what she wanted?" asked Amri.

"I think she said to meet her by the woods."

"You mean meet her at the trail by the woods."

"I guess. I'm still learning the language."

Amri noticed his mother was laying down with her hand resting on her abdomen. "Are you alright, Mother?" he asked.

"Yes, child. Don't worry about me. Go see what Nsia wants with you," Furaha said softly. Amri kissed her warm, moist forehead and left to meet Nsia.

Amri made his way to meet Nsia at the entrance to the trail.

He found her picking through a bush for berries in another intricately woven grass dress. Her long, curly black hair barely covered her breasts, and a series of seashell necklaces added to her beauty. When Amri arrived, she smiled softly. "Hello," she said to him in her language.

"Uh...*Hello*," Amri awkwardly replied in the Kuno language.

"Come this way." She took Amri's large hand and guided him into the lush wooded jungle. This terrain was much different from the beachfront village of the Kuno people. The ground was moist and unstable. Amri was unsure of his footing, and Nsia had to remind him to step where she stepped.

Marvelous sounds of birds and creatures filled the air. Amri's senses were overwhelmed by the scenery and various forms of vegetation. Every so often, Nsia would look back at the massive man behind her and smile to herself. She knew, no matter what they faced in the jungle, she was completely safe. That was a great feeling for Nsia. She loved the fact that this supposed monster was now relying on her for direction as they walked through the jungle. She did not believe Amri was incapable of love or tenderness. Amri's awkwardness was evident even when words were not spoken.

After a while, the couple approached a fabulous waterfall. Amri looked up in awe at the massive waterfall that was nothing like the waterfall he had seen in the Ema territory. The waterfall seemed to rise into the sky. Nsia looked at Amri, and walked along the edge of the pool at the bottom of the waterfall. She then stepped out of her grass skirt, walked out onto a rocky ledge that led behind the waterfall, and slowly moved into the stream of cascading water. Her hair glistened as the water rushed over her brown skin. She motioned Amri to join her, but he stood motionless.

Not because he did not want to join her, or the fact that he enjoyed the sight of her naked body under the waterfall—he was simply afraid of the water.

Thoughts of the dream he had back in the Sefu village ran through Amri's mind, and his feet would not comply with his desires.

Nsia could see that Amri was not comfortable with being under the massive waterfall, so she jumped from the ledge into the pool beneath her. It was shallow enough for her to stand in, so she walked toward Amri and reached for his hand. He extended his hand out to her, and she led him into the pool. The water came up to his chest, so Nsia had to maintain her position in front of Amri. He noticed her struggling and placed his hands on her hips as he walked backward into the deeper portion of the pool. Once again, feelings of security rushed through her mind as her monster of a friend came to her rescue without prompting.

"This is nice, yes?" Nsia asked Amri in her language.

"Yes," he replied.

"This is my favorite place."

Amri did not understand what she said, and Nsia did not repeat herself. She just smiled to the point her teeth were peeking from between her lips, and gave Amri a deep kiss. He did not know how to react. No one, other than his parents, had ever gotten so close to his face, and parents do not kiss like Nsia did. Amri's instincts took over, and he responded to Nsia's kiss appropriately. Afterward, the two shared a deep embrace, then she motioned him to take her to the edge of the pool.

Back on her feet, she reached under her wet hair, and presented Amri with one of her many seashell necklaces.

Unfortunately, Amri's neck was larger than Nsia expected, and the necklace that draped Nsia's bosom barely went around Amri's neck. He did not mind because he thought it was an extremely thoughtful gesture, and knew he would treasure the gift Nsia gave him at the waterfall.

She looked into Amri's eyes while caressing his scarred face and said, "Not a monster" in the Sefu language.

She then raised both of Amri's hands to her lips and kissed them gently. "We go home now," Nsia said as she walked along the edge of the waterfall to retrieve her grass dress.

Amri replied, "Yes" to Nsia in the Kuno language. She took his hand and led him back to the Kuno village.

In the hills that surround the waterfall, Amri and Nsia were not only being watched by nature, but Chike was also monitoring their aquatic interlude. He was not pleased with what he saw. Feelings of jealousy entered his heart, and Chike felt slighted by the fact that Nsia so willingly chose Amri over him. Chike and Nsia grew up together, and their parents had made an agreement that the two would wed soon. After observing the interaction between Nsia and Amri, Chike knew he did not have a chance with her. Anger started to swell within Chike's spirit. He stood from his perch on the hill, took the stick he had in his hands and angrily broke it across his knee. As he turned around, to his surprise, he saw Endesha leaning against a tree, looking directly at him.

"You saw something you did not like?" Endesha asked in the Kuno language.

Chike was further shocked that Endesha spoke his language so easily. He decided to say something complicated, so Endesha would not understand.

"I was just going for a walk along these hills, and stopped to look at the waterfall below," Chike said quickly in his native language.

"Oh really? I thought you were looking at my brother and Nsia in the waterfall below just now," Endesha replied quickly and easily in the Kuno tongue. "That is what *I* was doing, and I think that is what *you* were doing when I found you up here with me."

"Does the little brother always follow the big brother when he is in the company of a woman?"

"No. I am a Sefu man, we are natural explorers, and I am learning these lands just like I am learning your language. I have been exploring this area for several days, and I knew where they were going. I was following them because I was hoping to find something. What was *your* reason?"

"I do not have to answer to you, boy!" Chike barked as he walked past Endesha and intentionally bumped his shoulder with Endesha's. The Sefu man did not yield any movement.

After walking Nsia back to her hut, Amri returned home to see his mother lying in his father's arms crying softly. "Mother, what is wrong?" he asked.

"She is sick, Son," said Zuberi. "She has a fever, and it is getting worse."

"I will get Nsia. She will have something that can help her." Amri rushed out of the hut and ran to get Nsia.

Within seconds Amri arrived at her hut and said, "I need your help, my mother is ill!" Nsia had a confused look on her face, and he remembered that

129

he was talking to her in his language. "I need help," Amri asked desperately in the Kuno tongue.

He took her hand and they ran to Amri's hut. Nsia looked at Furaha and told them she would be back. When she returned, she had two elder women with her, along with Chief Chipo. Nsia asked for the men to leave them for a moment, and they did.

Endesha was returning from his confrontation with Chike when he saw the three Sefu men outside of the hut. "What is going on?" he asked.

"Mother is very ill, Desha. Nsia and some of the Kuno mothers are tending to her," Amri said.

"They asked us to leave for a moment to give them some space so they can help her," said Zuberi.

"Then I will sit here with you until they tell us we can go inside," Endesha proclaimed.

Zuberi was visibly disturbed by his wife's illness. Chief Chipo knew Zuberi did not want to show his emotions in front of their sons and told the boys they would return later.

Amri wanted to know what the Kuno mothers were doing to his mother, and was praying Nsia had something that would make his mother feel as good as she made him feel. Amri could not process what was happening; the only two women he had cared about in his life were in the same room. One he could protect with his hands, the other he could not protect from illness. Feeling helpless, Amri looked to the sky for some form of comfort.

A gentle breeze passed along the sandy ground where the Sefu brothers were sitting. Sensing his brother's concern for their mother, Endesha put his hand on his older brother's shoulder. Amri tapped his brother's left knee twice with his hand as the two brothers exchanged acknowledgement of each other's fear.

"I saw you and Nsia at the waterfall," Endesha said as he looked at the seashell necklace around his brother's neck.

"What did you see?"

"I saw enough." He would never reveal all of what he saw.

"Why were you following us?"

"I was hoping Nsia would take you somewhere I had not seen yet."

"So, you saw her in the waterfall?"

"I saw you stand there like a rooted tree," Endesha replied sarcastically.

The two brothers enjoyed a small moment of laughter that gave them temporary relief from the worry and fear their family was experiencing that dreadful evening.

Long after the moon was visible, Nsia came outside to talk to the Sefu men. Zuberi and Chief Chipo had already returned and joined Amri and Endesha outside. "You can come inside now," Nsia said in the Sefu tongue. The Sefu men looked at Amri and smiled softly as they walked past her into the hut.

"How are you, my wife?" asked Zuberi.

"I am happy to be able to see you, dear husband. That is all that matters."

"Mother, we are glad you are feeling better," Amri said as he and Endesha kissed her cool forehead. "Let Father be with Mother alone, Desha." The two brothers left the hut and found Nsia waiting outside.

"Thank you for your help with our mother," Endesha said in the Kuno tongue.

"I see you have been paying attention to my lessons lately," Nsia said with a big smile. "Let us go for a walk." She took both brothers hands and walked toward the beach.

17

The ocean crashed violently against the Kuno coastline as the Sefu brothers and Nsia sat on top of a large sand dune that shimmered gloriously in the clear moonlight. "What did you and the Kuno mothers use to heal our mother?" Amri asked.

"Your mother had a fever, and we have herbs and potions that we used to help heal her," Nsia said.

"Do you think she is cured?" Endesha asked.

"One of our mothers said your mother cannot be cured, and she will become ill again."

"Is there anything else we can do to heal her?" Amri asked.

"I'm sorry, but there is not," she said. "But, there may be someone that can help us."

"Who? Where do we have to go to find this person? I will go tonight," Amri said.

"No. This person cannot be found in this land," Nsia said.

"I do not understand what are you saying," Endesha replied.

"There is a man that comes to us from there." Nsia pointed to the ocean in front of them. "The man with the floating hut made from trees."

"Who is this man?" Amri asked.

"I do not know him. He comes once a year to see my father, and when he comes, he brings items to trade."

"What does he look like?" Endesha asked.

"He is old and crippled, and his skin is as light as this sand. The secret amongst the villagers is he is my true father, not Olamide," Nsia said while looking down into the sand. "I have heard stories that the man from the ocean laid with my mother, and she had me. When he came back and saw my mother had a girl and not a son, he killed her." She started to cry as she spoke. "My father will never admit what happened. He would never admit he allowed this man to kill his wife and ruin his family, because he valued the things this man gave him in return more," Nsia said as tears now raced down her face.

Amri took Nsia's hand, and she dove into his massive arms, sobbing. As she wept, Amri looked to Endesha for guidance, and his younger brother motioned for Amri to embrace her. He did, and Nsia shrunk further into his chest.

After a few moments, Nsia calmed down and said, "The man from the ocean should be coming soon, and he may have some potions that could cure your mother."

"Let us hope he comes quickly. We do not know how much longer our mother will survive this illness," said Amri.

The burning of exotic herbs filled Chief Olamide's hut with thick, aromatic smoke. The herbs were a personal treat given to him by the visitor from the ocean. Such pleasures were awarded to Olamide in trade for many things. Most frequently, the access to the Kuno women, and occasionally a prisoner from another tribe had been exchanged for medicines, fabrics, spices, and wine. The latter was not shared with anyone; it was Olamide's personal gift from the visitor.

The Kuno chief was sitting in his hut calmly, his legs crossed under him, when Chike asked for permission to speak with him. "Yes, Son. Please join me." Olamide replied. Chike sat down in front of his chief, and tried not to cough from the smoke. "What is on your mind, Chike?"

"I have concerns regarding the Sefu man, Amri," Chike said with a frown on his face.

"What concerns you, my son?"

"I believe he is a threat to us and our people."

"We know very well what he is capable of, and we should not risk our people's safety by having him here."

"I understand your concerns, dear Chike, but I have known the elder Chief Chipo for many years, and the Sefu people are our allies."

"I agree with you. The Sefu people are our allies, but what is preventing Amri from destroying our village on his own? Amri is known to be an out of control menace to anyone he thinks is a threat to him, or what he *believes* is a threat to his people. If something happened to Chief Chipo, or any of his people, would we be able to keep Amri from taking it upon himself to make the Kuno land his?"

"Are you saying *you* could not defeat Amri if he tried to challenge us for our land?" Olamide asked with a stern look on his face.

Surprised by the severity of the question Chike replied, "Of course I would defeat Amri if he challenged you for our land, but I am only *one* person, and what would prevent the rest of his tribe from following him if he desired our land?"

The Kuno chief pondered the words shared with him by his first in command. Olamide truly loved and respected the Sefu Chief Chipo, but Chike had valid concerns, and they weighed heavily on the smoke-altered mind of the Kuno chief. He remained in deep thought long after the smoke from the ocean visitor's herbs stopped burning. Chike did not move either. Both men thinking different things within the mutual silence they shared.

Chike's motivation for the talk with his chief was rooted in jealously. Nsia had never shown him the same level of care and interest as she has with Amri. This seemed to be a greater threat to Chike than an Amri-led Sefu takeover, or anything else that could happen.

As Olamide sat, he pondered the potential for a Sefu uprising. He did not believe, under the leadership of his friend Chipo, such an event would occur, but he could not discount the famously volatile nature of Amri Sefu. "Do you have a plan of action regarding Amri?" Olamide asked Chike.

"I believe the best way for our two tribes to survive together is for Amri to no longer be a threat. I think we should offer him in trade to the man from the ocean."

"Yes, that could be a viable option, but we would have to talk with the Sefu chief. Such an action without his blessing could lead to a painful war on our own land.

We would have to be cautious with our words, and convince the Sefu chief that it is in both groups best interest that Amri should go with the man from the ocean."

"What of his parents and brother?"

"They may be the only people capable of quelling his anger, and the brother may prove to be just as unstable as Amri. Unfortunately, it may be best they travel with Amri.

"When do you expect the man from the ocean to return to us?"

"I expect to see him soon." Chief Olamide stood and raised his hands above his head to stretch. "We cannot discuss this with Chief Chipo until the man from the ocean returns to us. Any possibility of Amri discovering what we have discussed could endanger us all. We must be careful with our actions going forward."

"Agreed. We have a plan," said Chike.

Moments after Nsia left the brothers at the beach, Endesha believed it was the right time to inform Amri of his confrontation with Chike. "I was not the only one watching you earlier today. When I was looking down on you from the hills above the waterfall, I noticed something moving on the cliffs. It was Chike."

"Chike? What was he doing on the cliffs?"

"Watching you more than me. He did not detect me until he had seen enough of you two, and turned around to go back to the village. I was standing behind him."

"What did he say?"

"Nothing important. Chike cannot be trusted. Do you think Nsia was with him before we came to the Kuno land?"

"I don't care. She wants to be with me now," Amri replied with a renewed sense of purpose.

"You should be careful, Brother. Chike has the Kuno chief's ear, and that could be a problem for our tribe."

"You are right. We are in their land, and cannot afford to have any problems with the Kuno people. We have nowhere else to go."

"So, what do we do?"

"Nothing." Amri stood and looked toward the Kuno village behind them. "We do nothing."

"Let us go check on Mother," Endesha said.

"Yes. Let us go home," Amri replied.

The Sefu brothers became more guarded with their actions. Amri continued to learn how to speak the Kuno language, and Endesha continued learning more about the ocean and the Kuno lands. Chike kept his distance from the brothers, and, unfortunately, Furaha was not getting any better. If she were going to survive, she would need the potions from the visitor from the ocean.

## 18

Weeks went by, and the Sefu people were thriving in their new territory. Chief Olamide had offered to make them honorary Kuno, which was graciously denied by the elder Sefu chief. The two tribal leaders proved that with much grace and diplomacy the two tribes could blend together and thrive in the same space. The Kuno people were experts in crafting and fishing, and the Sefu's strengths were in tracking and hunting; the two tribes collaborated on many things and shared thoughts on how to retain their own unique identities while working together to ensure their mutual success. A success that could be lost in an instant if Amri Sefu had his way.

During the evenings, after everyone went to asleep, Amri would fantasize about the ways he could kill Chike. He replayed the special moments he had shared with Nsia in the water, and when he thought about how Chike had been above the two of them watching, it filled Amri's mind with rage, glorious rage.

It had been almost a year since Amri had killed the Ema's chief, and he delighted in the notion that he had another foe standing in his way. But this time he could not act on his desires. He would not willingly destroy or kill without need or cause. He had to remember his people were now a part of a new tribe, and his actions could disrupt all of the progress the two tribes had made.

With this conclusion being realized, Amri became even more upset, more rage-filled because now he knew he could not act on his desire to destroy Chike.

For the first time, Amri had to consider his actions and the consequences that would be shared not only by him, but his people as well.

Aggravated and annoyed, Amri decided to seek the only thing that could quell his intense anger—Nsia's beautiful heart, long flowing hair, and comforting bosom. He left his hut to find her.

Within moments, he was outside of her hut, and when he gently tapped the outer wall, she came out to see who was there. "Oh, hello Amri. It is you."

"I'm sorry to wake you, but I need to speak with you."

"What is wrong? You look like something is bothering you."

"Can we go to the water to talk?"

"Of course, we can."

As they took the short walk to the Kuno coastline, Amri looked around, suspicious that Chike was lurking in the beachside darkness.

When they arrived at their favorite sand dune, the two sat, and Nsia noticed Amri's face showed distress. "What is troubling you Amri?" she asked.

"Tell me about Chike. What is he to you?"

"Chike is supposed to be like a brother to me, but he is not." She started. "Chike's mother is one of my father's wives.

When he was much younger, my father learned he was not his son, and when he confronted Chike's mother, she struck him across his face.

When the man from the ocean came, my father sent Chike's mother and her lover away with him, and since then, he has been raising Chike like he was his own son." Nsia looked at Amri for a visible reaction.

"So, you are not allowed to be together?" he asked.

"If my father desired it, then yes, but my father believes Chike's blood is cursed with his father's seed, and he forbids Chike from being with any of his children."

"Now I understand."

"What do you mean, Amri?"

"The other day at the waterfall, Endesha caught Chike watching us from above in the hills."

"What did Endesha say?…And why was he at the waterfall at the same time we were?" Nsia's look of surprise turned into a curious frown.

"He was trying to see where you were taking me. He was hoping to learn of a new place to explore, and that is when he found Chike looking down on us."

"Why are you so troubled about what Chike was doing at the waterfall?" She looked at him with a glowing smile. "Are you looking for a fight or protecting what you think belongs to you *mighty Sefu warrior?*"

"If we were in my village, I would tell you immediately that I am *always* looking for a fight. But here, in this place, this village—I find myself only thinking about you."

Amri was looking out onto the moonlit ocean, then laid on his back and turned his face toward the sky. Nsia placed her head on his scarred chest and gazed at him adoringly.

That night, the wind moved in and out mimicking the movements of the waves crashing below, a perfect symphony of nature that enticed the young lovers to fall asleep.

The crashing waves of the previous night had softened as the sun eased over the coastal horizon. Nsia slowly opened her eyes, and as she looked toward her and Amri's feet, she saw a frightening sight afar off in the ocean.

It was a ship with open sails heading toward the Kuno coastline. She could tell, given its distance, it would arrive by early afternoon. "Get up, Amri! We must go!" Nsia shook him awake.

"What? What is going on?" he asked.

"Look to the water. He is coming." She pointed at the ship in the distance. Nsia attempted to run toward the Kuno village to alert her father and noticed Amri did not follow her. He continued to look at the ship.

He could not seem to look away—amazed that something could float on water like that. Remembering he had been told the man from the ocean could have what his mother needed to improve her health, he joined Nsia, and set off to inform his family that the ship would soon arrive.

Nsia entered her father's hut, and tried to capture her breath before saying, "Father, the man from the ocean is coming. I can see his boat from the coast!"

"Excellent! I will inform the elders and the tribal leaders to prepare a great feast for our returning guest! Chike!" Olamide bellowed.

Chike swiftly entered the hut. "Yes Chief?"

"It is time to talk with Chief Chipo about our concerns. But first, go to the beach. My daughter believes the man from the sea will be here by early afternoon—see if she is correct in her prediction."

Amri ran into Endesha as he made his way into their hut. "Where have you been Amri?" he asked with a silly look on his face.

"This is not the time, Desha," Amri barked. He went over to his where his mother was lying down to rest. "How is she today?" he asked his father.

"She is not feeling well, Son. She is becoming weaker as the days go by," Zuberi said while caressing his wife's face gently.

"Remember the man with potions and herbs that the Kuno spoke of?"

"Yes, I do."

"His ship is almost here. You can see it in the distance from the beach. Maybe he has a potion that can heal Mother," Amri said while trying to figure out how to get the Kuno Chief Olamide's assistance for his ailing mother.

Chike returned to Chief Olamide after investigating Nsia's claim that the man from the ocean was returning. "Yes. It is him, and I agree he will arrive early in the afternoon, as you were told."

"Wonderful. Alert the village mothers to prepare a glorious meal for our visitor, and send for our offerings to him."

"Offerings? Oh, you are speaking of the prisoners we have in the woods?"

"Yes. Have them cleaned and presentable for our guest. I am hoping they will get us something nice from him in return," Olamide said with a great

143

smile on his face. "We must go and talk with Chief Chipo to discuss the other offering for our returning guest."

"Do you foresee any problems with the Sefu chief?"

"I am not sure, but we must go see him now," Olamide said as he looked in direction of the beach.

Chief Chipo was sitting on the sandy ground in front of his hut, amused by all of the activity within the village. The Kuno people were moving hastily from one point to another. He did not stop anyone to ask what was going on, he was more interested in watching their hustle. Moments later, Chief Olamide, Chike, and two other Kuno leaders arrived at the elder Sefu chief's hut. "May we talk to you...alone, old friend?" Olamide asked.

"Of course. Let us go inside," Chipo replied. The men entered, and sat in a large circle.

Chief Olamide sat directly across from Chief Chipo, and the Sefu elder could feel in his spirit, something was wrong. "What troubles you and your people today, old friend?" he asked.

"We have a visitor coming today. A man from a faraway land. He brings many items with him for trade; food, potions, medicines, and weapons. In return, we trade with him our food, women, and our prisoners."

"Prisoners?"

"Yes. I have prisoners from wars fought with other tribes deep in our woods."

"Then why are you here talking to me about this visitor? My people do not have anything to offer." Chief Chipo wondered, with a suspicious tone in his voice.

After a short pause, Chief Olamide gathered his words and spoke very softly with emboldened confidence. "You do have something to offer our visitor, old friend." He cleared his throat and continued, "We believe that Amri is a danger to our people. We know the story of his fury in the Ema village, and what happens to those who oppose him. We believe he could be a threat to our people. His ability to kill at will with the level of destruction he is known for is something we *cannot* allow on Kuno land." Olamide looked the elder Sefu chief directly in his eyes.

"Amri would never do such a thing. I would never allow it." There was a stern confidence in his voice.

"My friend, we are old, and Amri is very young. If you were not with us, who would be able to calm the storm he brings when his fury is directed at my people?"

"The boy comes from a good family, and he has a good heart. Yes, he is a warrior, but he would not slay the innocent, nor would he jeopardize his people here on Kuno land."

"I believe you, dear friend, but the consequences of taking your word on this matter could be my people's safety. I welcomed your entire tribe into our land, and in order for your people to thrive you must take what I am proposing into consideration."

"What you are proposing is to send Amri away from here when he was the one person that protected us from danger, ensured we made it out of our village safely, and led us here to the Kuno land? That is the reward you believe he should have?"

Chief Chipo's brow was heavily furled on his wrinkled face. "He has not given you any reason to believe he is a threat. He has only been an asset to your tribe because he not only protects us, but your people as well."

Suddenly, Chief Chipo started to laugh uncontrollably. "What is amusing to you?" Chief Olamide asked.

"I would not want to be you when you *ask* him to go with your visitor," he replied with a glorious laugh.

"This is why we are here, dear friend. I need you to help me talk to him; explain to him why he must go with the visitor."

"What if he refuses? What if he wants to stay here with us?"

"I'm afraid to tell you dear friend, but if he refuses, the Sefu people cannot stay on Kuno land. Do not allow one man to make your people perish as they wander across the sands beyond our land."

Chief Chipo's laughter was quieted by the seriousness of the situation presented to him. He knew his good friend was serious, and was also aware that his threat to send the Sefu people into the sandy wastelands was said with veracity. Thoughts about how to tell Amri flooded Chief Chipo's mind.

Chief Olamide could see that his dear friend was in duress and told him, "I will leave you now, as we have more arrangements to make before our visitor joins us."

"Yes, that would be good," Chipo replied. As Olamide and his group left the hut, a violent crack of thunder sounded in the sky. Chief Chipo stood, made his way slowly to the mouth of the hut, and looked toward the western sky. He could see a storm approaching from behind the ocean horizon.

A strong gust of wind whipped the sand throughout the village as if the land was preparing for the fury Amri would feel once he was told the news of his forced departure.

***

Several miles off the coast of the Kuno village, the ship called *The Kingmaker* dropped its mighty anchor as her crew prepared to depart for land.

The ship's captain, James Burton, was filled with anxiety. His crew was weary after their seven-month trek down the coasts of France, Spain, and northern Africa. Captain Burton surveyed the Kuno land in the distance, and commanded his crew, "Prepare the skiffs. We must depart for land before this bloody storm catches us from the west."

"Aye captain," the crew replied.

"Load the supplies into the skiffs and bring plenty of wine. Welcome to paradise!" He let out a hearty laugh as his crew cheered with lustful enthusiasm.

The sky was darkening quickly as Captain Burton and his crew climbed down into four medium-sized skiffs. The men started to row vigorously through the swelling water as the storm seemed to chase them to the Kuno shores. "Row like your bloody life depends on it! These waters are turning us away from the coast, row harder!" commanded the captain.

Back in the Kuno village, Chike could see the skiffs approaching the beach, so he sent one of his aids to alert Chief Olamide that the visitors would be arriving soon. Most of the villagers had joined Chike on the beach, and watched as their small boats battled the violently churning waters.

The sky erupted with dazzling bolts of lightning that frightened the young children. Darkness covered the Kuno village and rain started to fall as the wind whipped violently across the beach, sending sand and salty water into the onlooker's eyes.

As the men of The Kingmaker approached the beach, the waters became more turbulent—as if the land did not want Captain James Burton and his crew to make shore. The sky continued its fantastic display of lightning, and the accompanying thunder was so loud it shook the sandy ground the Kuno people were standing on. Amri and his family could see the men struggling to row themselves ashore. "Look at them, they are battling the water as if they are being pushed away from us," said Zuberi.

"I don't know if this is what I wanted for Mother," Amri said as he looked at the sandy-colored men in the boats Nsia described earlier.

The storming waves crested and crashed into the skiffs. "Brace yourselves men!" commanded Captain Burton. The boats became temporarily airborne amongst the waves. As the men approached the beach, a strong wave rushed the side of one of the boats forcing the men overboard. Another wave drove the men against the bottom of the boat, knocking two of them unconscious.

The crew of The Kingmaker finally made it to shore, and the sky cracked with mighty clap of thunder as James Burton and his crew stumbled onto the sandy beach.

A torrent of rain welcomed the visitors as they gathered their injured men and collected the skiffs to bring them ashore. A strong yell could be heard from the distance as the men lumbered their way toward the Kuno village.

Suddenly, the sounds of drums pounding rhythmically could be heard along with sounds of women and men singing.

Chief Olamide was giving Captain James a hero's welcome. However, the sky was not willing to comply with the Kuno people's welcome.

Sheets of rain were falling as the captain and his crew walked up to the Kuno chief. "Hello," said Burton in the Kuno tongue.

"He-llo," Chief Olamide replied in the language of the captain and his crew. "Welcome. We have been expecting you for many months. Come rest yourselves in our village." He motioned the men to follow him.

"What did he just say?" asked one of The Kingmaker crewmen.

"I do not know. Just smile, and do what the captain does," replied a shipmate.

The rain from above had not extinguished the raging fire at the center of the Kuno village, and the storm was waning. The Kuno leadership ensured their guests were comfortable and entertained.

Small drums and singing could be heard as the men shared the visitor's rum and laughed heartily. The rum was Chief Olamide's favorite, and he drank sparingly.

He had also poured a portion of what he was given by Captain Burton into a small container to be consumed in private.

The men were sitting in the largest of huts in the village. It was open on three sides, with a high roof, and the tribeswomen had lain fresh palm leaves on the ground.

Olamide commanded all of the daughters he felt were of age to join the group of men and sit along the perimeter of the hut. He wanted James and his crew to see the wealth of flesh the Kuno people had to offer. The men stared at the half-dressed, bronze-skinned Kuno women with lustful hunger in their eyes.

Their supple breasts and attractive faces were a pleasant sight after such a long voyage—a welcomed change from the coarse beards and sun-stricken skin the men of The Kingmaker were used to seeing. After reviewing the display of young women for the crew of The Kingmaker, Chief Olamide noticed that Nsia was not present, he discreetly asked Chike to find her. "Nsia is not here. I wanted to introduce her to our visitor. Go find her for me." Chike nodded and left to search for Nsia.

In the distance, Endesha and Amri could also see something was missing from the display of flesh Olamide was showing his guests. "Amri, where is Nsia?" Endesha asked.

"I do not know. She ran away when she saw the boat in the distance this morning, and I have not seen her since," Amri said with a puzzled look on his face.

"You should find her, Amri. I believe she needs you," Furaha said.

"Mother, you are weak, and I want to be here with you," Amri replied.

"No. Be with Nsia. She would not have left you if she felt safe here. Something is wrong. Go find her," Furaha commanded.

"Ok, Mother. I will go." He conceded.

"Desha, stay with our parents. I will return once I find Nsia and make sure she is all right.

"I will, Brother."

Amri set off to find Nsia, first stopping by her hut to see if she was there. No luck. He took a moment to think of a place where Nsia would go if she was frightened. He then remembered the special place in the woods. So he set off into the nearby wilderness, fully aware that his vision would be challenged so late in the evening. Thankfully the storm had passed.

## 19

The sky cleared as the storm that arrived with Captain Burton left the Kuno land. The bright moonlight was a welcomed aid in Amri's search for Nsia. He was not sure where she was within the woods, but hoped she was at the waterfall where she had taken him before.

Amri did not have much trouble retracing his steps as he found things that reminded him of the path Nsia had taken to get to her special place. Amri's bare feet avoided every imperfection he could remember in the terrain. After a few minutes of walking, he heard the rushing water in the distance. Not wanting to alarm her, he did not call out to her. Instead, he decided to be still, and set himself on one knee to take in what the land was giving him. It was time to listen. Amri calmed his breathing, and steadied his heartbeat. He closed his eyes and breathed quietly—smoke—Amri could faintly smell smoke. Then he heard a small crack to his right. Something was moving, and all of these clues were coming from the same direction—Amri quickly open his eyes. He knew where to go, and like a swift gazelle, he ran through the woods toward where he thought the sounds were coming from.

Within moments he was behind a shadowed figure that looked to be collecting sticks from the ground. With a sigh of relief, he found it was Nsia. She was cold, and attempting to restart the small fire that had been doused by the storm. Instead of approaching her, Amri decided to remain in the shadows, taking too much delight in his hunt for her.

He watched her as she searched for sticks and twigs dry enough to light her fire, and once she had enough, she turned to go in the other direction and Amri casually said, "Do you always play with sticks in the dark?" Nsia jumped off the ground, dropping all of the items in her arms, trying not to scream.

"Amri!" Nsia exclaimed in a violent whisper. She hit his massive chest with her hand, then tenderly embraced him.

"Where were you going just now?" He laughed.

"I was going to a cave near the waterfall. I had a fire, but it went out when that storm came earlier." She smiled at him.

Amri collected sticks, and said, "Show me."

The cave Nsia was hiding in was more like a small alcove. It was large enough for two people, but it left her exposed to the elements. She was cold, wet, and hungry, and was very glad to see Amri. He gave her some fruits from the satchel he had tied across his shoulder. "Eat. I will be back with some things to help us stay warm," Amri said. He left her to collect several items for the night.

Soon after, Amri returned with a large tree trunk. When he dropped it, it made a solid thump on the ground. "What is that for?" asked Nsia.

"My Uncle Coffa taught me how to survive with what the land gives you. This land has much for us to use tonight." Amri quickly went to work as Nsia gazed at him adoringly. First on his list was to get the fire started. He used his large, strong hands to pry open the old tree trunk. He then tore off the bark and peeled away the stringy fibers to fuel the fire. Amri, using the stones Nsia had found, quickly struck them together to light the fibers, and before long, there was a fire large enough for both of them.

Once satisfied, he decided to place the two large pieces of wood along the perimeter of the alcove, shielding them slightly from the cool air.

Next on Amri's list was to make Nsia comfortable. He went to his stack of supplies that he gathered earlier, and before he set some large palm leaves down on the ground he used his hands to smooth the land under them. "You can sit here," he said. Swelling with gratitude, Nsia complied.

Pleased with his work, Amri laid down on his back and exhaled deeply. Nsia, exhausted from the day's events, quickly coated Amri's body with her own, seeking warmth and safety. He placed the remaining palm leaves over them, and they slept comfortably through the night.

Back in the Kuno village, Chief Chipo had not been invited to greet Captain Burton and the sailors of The Kingmaker. Instead, the elder Sefu chief decided to visit his dearest friends after observing Amri venture into the forest moments earlier. As the elder Sefu chief slowly approached, Endesha noticed his presence, and immediately assisted the elder leader toward his parents. "May I have a word with all of you?" Chipo asked politely.

"Of course, Chief Chipo. We can go inside and leave Chief Olamide to his friends over there." Zuberi said as he looked at the gathering of people across the Kuno village. The group sat down, and Chipo noticed Furaha did not look like herself. "Are you well, dear Furaha?"

"No, I have not been feeling well lately, but I will be all right."

"Good. I have something important I need to discuss with you all."

"Amri is not here," Endesha said quickly.

"I know Endesha. I saw him go into the forest earlier," Chipo replied. "Which is good because I have to talk to all of you about him."

"What about Amri must be discussed?" asked Zuberi.

Chief Chipo took a deep breath and recalled some of the bravery he had suppressed in his old age, and said, "Amri must go with Olamide's visitor."

A few moments passed as the three family members processed what they had been told. "That will never happen!" Zuberi replied.

Chief Chipo had braced himself for the reaction, and had more to tell, but he wanted to give the family a chance to receive his words before he moved on.

"*Why* would Olamide want Amri to go with his visitor?" Furaha asked with renewed energy.

"He believes Amri is a threat to the Kuno people."

"How can Amri be a threat to his people? He has shown nothing but true leadership since we have been here," Zuberi said.

"I understand how you feel, and I told Chief Olamide the same words, but he believes Amri's reputation and temper are something we cannot control."

"I know my child, and he is under control. At least, I believe he is under control," Zuberi replied.

"That right there, that small portion of doubt, is the only reason I continued to listen to Olamide today. Zuberi, we both know what your son is capable of, and if something happened to any of us, who would be able to stop him?"

"Amri is a good man, and he knows who his enemy is, and who is not," Furaha said.

"Yes, I know this, but Olamide insists Amri leaves."

"What if Amri refuses?" Endesha asked.

"He cannot."

"Why could he not refuse the chief?" Zuberi asked.

Chipo put his right hand over his mouth, his eyes welled with tears, and he started to cry uncontrollably. His gray hair and wrinkled skin shook as he tried to control his emotions. Chipo looked his good friend in the eye, and said, "If Amri refuses, all of our people will be sent into the eastern sands where we will all surely die."

"This is really what he told you?" Endesha asked, with a newly discovered bravado in his voice. "What do you think he is going to do once he finds out what they want to do to him? He is not going to accept this. I know him, he is my brother!"

"There is more, Endesha," said Zuberi quietly.

"What do you mean, Father?"

"Think about it. Who would be able to stop Amri from destroying this place?" Zuberi replied.

Endesha took a moment, and said, "*We* are supposed to tell Amri he must go?"

Furaha looked at her husband, and as tears started to slide down her cheeks said, "Endesha, *we* will have to go with Amri as well. That is the only way he will not attack the Kuno people and their visitor."

"It is the only way for our people to survive," Zuberi said.

156

Endesha's burgeoning intelligence could not come up with a solution to the problem in front of him. He tried to think of every possible way to solve the issue, yet he could not see any other way. Frustrated with the situation, he said, "We are not going to leave with the visitor. Amri and I will defeat him, his crew, and all of the Kuno people by ourselves!"

"No, Son. You cannot think that way," Zuberi warned.

"The Kuno people have always been a great ally to the Sefu people, and it would be dishonorable to start a war on their land after they have been so kind to us," said Chipo.

"Endesha, this is something we must do together," Zuberi said. "We cannot put our people's lives at risk, and leaving with Amri is best for *all* of us."

"What about Mother? How can she go with us? Where would the visitor take us?" Endesha asked.

"Our job would be to ensure Amri complied with the visitor's commands, Son," Furaha said.

"If Amri did not comply we will be used as a way to control him," Zuberi said softly.

"I am so sorry to tell you this," Chipo said as his body trembled with fear and sadness.

Chipo attempted to approach the family on his knees with his arms open wide, hoping for an embrace with understanding and love returned to him. Endesha pushed his arm aside and left the hut. Furaha reached out to her youngest son, but he walked away.

"Let him go, my love," Zuberi said as he held his old friend and mentor with one arm, and his weakening wife with the other.

The next day, the Kuno people woke to sounds of glorious laughter as James Burton exited his hut nude and pleased with himself. He stumbled to the beach and into the ocean, splashing his face with the cold salt water. "Ah, paradise indeed!" James said to himself. Feeling refreshed, he made his way back to the coastal village, and to dress himself for the day.

Captain Burton was in awe of the beauty the sunny beachfront village had to offer. He then looked down at the nude Kuno women he inefficiently entertained the previous night and thought to himself, *Is this place heaven?*

Peter, one of Burton's men approached, and asked, "What would you like for us to do with The Kingmaker's supplies Captain?"

"Aye, bring them to me, and I will exchange them for supplies for our return trip," Burton replied.

"Captain, what are we taking back with us?" Peter asked.

"As much as we can Master Peter. Send word to The Kingmaker to prepare to depart in a few days. They should have collected much water with last night's rain, and we will need it for our long trip home."

"Home, sir?" Peter asked.

"Aye. It is time for The Kingmaker to return to her home in England."

Zuberi awakened with much sadness in his heart. Endesha was sitting at the huts entrance. "Are you scared, my son?" Zuberi asked.

"No, Father. I am not," he said confidently. "We are not thinking about the other person that will be affected by us being sent away with the visitor."

"Who else will be affected son?" Furaha asked softly, removing the night's sleep from her eyes.

"Nsia. She is the only woman Amri has ever loved—other than you, Mother. Leaving her will tear him apart, and I feel it will do the same to her."

"He feels that strongly for her? How do you know, Desha?" Zuberi asked.

"I know him well, he is my brother. Nsia is the reason why I am not sure he will agree to any of this madness."

"Where *is* Amri?" Furaha asked.

"I know where he is. We should allow them to be together while they can," Endesha said.

"How could he find her in the dark and during a storm?" Furaha asked.

"He found her easily, I am sure. Nothing could keep him from her. At least, that is what I used to believe," Endesha said with finality.

The fire lost its warmth hours before Nsia and Amri woke from their long night together.

Amri had woke hours before Nsia stirred from her blissful slumber. He looked at her and began to laugh, softly at first, then he couldn't help himself and his laugh grew heartily louder. "What is so funny?" she asked.

"If you could see your hair, you would be laughing too."

"What is wrong with my hair?"

"It is all over both of us. How do you think we stayed so warm last night?" He picked up a section of the straight, black hair that covered Nsia's head, and a portion of his chest.

"How long have you been awake?"

"I've been up for a while now."

"I did not feel you move."

"I tried not to, so I would not wake you."

"How nice of you."

"I have never been called nice before." Nsia adjusted her position, and rested her head on her elbow. She pushed her hair back over her head, looked at her lover, and said, "Why are you so nice to me?"

"You are the first person that I met that was not scared of me," Amri replied.

"Why do I not scare you? You said you heard stories of my battles before?"

"Yes. But after meeting you, I learned that you are more than a warrior."

"You said I was not a monster many moons ago. Do you still believe that?"

Nsia gently traced her fingers across the many scars on Amri's chest, and replied, "You are more than a warrior or a monster.

You are gentle with me when you are brutal to others. You move quickly when you are threatened, but you move very slowly with me. How can I be scared of you when you are changing your behavior for me?"

"When I am with you I do not feel the pain and the burden of being me," Amri said. "I forget about the anger, I forget what *my* world is when I am with you. That brings me much peace, and it shows because I can rest when I am with you."

Amri and Nsia ventured into the woods to collect food and wood for the fire as the daylight grew stronger by the minute. Once they had eaten, the two young lovers took a swim in the small lagoon at the bottom of the waterfall.

Amri's heart was defenseless against the onslaught of love from Nsia, and as strong as his will was on the battlefield, he willingly gave his feelings away to the girl he met on the beach. In Amri's mind he wondered if he could put aside his lust for battle and transform those thoughts into a desire for love in the new land he brought his people to.

The day could not have been more perfect for Amri. He was with a woman that loved him in a way he could not even comprehend. He was so involved with Nsia he had not though once about his ailing mother or his younger brother. For a brief moment that day, Amri Sefu was just a man—normal on the inside and out. His size, strength, and past had no relevance with Nsia.

She did not care how many men Amri killed, nor was she concerned with what harm he could do to her. She just wanted to be with him.

When they were done in the water, they realized they were hungry once again, and went foraging within the shady forest.

Nsia found some fruit she was sure her warrior man had never eaten before. "You are going to like this." She took a small bite of the dark berry that only grew in the area, and placed the other portion in Amri's mouth. "Well?" Nsia asked.

"That was good. More please."

"Sit down. I found enough for you, and maybe a few for me if you don't eat them all," she said with a smile on her face. Amri complied and sat down to enjoy the late lunch.

While the couple ate, the *Black Lion* playfully bounced a berry off Nsia's head—making him laugh gloriously. Nsia smiled, and joined in the laughter. She tried to push Amri over in retaliation, only to find herself almost on her side due to Amri not being easily moved.

"You almost tipped yourself!" He laughed.

"I am stronger than you think!"

"Not strong enough to move me." He chuckled.

Amri laid down on his back and closed his eyes. He took in a deep breath of fresh air, enjoying all of the smells and sounds he could hear.

Suddenly, Nsia pounced on his torso, which caused him to cough violently. "I told you I am strong!"

"You are the only person that has ever caught me off guard."

"That means I am special?"

"No. It means you are lucky." He smiled genuinely at her, as she laid on his chest. "I could live in these woods with you forever."

"No, you cannot. You have a little brother that needs you and a family that loves you."

"He is not so little anymore. He is changing, and is no longer looking to me for protection. He is going to be a mighty warrior in his own right one day."

"He will always need his big brother. I think we should get back to the village soon. I am sure they are looking for us."

"Let them wait for us. We will return when we are ready."

Four days later in the Kuno village, Captain Burton was thrilled to see Chief Olamide's offerings and for trade. He had presented: six enemy prisoners, four young Kuno women, several large baskets of fruits and berries, and multiple pounds off dried and salted fish. In return, Olamide wanted as much rum as the crew of The Kingmaker could provide, along with their knives and fine fabrics. "Aye, this is a mighty fair exchange here boys," said the captain, knowing his take was greater than the half-dressed tribal leader. "We must take our lot to The Kingmaker and prepare to depart by first light. No need to stay here any longer. We need to use this good fortune to carry us home quickly."

"Aye, Captain," the crewmen said as they loaded the skiffs.

That evening, Amri and Nsia arrived back in the village, and as they walked across the village center, Captain Burton could not help but notice the massive Sefu man. "Aye, look at that ghastly Moor right there! Hey, you. Come here!" Nsia tried to pull Amri's hand to continue walking, but Amri was still. "I want him to come with me," Burton said to Olamide.

"Yes, yes. Of course," Olamide said while motioning Amri to come their direction.

In the distance, someone yelled loudly in the Sefu language, "Tell, Zuberi and Furaha he wants to take Amri!"

Endesha heard this and rushed to the center of the village. "Amri, do not go to him! He wants to take us away from here!"

"Away from here?" Amri repeated. "We are not leaving this place." He looked to Nsia and saw tears beginning to moisten her face. Elder Chipo walked up to Amri and said, "Talk to your father, my son."

Captain Burton had been calling for Amri to come toward him for some time with no response. "Hey, does your giant Moor have a problem with hearing? Bring him to me," he ordered his crew. Sensing their inevitable death, Olamide motioned the men to stop and ordered the six prisoners to escort Amri to the captain.

Amri's family was talking to him, trying to explain what was going on and why they had to leave. They explained to him how their entire tribe would perish if he did not comply. They also told Amri that chief Olamide was worried he would ravage the entire Kuno village. None of what his family said to him mattered. All he knew was at that moment in his life—a life complete and filled with happiness and love—was being taken away from him.

As Amri tried to understand what was happening, he looked to Captain Burton in the distance to his right. He saw the six men coming toward him in a threatening manner, and his eyes closed slightly.

Nsia could see the man she loved quickly retreat inside of his own skin, and without knowing, she witnessed the rebirth of the *Black Lion* right before her eyes. Amri had his target, Captain Burton, but the six men in front of him would need to be dealt with first.

The first man to reach him tried to grab hold of Amri's right arm. He jerked his hand quickly toward his body, and used his left hand to grab hold of the prisoner's neck. Lifting him into the air, then violently slammed the prisoner's head backward into the sand, breaking his left leg at the same time.

Amri reset his footing in the sand and struck another prisoner in the face with his right hand, rendering him unconscious.

The next two prisoners came at him from either side, and tried to grab hold of Amri's arms. With little effort, he threw one man off to the side, and in full-rage, tore an ear off of the other. Nsia looked on horrified. She had never heard such screams of pain.

A prisoner successfully struck Amri in the face, but this only made him more upset. He flipped him over his shoulder, bent to pick up a large rock, and pummeled the prisoner's face with it. Amri then turned to the one-eared prisoner, yelling in pain, and threw the rock at the man, killing him instantly.

Furaha screamed, "No! Amri stop. Stop before you are the death of our people!"

His mother's words never made it to his ears. Deaf with glorious rage, only two more prisoners stood between him Captain Burton. One very large, impressively built man, and one much smaller that was too frightened to move from his position. The large prisoner approached Amri, slapping his chest violently with both hands, left first, then right. Amri started to walk toward the man, looking through him to his goal.

As he approached the large man, he struck him with a mighty backhand blow to the chin so powerful it lifted the large man off his feet.

The prisoner fell backward onto the sandy ground, started shaking violently and foaming at the mouth.

Amri was almost within range to attack the man from the ocean, when he heard the love of his existence scream, "No! They will kill me! They will kill me, Amri." He stopped mid-stride and turned to see Chike and his Kuno warriors holding spears to Nsia and his family's throats.

## 20

"Enough!" Chief Olamide yelled. "Do you see now, Chipo, why we cannot have such a beast living within our village? Look at the ease in which he delivers death. It is as if it is pleasurable to him."

"Let his family go. They will ensure Amri does not kill again," said Chipo.

Olamide looked at Amri breathing heavily and staring at Captain Burton with purpose. The captain and his crew tried to maintain their masculinity, but Olamide could see yellow fear cascading down the legs of some of Burton's crewmen. "Father!" Nsia yelled. Chief Olamide motioned Chike to let her go. She immediately ran to Amri, but he did not respond to her—the man she loved was not present.

In his absence was the monster everyone knew he was. The *Black Lion* stood before her now, the swift, efficient killer of five men. "Amri, listen to me. You must stop! Your people will perish if you do not stop fighting," Nsia begged him. He still did not respond to her.

The Kuno men brought Zuberi, Furaha, and Endesha to stand beside him. "I am so sorry, Amri," Furaha said, sensing the pain Amri was going to feel leaving his Nsia.

"This is the only way our people can survive, my son," Zuberi said while holding Endesha's arm for support.

Amri looked at Endesha and could see in his eyes the same rage that swelled within him.

Seeing this, Amri understood he could not fight any more for his family and his tribe's sake. "I will not resist anymore," he told Chief Olamide.

"Good. Too much blood has already been spilt this evening, and as promised, your people will continue to live in peace with us," Olamide said as he faced the village and the crew of The Kingmaker.

"Steady men," Captain Burton ordered.

"What is going on with the big one? I thought he was about to tear our heads off, sir," said one of The Kingmaker's crewmen.

"Aye, I thought he was too for a moment there. Put down your swords men. It looks like he is coming willingly," the captain ordered.

"We need to gather our things from our hut. That is the least you could do for us Olamide," Zuberi bellowed.

"Be with your people tonight. In the morning, you will gather your belongings and leave with the visitors," Olamide commanded.

The mood was somber in the Sefu portion of the Kuno village as the tribe gathered around the hut of Zuberi and Furaha's family. Many people were crying, devastated at the horrific sacrifice their fellow kinsmen were making. They offered the family clothing, and other items to take with them, but Zuberi refused it all.

He only wanted to take the things he would need to tell his story; his tools to carve and some other items he wanted to share with his sons as they matured. As the Sefu people sang the songs of their village, Zuberi wrapped his possessions delicately in fabric and strung rope around it so it could be worn across his shoulder.

Furaha could not take the stress of the day, and she laid in her bed watching her family prepare for a trip she dreaded accompanying them on. Thoughts of her family and their path to this point crossed her mind.

She wondered if they would have been better off if they'd stayed to fight the Ema. Maybe they would still be in their village. Such thoughts stole the remaining energy she had, and Furaha willingly surrendered to her body's request for sleep.

Endesha would not find any comfort in sleeping on his final night on Kuno land. His spirit was filled with a rage. He desperately wanted the chance to fight for his family's freedom, but he knew he could not. So, he decided to sit on the sandy ground and wait for the sun to rise in the morning.

Amri was not inclined to sleep either. He was sitting in the hut watching his ailing mother sleep when Nsia came to him, and sat at his side. "Are you worried about her?" she asked Amri.

"Yes, I am," he replied.

Nsia noticed he had a swollen hand, took it in her own, and held it close to her heart. "I am so sorry, Amri. I did not know my father would do this to you and your people," Nsia said softly.

"It is not your fault, Nsia. Do not blame yourself."

The scowl on Amri's face did not change. This confirmed Nsia's fears that she would never see the Amri Sefu from the woods ever again.

However, Nsia did not give up on her attempts to reach her warrior lover. She continued to hold his hand and caress his shoulders. Deep in his spirit Amri could feel Nsia's love. But his hate for her father and James Burton overpowered his newly exposed inner emotions. Like his younger brother, Amri decided to welcome the sun awake and with pride.

"What the bloody hell was that?" Captain Burton yelled as he paced the sandy ground near the center of the village.

Chief Olamide walked over to the captain and said, "The big one, I want more."

"More of what?"

Chief Olamide pointed to the skiffs down by the water's edge, then looked back at Burton.

"You want a boat? For the big one? That is a fair trade, so yes. You have a deal." The two men shook hands awkwardly, and Burton left to meet his men at the beach. As he approached, he laughed loudly to himself. "Men, we have to make a change to our plans. I figure we can get a great bounty for the big Moor back at port. We will sail for Lisbon in the morning. If we don't get what we want in Portugal, we will sail home to Brixham. I know he will command many pounds back home. Listen men, that beast is of no value to us dead. He must not be harmed. We will use his family as a means to control him. Do you understand my orders men? Do not hurt my big Moor!"

"Aye, Captain!" replied the crew.

The next day, the sun did not show itself, and the sky was gray again. Amri carried a weakened Furaha to the beach, and Zuberi leaned on Endesha's broad shoulder.

The Sefu people followed them, still singing their tribal songs as their former chief wept uncontrollably. Nsia ran from her father's side to be with her lover one last time. She kissed Furaha on her forehead and hugged Endesha and his father. Lastly, she looked at Amri and could not stop her tears from flowing. "You are not a monster, my love.

You are my wind, my shield, my Black Lion," Nsia said. With his mother still in his arms, Amri kneeled down so Nsia could embrace him. She kissed his emotionless face one last time and rubbed the scars on his face one last time. For a split second, Nsia thought she saw a glimpse of sadness in Amri's eyes, but he only looked at her, then to her father, Olamide.

As Amri stood he told Nsia, "One day, I will come back for you, and I will wash the land with the blood of anyone that comes before me."

Thunder boomed in the distance as the Sefu family continued their walk toward Captain Burton and his men.

Nsia went to her knees as tears fell so violently she could not see Amri and his family board the skiff or the crew of The Kingmaker push off and row out to sea. Amri did not take his eyes off of Nsia as the waves rocked and heaved the skiff as they headed toward The Kingmaker awaiting them in the distance.

This was a terrible day. Far worse than the day the Sefu people were forced to abandon their village. Worse than the pilgrimage to the Kuno land, but nothing was as bad as this; their protector, their champion, and the human symbol of the Sefu people's strength was leaving them—floating on a boat to an unknown destination.

The ocean lost its energy that day. The waves settled as the skiff with the Sefu family made its way farther from the Kuno coastline.

It almost seemed like the land Amri loved so much gave its energy to the sea and in response the sea took on Amri's energy. The waves became still and motionless just like him.

As the crew came upon The Kingmaker, Amri Sefu understood his actions would have a direct result on his family's survival. After Amri climbed up a tattered rope ladder, he turned and pulled his parents up and aboard as Endesha ensured their safety from below. As soon as he turned around Amri was met with a crushing blow to the face. "That is just a reminder of what will happen to you if you attack any member of The Kingmaker," said Captain Burton.

Amri did not understand what had been said to him, and thus, did not respond. What he did know, is he would have to travel deep within himself in order to survive the journey to a place unknown to him and his family.

The family were given wrist and ankle shackles, and escorted down into the bowels of The Kingmaker. The ship was a miracle in the fact that it remained buoyant considering its tattered and poorly maintained status.

The wooden floors of the ship were uneven and squeaky, and the stench of urine and other putrid smells dominated the Sefu family's senses as they walked down into the lower portions of the ship.

"Lay down here!" one of the crewmen told Amri.

Once again, he did not understand, so he stood motionless, and again, was hit with a blow to the face causing blood to rush out of his nose. The crewman pulled on Amri's chains to guide him where to go, and he complied.

Endesha could not hide the anger on his face as he took his position on the floor next to his bloodied brother. The crewmen climbed up the rickety stairs, and closed the hatch above.

Now in complete darkness, Furaha laid a hand on her youngest son, and held her husband's hand with the other. No member of the Sefu family showed any emotion in that moment. Yet hearing the metallic clank of the lower galley's door shut and lock was a relief; it meant they could cry to themselves without anyone seeing or hearing.

## 21

The voyage on The Kingmaker was just as Amri dreamed that night when he met the lion in his dreams. The motion of the water was precisely what he saw and felt in his dream. Everything that was in Amri's vision that evening came true.

Deep in his mind he knew he had to be strong for his family. It would be all too easy for Amri to dive deep within himself during this terrible voyage, and cruelly leave Endesha to fend for himself, but he knew his brother, lying next to him, needed him to stay with him in spirit.

Furaha's condition had not improved since they had boarded The Kingmaker. Her fever had returned, and she would have fits of uncontrollable coughing. Zuberi was not as ill as his wife, but his spirit was full of despair. Many days and nights he thought about how his life had gotten him to this point and if he would survive this voyage. He missed his brother, Coffa, and welcomed the opportunity to see him again in the afterlife; the thought of which seemed much better than the life they were living on The Kingmaker.

Eventually, the ship made it to Lisbon, Portugal. Several of the slaves already aboard before she had dropped anchor on the Kuno coastline had perished during the voyage. Fortunately for the Sefu family, Captain Burton's crew ensured Amri was well fed, and he shared those meals with his brother, father, and now gravely ill mother.

Captain Burton knew if he were to get the best price possible for a man of Amri Sefu's size, he would have to be well kept and in the appearance of good health. While at sea, they occasionally brought the Sefu brothers up to the main deck. Amri and Endesha liked it at night the best, and would look up into the stars that seemed to go on forever.

Their father declined going on deck with his sons because Furaha was too ill, and he would not leave her. The crew was gracious in noticing her condition, and allowed Zuberi to remain with her.

While at sea, Endesha had marveled at the vast nothingness of the dark and moonlit ocean, but at port in Lisbon there was so much activity. People that did not look like him moved swiftly, off-loading supplies from The Kingmaker. There were conversations between men that he could not understand, and smells that were both unpleasant and unfamiliar at the same time.

On the second day of the four days in the port of Lisbon, Endesha was watching the people in the distance on the dock, and whispered to his brother, "Do you see them over there, Amri? There are people over there, and they look like the man that all of these men follow."

"I see them," Amri replied quietly.

"Maybe if we can get away one of them would help us."

"No one will help us, Endesha. Notice, no one here looks like us," he said with a blank look on his face. "Besides, anything we try to do will put our parents in danger, Endesha, you must understand that."

"I do not want to die and have my body thrown into the water like we have seen with the others, Amri," Endesha said angrily.

Amri's anger surfaced from deep within his spirit, and he angrily told Endesha, "I do not want to be here, and I do not want to die here either, but

175

you *must* understand that we do not have any control over these men. There is *nothing* we can do to free ourselves. It will only make it more difficult for all of us to fight these men. *Do as you are told, so we can survive!*"

Deep in the bottom of The Kingmaker, Furaha could feel her son's concerns deep in her spirit. "Our children did not deserve this fate. Their destiny was to do more than this."

"They will survive this and fulfill their destiny," said Zuberi. "I believe we are all alive because of the restraint and wisdom of our sons. We have done well in raising them, and we should be proud of the men they have become."

"Yes. I am proud of our boys, and I am so glad I had them with you. I am so tired, and I want to rest husband," Furaha said as she started to close her eyes.

"Then rest, wife, and take back your peace."

A few moments went by when Furaha said softly, "Hello Coffa. Why are you here? Are you here to take me with you?"

Sensing what was happening Zuberi started to cry uncontrollably. He gently gathered his wife into his arms and kissed her on her forehead. "Don't worry husband, Coffa will take good care of me until you can be with us," Furaha whispered.

"Tell him I love him, and to take good care of you until I get there," Zuberi mumbled as tears blinded his vision. Streaks of sunlight made their way into the bottom of The Kingmaker, and Zuberi held his wife as close to him as he could.

After a while, he stopped crying and looked down at his wife's face. She was not breathing, yet her body was still very warm. Zuberi gently caressed her face, hoping to draw some movement from her eyes, but nothing happened. He had lost his best friend, and the mother of his children. So many feelings were running through his mind; thoughts of fear and intense sadness filled Zuberi's spirit. When it all became too much for his mind to handle, Zuberi wailed so loudly in sadness it could be heard along the docks of Lisbon.

Amri heard his father and immediately knew his mother had passed away. He stood to his shackled feet and tried to go toward the area that led to the bottom of the boat.

"What the bloody hell was that?" asked Captain Burton.

"I do not know, Captain, but the Moor is trying his best to get below deck for some reason," said a crewman.

"Well, *maybe* you should go see what is going on down there," said Burton with a befuddled frown on his face.

The crewman went below deck and found Zuberi sobbing, and holding his dead wife in his shackled arms. The deckhand climbed back up the ladder to the main deck to report his findings.

"Captain, the big one's mother has perished."

"Oh. Bring her body up, and we will give it to the harbor master," ordered Burton.

"We cannot throw her into the harbor. They will most likely burn her body with the rest of the sick and dead."

"Aye, aye, Captain," the deckhand replied.

Endesha and Amri looked on with great anticipation as the deckhands went down below, hoping the noise they heard was not from their father. But when the deckhands reemerged with the body of their mother wrapped in a dirty white sheet, Endesha screamed in agony. Amri stood to his feet as the men carried his mother's body past him. Filled with rage, he broke the chain holding his hands together, and lunged at the men with his mother's body. His intent was not to harm the men, but to retrieve his mother's body so he could say goodbye. The crew of The Kingmaker did not see it that way, and it took several men to keep Amri at bay as they removed her body to the dock.

Endesha could only watch his older brother and wonder why he did not kill the men when he had the opportunity. He cried to himself as the crew wrestled with Amri, resorting to violence—a blow to Amri's back with a boat ore to calm him down.

Thunder was heard as The Kingmaker bowed and listed to the left and right with the swelling of the harbor waters. Amri was brought below deck and saw his father and brother lying together. He was made to join them, and as he lowered himself to the ground, he felt the pain from the ore used to submit him. "Try not to move, my son," Zuberi said softly.

"Mother is gone," Amri whispered.

"Yes, Son. She is gone from us, but she remains with us in spirit."

"How can you say that, Father?" Endesha asked.

"Your mother has joined the world outside, and you can see how the waters are unsettled now. She is letting us know we will have a safe passage to our destination."

"You believe that?" asked Endesha.

"Desha, I know it. Remember when Coffa taught you about putting back what we take from the land? This water is no different," Zuberi said while holding a piece of fabric from Furaha's dress he had managed to tear away before the crewmen took her body away.

"I wonder if it would be better for us to be with her," Amri said softly.

"No, my son. That is not your destiny. I will be with her soon, and you boys will have to depend on each other."

"Stop talking like that Father," Endesha said angrily.

"Understand this, my sons; you will survive this, and in the end, both of you will be victorious.

All of the things that have happened to you two were for a reason. Amri, you have been groomed to be a mighty warrior, and your greatest battle has yet to come.

"Endesha, your time to rise up and become something more than what you could ever believe you are is coming. I see transformation in both of you, my sons," Zuberi continued. "It is time to rest. Think about your mother now. She is watching over us, and I want to be with her in my dreams."

Zuberi began sobbing, and Endesha could not hold back his sorrow, but Amri did not join his father and brother in crying; he thought about the loss of his mother as the boat rocked gently within the harbor. Curiously, the winds did not stop blowing that evening.

The next morning, The Kingmaker set course to Brixham, England.

This particularly long leg of the trip would be a challenge for any seasoned sailor, but Captain Burton was more concerned about the status of his prized, and potentially injured, possession. "What of the Moor down below?" he asked.

"Aye, Captain, he is fair," said a crewman.

"What of his back?"

"He is bruised, but he appears to be all right."

"Bring him above deck, so I can take a look at him."

A couple of crewmen left to gather him and brought him above deck. Once there, Amri's eyes needed a moment to adjust to the brightness of the sun. The men of The Kingmaker looked like pale-skinned monsters to Amri with their gray and matted or sun-scorched blond hair.

The sky was amazingly blue with clouds larger than any Amri had seen before. The wind was so strong it whipped the sails violently, causing the crew of The Kingmaker to constantly readjust to ensure they stayed on course.

Amri was led to Captain Burton, and at an easy foot taller than the captain, had to look down at him. "Aye, this one is a killer," Burton muttered.

"I can see it in his black eyes." The captain took a step back, and said, "Look at the scars on his face and body, lads. This one has fought a beast."

Amri stood still during the inspection, absent of mind and thought after he had finished noticing his surroundings. He believed at any moment he would be thrown overboard, and the terrible life he was living as a spectator would come to an end. "Turn him around so I can see his back," Burton commanded. He traced the mark from the ore with the blunt side of his dagger. "Get him cleaned up. We need him well before we dock at Brixham."

For the next several weeks, the crew of The Kingmaker rubbed ointments and herbs onto his back to take care of Amri's wound. During this time, the ship was sailing faster than Captain Burton expected.

Ominously strong winds propelled the ship quickly throughout the day and night. "We will be getting to our location quickly, I believe," Endesha told his father.

"What makes you think that, Son?" Zuberi replied.

"I can feel us cut through the water when the wind blows. I can also tell when we slow down because the wind is not as strong. But it never goes away, it just calms for a moment, then picks up again quickly."

"She wants us to get to solid ground." Zuberi smiled to himself with pleasure. "That is her gift to us."

"Why do you think Mother wants us on land so badly?"

"Because she knows if we do not get off of this thing soon, Amri will kill all of those men."

## 22

Even with the spiritually assisted winds pushing The Kingmaker along the seas, it still took almost two months' to finally arrive at the port of Brixham, England. Their trip had been shortened by nearly two weeks with the heavy winds pushing them toward land, and Captain Burton was glad to make it home in record time. "Aye, men, we are back home!" he said joyously. The men laughed and clapped with enthusiastically. "We shall offload our supplies, and meet at the pub where you will receive payment for such a fine job sailing us home to Brixham!"

With renewed energy, the men went to work preparing the ship for arrival. The constant movement was unsettling for the Sefu men. Several of the remaining prisoners were ordered to assist with off-loading items, but the Sefu men remained unseen. After a while, the activity on the upper-deck of The Kingmaker subsided. The men were gone, and the once-noisy ship grew silent.

After dark, the Sefu men heard someone stepping down to the lower deck. The hatch to their hovel opened, and down came Captain Burton with a stack of clothing for the Sefu men to wear. With his sword in hand, he pulled Zuberi toward him, and removed his shackles so he could assist him with putting on a relatively clean white shirt and dark-blue pants.

After he was finished dressing the elderly man, Burton looked to the brothers, and said, "Your turn, the both of you." He motioned to the floor with his sword, pointing at the clothes.

The Sefu brothers extended their arms toward Burton, and he unlocked their shackles with his free hand. While the younger Sefu men dressed, Captain Burton kept his sword near Zuberi's neck.

He knew what he was doing was unsafe, but he did not want to share his human bounty with any of his crewmen. He figured, under the cover of night he could smuggle the Moors off The Kingmaker, while he negotiated a price for their purchase.

When Amri and Endesha were dressed, Burton put the shackles back on awkwardly with his left hand, and ordered the men to go above deck. Closing the galley door behind him, Burton nervously looked around to see if anyone was watching. Certain they were alone, his jitters were calmed, and he guided the men down the board plank onto English soil.

The city of Brixham was a cold place; the Sefu men had never felt such weather. The air smelled foul to the brothers as they were placed into the back of a carriage and told to lay down and be quiet. When the carriage stopped, the three men were led into a small cottage alongside an alley; home of Morris Peters and his wife Emma. "These are the men I told you about earlier, Morris," said Burton. "Fine looking Moors, aren't they?"

"Yes. The large one is unlike anything I have ever seen," Morris said.

"Aye, they are from far in the south seas. I've seen the big one kill five men right before my eyes."

"Are you sure it is a good idea to bring them here? I am a member of Parliament, not a warrior."

"I will return for them after I take care of my crew and meet with my buyer. Please have Mistress Emma provide food and water for the men, and keep a sword near your side."

Morris went into a closet and retrieved a small sword not suitable for cutting meat let alone fighting.

"Here, you can have mine," said Burton, shaking his head in disgust as he left the cottage.

The tavern where the crew of The Kingmaker gathered was full of people. Sounds of singing and laughter could be heard from outside the thick wooden doors. Many crewmen had long since washed the stench of the sea off of their bodies, and thankful bar maidens gladly passed drinks to the crew, hoping to cash in on the sailors newly gained wealth. "What a voyage men!" Captain Burton said as he entered the tavern. "We made it home in record time! Take this time to rest and restore yourselves."

"We will restore our glasses with mead for now," a crewman replied with the room laughing together.

"Indeed, drink and enjoy your night, lads. It is yours for the taking." Burton nabbed a tankard of mead from the table, took a deep swig, and as he swallowed, he noticed a rather sinister looking man watching him from the corner of the room. Deciding to disregard the fellow for now, he made his way to each of his crewman to give them their cut of the profits.

Burton made his way toward the stranger, obviously a man of wealth and distinction by the way he was dressed. His hair was clean, combed and parted on the left side of his head.

He wore a fine black coat with matching trousers, and his black boots shined to perfection. As Burton approached the man, he motioned to the still-uncleaned captain to sit with him. "James Burton, correct?" asked the man.

"Aye, I'm him."

"My name is Horace Darlington. I was sent here to meet you by my associate, Mr. Peters."

"Morris says you are a man that enjoys collecting fine items."

"Indeed, I have some of the finest items in the world in my personal collection, and since I do not have much time, I would like to get to business quickly, if you don't mind. I was informed you arrived this evening from a voyage, and have two Moor beasts in your possession."

"I do, and there are three of them, not two. One is elderly, and the other is large, but not as big as the one I would refer to as a beast. He is as large as the door at the front of this tavern, Mr. Darlington." Burton deftly muted his enthusiasm.

"Well, that is your opinion, but in order for me to do business with you I must see these men for myself." Horace took a drink from a flask hidden within his coat pocket.

"Absolutely, but before we do that we should discuss the price."

"Very well. What price would make the three beasts mine, Captain Burton?"

"Three pounds twelve shillings for all three is a fair price."

Horace laughed mightily. "You are wasting my time with pricing only a thief would ask for.

You only just mentioned a moment ago that only two of the three men were of able body. The elder should be included at no additional cost. The most I would ever give to you for the lot would be one pound ten shillings, and only if the men are in the best of condition."

"They are in excellent condition, Mr. Darlington. We can go take a look at them now." The two men shook hands, left the tavern, and started walking down the cobbled street toward the Peters' cottage.

***

Back at the Peters' home, Amri and Endesha were whispering to each other. "What is this place?" Endesha asked.

"I am not sure," Amri said.

"We are far from our land, my sons," Zuberi said.

"Endesha, listen to me, we must protect Father. Do you understand?"

"What do you mean, Amri? Our hands are tied together and so are our feet," Endesha replied.

"I know, but we need to let these men know we will not let anything happen to our father. So, if we are stood up on our feet, and danger is present, we will shield him with our bodies. Maybe this will prevent them from harming him."

"Boys, I do not need such covering. My time to be with your mother is coming soon, and your destiny will be fulfilled in this place. You will see."

The Sefu men heard a knock at the door. Muffled discussions could also be heard in the adjacent room.

The Sefu men heard Emma Morris scream, followed by a loud crash of plates, and two large thumps on the floor. The door to their comfortable prison swung open, and it was not Captain Burton who came into the room. With a rotten-toothed grin, the captain's first mate, Roderick made his entrance, followed by a second unfamiliar man.

Amri recognized him immediately. He was the man that had struck him with the ore. "Get up you filthy Moors, we don't have time to waste," Roderick commanded.

The Sefu men complied. They stood and walked as quickly as their shackled feet would allow. As the three men left their room they saw the bleeding bodies of the Morris and Emma Peters on the ground. Morris was still alive and reaching for the sword his friend James had given him, but his throat was filling with blood and was dead before Roderick and his accomplice closed the door behind them.

The Sefu men were placed in the back of a cloth-covered carriage lined with hay. Roderick and his accomplice took off quickly, hoping no one had seen them leave the residence. "We have to take their shackles off, Master Thornton. We cannot move them swiftly with their feet shackled like they are. Where you able to get the key?" asked the accomplice.

"Aye, of course. I was able to nab it from him at the tavern after he had a few pints of ale," said Roderick.

"Where are we going, sir?" asked the accomplice as he steered the carriage through the dark stone streets.

"We are going to see an old friend in the north. We shall head to a village called Tawny. I have business with man there."

Moments later, Captain Burton and Mr. Darlington arrived at the Peters' home. When they knocked on the door and no one answered, Burton opened the door to find Mr. and Mrs. Peters lying on the floor in a pool of their shared blood.

Without thought of his friend's condition, Burton ran to the back room to see if his prized possessions were still in the residence, but they were not. Even with his alcohol-clouded mind, James Burton knew he would not recover the men he had taken as slaves.

## 23

As the single drawn horse carriage made its way northwest out of Brixham, the Sefu men did not know what was in store for them on this cold late-fall night. The ride was bumpy and harsh. They did not dare make a sound even as their heads and legs banged into the wooden sides of the carriage. Amri could see Zuberi was having difficulty with the severe movements, and placed his father's age-weakened legs in between his hoping to provide a buffer against the hard wood surfaces surrounding them. Endesha used one of his arms to brace their father's head.

The horse neighed in protest of the hastened pace set by Roderick. The dense cold of the English night was frightening to the Sefu men. They could occasionally see their own breath under the fabric sheet when the lantern shined light over the carriage's imported cargo.

As the carriage approached the outer perimeter of Aveston. Roderick commanded his accomplice to slow his pace and extinguish the lantern. It would be prudent to afford caution as they were now in King Phillip Miles' Midland Kingdom.

"Steady your beast, or we will be bloody discovered," Roderick whispered loudly. "Slower! We mustn't be seen. We are close to Tawny. The carriage slowed and was being led down through a shallow ravine, when a voice spoke out from within the woods.

"Halt! What brings you to the kingdom of his Royal Majesty King Phillip Miles?"

The man within the woods continued, "My name is Fitzgerald Singletary. I am a captain of his Majesty's Red Guard. Why are you traveling at night without the light of a lantern?"

"Oh, I am headed to a small village north of here with my brother … Charles," Roderick replied.

"And what of the goods in the back of your carriage, sir?"

"You are seeking money for taxes? Yes, yes, I will gladly give you three shillings." Roderick made show of untying his coin purse.

"I did not ask for three shillings because I have not viewed your cargo in order to determine your tax, sir." Singletary lit his lantern, revealing two more Harkstead riders. "Light your lantern, Master …?" Singletary asked while waiting for Roderick to share his name.

"Roderick, sir. Roderick Harris is my name."

"Master Harris, please light your lantern, and step down so we may view your cargo and collect your tax. Then you and Charles shall be on your way."

Roderick took a moment to determine his options; they were outnumbered, so they could not challenge Singletary and his Hearksteadian soldiers; they could not outrun them either considering the nighttime darkness would prevent them from finding their way through to Tawny.

Realizing they had no other alternative, Roderick looked to "Charles," and stepped down from his less-than-regal carriage.

He walked to the back of the carriage as Singletary positioned his horse to see the contents. With a small breath, Roderick removed the fabric to reveal the three intertwined Sefu men.

"What is this madness?" Singletary yelled in surprise as he and his fellow soldiers unsheathed their swords. "What kind of men are these you have in your carriage?"

"They are men my captain and I took as prisoners from a faraway land, sir."

"You do not look like a man from the waters. I do not believe you. Bring these men to their feet," Singletary commanded. The Harkstead soldiers dismounted their horses and assisted the Sefu men to their feet. As they stood, Singletary was awed by Endesha and Amri's size. These men of the Red Guard had never seen a man as massive in size as Amri in or out of battle.

"This one is mighty large," Singletary said to his men. The two brothers stepped closer to each other to shield their elderly father. Noticing their movements, he asked them, "What are your names?" The men did not reply. "No matter, we will talk again later. Have them get back into the carriage, and we shall head to Harkstead Castle."

"And what of us, Captain?" Roderick asked.

"I do not know where you were taking these men, but I believe you were not traveling within the shadows because you wanted to be seen. Considering what you were hiding, my assumption is you were headed to Tawny to relieve yourself of these men, collect your payment, and return to the coast—if you are in fact a man of the waters. But that is not going to happen.

You, sir, will spend the rest of your days in the dungeons of Harkstead Castle for bringing these *things* to our land." Singletary's soldiers redirected Roderick and "Charles" toward the path that led to Harkstead Castle. One soldier rode in front of their prisoners and the other behind them while Singletary brought up the rear.

Even though the night was bitterly cold, the Sefu men did not notice. Finally, free of rooms and covered confinement, they were too busy looking at all that was around them. Everything was new. The air was crisp and smelled of plants they had never seen before. The sheer size of the horses with their grunts and the clatter of their hooves with every stride made them seem like monsters to the Sefu. The mounted men looked menacing with their long shiny weapons, fine armor, and bascinets on their heads.

Endesha looked up to the sky like he used to back in their village, and, to his surprise, the moon was right where it usually was. This gave Endesha a sense of comfort. He tapped his brother on the thigh and pointed up. Amri nodded in approval. He also understood that even though they were thousands of miles from home, the sky presented a landscape to the Sefu brothers they immediately recognized.

As the men rode under the heavy portcullis into Harkstead Castle, people stared in awe at the Sefu men that many had never seen the likes of. When Singletary and his men returned to the stables, he ordered them to take the two smugglers to the dungeon.

"Yes, Captain" the soldiers replied.

Singletary pointed to another guard and commanded, "You, come with me. We shall take these men to see King Phillip."

Captain Singletary removed his bascinet—revealing his thick blond beard, matching long locks and daylight-blue eyes—and handed it to a young stable boy. With his sword still unsheathed he led the Sefu men through the series of corridors and stairs that eventually led to King Phillip's chambers.

As the group approached the king's chambers two fully-armored soldiers stood guard outside.

When they arrived, Captain Singletary nodded to the guards, and promptly rapped on the door. Amri looked to one of the guards and noticed he could not see his eyes. He had leaned in closer to get a better look, when Endesha bumped his elbow and nodded toward the now open chamber doors.

"Captain Singletary, what brings you to my chambers at this time of the evening?" King Phillip asked.

"Your Majesty, I found these men on the outskirts of our land. Singletary motioned for the Sefu men to enter the chambers. "I believe they were being transported to Tawny by two men from the southern coast."

"What of those men?" Phillip asked.

"They are in the dungeons on charges of transporting prisoners without tax or papers with your royal seal, Your Majesty."

"Very well. Now, let me take a look at these…men." King Phillip walked toward them, impressed, but not awed as his people had been.

Amri noticed the king's fine white linen robe. His shoulder-length hair was pulled back behind his ears, revealing the finely woven crimson stitching along the collar of his garment.

Endesha had not noticed the king's clothing—he was more interested in the fruit on the table.

The king looked up at Amri and took two steps back to get a better look. He then looked to Endesha before noticing their father next to them. Again, the brothers took a step closer together to shield their father as the king walked toward him. "Do these men speak English, Captain Singletary?" Phillip asked.

"I do not think they do, Your Majesty."

"Take them to the dungeons as well, but place them in a space together and separate from everyone else. I believe these two larger ones are related to this older one. Maybe they are his children. See to it the three of them are well-fed and given water."

"Yes, Your Majesty"

"And Singletary, please ensure they are not seen as you transport them."

"Yes, Your Majesty."

As the group left the king's chambers the Sefu men were growing tired from the night's activities. The smell of the food on the king's table remained in Endesha's mind as they walked down the cold, damp corridors, and several flights of stairs. Finally making their way to the lowest level of the castle, they entered the dungeon, and were hit with the horrible smells that filled the dank air. Sounds of men groaning in pain echoed through the narrow halls.

Zuberi could not walk anymore, so the brothers picked him up by his arms and carried him into the small cell at the end of the long hallway.

Once inside, the Sefu men's shackles were removed, and, just as King Phillip commanded, they were given a large platter filled with scraps of chicken, half-eaten fruit, and chunk of bread the guard transporting the food had not finished.

Amri and Endesha offered their father the majority of the food, but he declined. Zuberi only ate what he thought his old body needed. The men drank their water in deep, gulping swallows, then used the rest to wash their faces—it was a welcomed refreshment. Afterward, the Sefu men took some time to look at their new surroundings.

Zuberi looked at his sons and said, "I told you your destiny would be fulfilled in this new land. It is time to rest now." Zuberi laid flat on his back.

"Yes, Father," they replied.

Within minutes, Endesha and his father were asleep, but Amri could not rest, at least, not immediately. Thoughts of the day filled his mind; the death of his mother, the home that he was in, and being taken away by Roderick—it was all too much to understand. Another thought came to Amri's mind, more pleasing and comforting than all of the others—Nsia. He longed to see her one more time, but he knew he may never. He took a deep breath, suppressing his burgeoning anger, and fell asleep.

Prince Stuart Miles stood in his chamber, admiring himself in mirror. It had been many years since his accomplishments over Carpenter's Army, he had not seen any major battle since, and his portlier frame gave evidence of his depleted athletic ability. "You are so handsome, *Your Highness*," said the maiden nestled under the white sheet on his bed. She quickly pulled the sheet to her neck when a knock sounded at the door.

"Enter," he said, motioning the maiden to keep her silence. The doors to his chamber creaked open.

"Your Highness," said a porter. "Your royal father has requested you be informed there are Moors imprisoned in the dungeons, and would like you to view them.

"Tell my father I will be on my way to the dungeons immediately."

"Yes, Your Highness."

Stuart got dressed and made his way down to the Harkstead dungeons.

He walked down the familiar corridors that led to the Sefu men. He truly did not know what to expect as he had not seen many Moors in his lifetime. However, once he arrived at the Sefu men's cell, he immediately knew these men were nothing like the Moors he remembered.

As Stuart stared at the Sefu men he did not understand the potential danger that dwelt behind those iron bars in the dungeon. He only saw three dark men, two of which were larger than any men he had seen before. One of which was exceptionally large and intimidating.

Upon exiting the dungeons, Prince Stuart went first to his quarters to remove the stench of the dungeons from his body before going to see his father, the king.

"Good morning, Father."

"Ah, hello, my child."

"I have just returned from the dungeons."

"What do you think of the Moors Captain Singletary found last evening?"

"I am not sure what I was looking at, Father. They are unlike any form of man I have ever seen. Shall we keep them as prisoners?"

"I'm not sure my child. Men that size would make excellent infantrymen."

"What men are you talking about, Father?" asked Harold Miles.

"None of your concern, little one," Stuart said.

"I am not little any more, I am nine years old!" Harold quipped.

"I know, Son, you are in fact not a little boy anymore. Run along. Your brother and I have many things to discuss," Phillip said with a large smile on his face.

As Harold left the king's chambers, the two men returned to the topic of what to do with the Moors in the dungeons. "Singletary believes they were being transported to Tawny. Perhaps they were to be given to someone as a gift. Or a weapon," said King Phillip.

"Tawny has returned to a haven for mercenary lancemen since we gave up control years ago," Stuart said.

"It is likely those men were going to become a part of the Carpenter's army if given the opportunity to be seen."

"Perhaps we were fortunate in intercepting Thomas Carpenter's secret soldiers."

"Go to the dungeon with Singletary, and talk to the men that brought the Moors here. Find out what their plan was so we can understand what and who these men are."

"Yes, Your Majesty."

Later that day, Singletary and Prince Stuart went deep into the dungeons of Harkstead Castle to question Roderick and his accomplice, "Charles." When they arrived at the prisoners' cell, they could see the two smugglers were asleep on the dirt floor.

Singletary used his sword's scabbard to bang on the iron bars, waking the two prisoners from their uncomfortable slumber. "Good morning, or maybe it is good evening to you both.

Either way, it does not matter because if you do not answer our questions you shall never see the light of day again," the captain said. "This is His Royal Highness Prince Stuart Miles of the Midland Kingdom, and he has some questions for you. If you are fortunate with your words he may allow you to retain your life. I would not waste his time if I were the two of you."

"You are in my dungeon because you were caught by Captain Singletary attempting to transport three Moors on Midland grounds without payment of tax or sanctioned documentation from His Majesty King Phillip Miles. I will ask you each question only once, and it is my expectation that you respond truthfully, or your lives may be lost with your answers withheld on your tongue. Firstly, what was your destination, and to whom were you delivering those men to? Secondly, who are the Moors you had in the back of your carriage, and where did you get them? Lastly, what do you know about those men?" Stuart finished, and waited for their responses.

Roderick thought for a moment about what he was being asked. He knew his life was, in essence, over, and his silence would only accelerate the time before his death would come. "We were headed to Tawny, Your Highness," Roderick said. "We were going to sell them to a friend of mine that works for a carpenter."

"A carpenter you say?" Singletary replied.

"Yes. My associate in Tawny works for a carpenter," Roderick said. Stuart and Singletary shared a small chuckle.

"All right, so where did you find these Moors?" Stuart asked.

"As I told your mate before—I am a sailor, and we found those men in a place very far from here."

"What else do you know about them?" Stuart asked.

"We had the whole family. The mother perished during the voyage to Brixham. The old man is the father, and the two large ones are the sons."

"Surely you would not take an entire family prisoner without cause?" said Singletary.

"The largest one of the three is a beast of a man. We both witnessed him kill five men with his bare hands."

"He does not seem to be very dangerous at the moment. Why did he not attempt to flee from you before you were caught?" Stuart asked.

"Probably because of the old man. Both Moors are protecting the old man, and that is why they are restrained."

"What you have told us seems to be understandable, and I believe it to be true," Stuart said. "However, your associate in Tawny that works for a carpenter is an unfortunate occurrence for you. The person you were meeting does not work for *a* carpenter; he works for a man *called* Carpenter.

Thomas Carpenter and his army are enemies of the Midland Kingdom, and anyone that does business with him is an enemy of mine, and of my father, King Phillip Miles.

199

"Your honesty is appreciated, but your associations have led you and your brother to your deaths. I am a just and fair man, so instead of having you beheaded or leaving you to rot here in my dungeons, I believe, based on what you told me, a more fitting death for you both would be at the hands of the very persons you took prisoner."

"Guards, take these men out of this cell and escort them to the Moors," ordered Singletary.

The guards unlocked the cell and quickly took hold of Roderick and "Charles." Stuart and Singletary followed as they escorted the two men through the corridor to the end of the long hallway lit modestly by torches.

Amri and Endesha heard many footsteps getting closer, and stood with the anticipation of bodily harm. Much to their surprise they saw Roderick and his accomplice outside of their cell. A guard opened the Sefu men's cell, and Singletary stepped inside, extending his hand toward Zuberi. Amri instinctively moved in front of his father. "No, no. I will not harm your father, large fellow. What is about to occur is not something an old man needs to see. I will return him to you in due course." He extended his hand again, and Zuberi moved slowly around Amri.

Zuberi could not walk without assistance, and had to hold the iron rods in order to make his way out of the cell.

Stuart could see the elderly man needed assistance, and offered his hand as he entered the hallway. Singletary unsheathed his sword, and motioned Roderick and "Charles" to enter the Moors cell.

Reluctantly, they stepped over the threshold, leaving barely enough space for the heavy, rusted-iron doors to be closed and locked behind them.

Amri understood what was happening, and started to smile with the enthusiasm of a child preparing for a day of play. Endesha remained stoic as thoughts of what these men did to his family charged his lungs with the desire for more air. Singletary and Stuart looked at each other with devilish smiles and started walking toward the opposite end of the hallway. "Guards, take this man to the stables, and see to it he is carried there.

Give him food and drink, oh, and if any of you tampers with it, I will see that you meet his sons in their cell, as well," Stuart commanded.

The two guards each took one of Zuberi's arms over their shoulders and walked him down the corridors of the dungeon; horrific screams could be heard behind them. Roderick and his accomplice's wails sounded as if their skin had been peeled off their bodies in one continuous piece. This was followed by violent sounding thumps, metallic clangs, and bones crashing against iron bars.

"Killed five men with his bare hands he said?" Singletary said in jest.

"Surely, two will be much easier," Stuart replied with a smile.

Eventually, the screams from within the dungeons were silenced.

Prince Stuart and Captain Singletary continued their conversation as they walked along the intricate stone walkway in the castle's garden. "What are we to do with the Moors?" Singletary asked.

"I am not sure. The large one may be too dangerous to be allowed to walk amongst our women and children. Perhaps they should stay within the dungeons until we learn more about them and their behavior," Stuart replied.

"What of the elder Moor?"

"He does not pose any threat to us, and that is why I sent him to the stables. I believe Roderick was correct in saying as long as the elder man is alive the son's will not misbehave fearing for their father's safety."

"I will return to the dungeons to check on the elder's sons, and will have them fed and their cell changed."

"Very well, Captain Singletary."

As ordered the dungeon guard took Zuberi to the castle stables. They did not have him sleep with the horses, instead they placed him in the upper-level of the stable, overlooking the cobblestoned courtyard, merchant's quarters, and the marketplace. From the front window, Zuberi could see the ironworkers in the adjacent armory, and from the window on the opposite side, he could see into an area that looked like a training hall for the palace guards.

The smell of the stables was unpleasant, but it was more acceptable than the foul stench of the dead prisoners in the Harkstead dungeons. *This place will serve us well*, Zuberi thought to himself as he looked around the space.

There were several bales of hay stored in the room, so he used some of it to create a soft place to sit and eat the strange food he had been given. After squeezing and smelling everything, he determined they were similar to the items that Amri and Endesha ate the night before, and since he was alone, ate as hungrily as his sons had.

After his meal, Zuberi laid down to rest—such a meal makes old men tired. Before falling asleep, Zuberi listened to the horses below, and thought about his beloved Furaha. *If only you could have made it here with us*, he thought.

He reached into his shirt and delicately lifted the piece of dress she had on the day of her death, and held it close to his nose. It still had her scent on it, and he found it soothing. Thoughts of their past came and left Zuberi as he traveled into a deep slumber. This would be the first time he had been able to rest without fear since his family left the Kuno village.

***

Was it sweat dripping from Endesha's face, or was it blood? Amri could not determine what the liquid was either. Both Sefu brothers sat on the floor of their cell with their backs resting against the wall. In front of them was a horrifying mess that consisted of their capturers Roderick and "Charles." Bits of their lifeless bodies were scattered across the floor of the cell, each bit resting in a pool of blood.

The Sefu men mutilated them in a way that would be considered cruel, even despite their terrible treatment of the Sefu family. Endesha did not care. He sat on the ground staring at his bloodied hands and noticed they were shaking.

Endesha looked to his right at Amri and noticed he was sitting with a blank stare on his face. His older brother did not seem bothered by their actions either.

Endesha thought he seemed to be *more* relaxed than he had ever been since leaving the Kuno village. In his opinion, Amri looked as if he just finished eating a huge feast—the satisfaction was visible in his eyes. "How do you do it?" Endesha asked.

"Do what?" Amri replied.

"Turn off your thoughts."

"What do you mean?"

"How do you turn off your thoughts when you kill?"

"I do not know. I just do not think when I am doing it."

"You ripped that man's arm from his body, Amri. You did not think about that when you did it? Look at what we just did to these men. You don't feel anything?" Endesha pointed at the various limbs on the floor of their cell as he spoke.

"I feel alive when I do those horrible things. I feel free when I am fighting. Remember the elder women back in our village?"

"Yes."

"Those old women sang songs because they enjoyed it. I feel the same way about fighting. It brings me happiness."

"I do not understand how you can get such satisfaction from doing terrible things."

"It depends on how you look at it. Those men *took* us from a place we had started to enjoy.

They caused us to lose our mother, and they took Nsia away from me. So, they had to pay for their actions, and I was glad to make them suffer like we did.

"You sit there judging me about what I did, when you have those men's blood on your hands too, little brother. You and I are *not* that different. We share the same blood, and eventually, you will see that you are much stronger than me."

Endesha huffed at Amri's speech. "I am not like you—I cannot derive joy from inflicting pain on others."

"You may not enjoy inflicting pain like me, little brother, but you can deliver terror with ease just like me if you are pushed," Amri warned. "You are not a warrior—you are too smart for that. Your strength is being smart enough to prevent a fight. Only if you are desperate will you then fight with the passion of a true Sefu warrior. I have seen this in you for years now."

"When did you first notice this?"

"I saw it a few times back in our village when you were younger. I really understood it when you told me about your confrontation with Chike in the woods.

You stood your ground with an older man, and you did not let him intimidate you. That is when I noticed you had changed, Desha."

The brothers were sitting in silence when Singletary returned to their cell. "Dear Lord, what happened here? Guards!" Singletary yelled. The guards came running to the end of the hallway. The first one to arrive looked down at the bodies and parts on the ground and relieved his stomach of its contents on the ground.

"Bloody hell is this?" said the other guard, forgetting his superior, Singletary, was standing next to him. "Apologies, Cap'n."

"Take these men to another cell, and give them water so they can bathe," Singletary ordered, bringing his kerchief to his face. "They reek of blood and excrement."

"Yes, My Lord," replied the guard as he lifted the other guard to his feet. The two guards motioned the Sefu brothers to extend their hands so they could be shackled, and they complied for fear of repercussions if they didn't. The guards escorted them down another long hallway within the dungeons of Harkstead Castle.

This time, other prisoners could see the brown-skinned men, bloodied and daunting, as they walked down the dimly-lit corridor. Prisoners retreated from the bars at the sight of the Sefu brothers, and some even shouted "*Demons!*" to them as they walked by.

Once they got to their new cell and were unshackled, the two brothers were given a large barrel of heated water and some tattered, yet clean, clothes. "Wash yourselves you bloody monsters," said the guard. They did not understand what the guard said so they just stood still. "Wash yourselves!" This time the guard made the motion of washing his body to them.

The brothers understood what he wanted and started to douse their bodies with the warm water from the barrel. "I thought they were going to kill us," Endesha said.

"I thought they were going to, also," Amri replied.

"They are treating us better here than that man on the water did."

"Our hands are still bound, and we are sitting behind these hard bars, so I do not believe we are better off here. We are alive because these men are trying to figure out how we can benefit them."

"What about Father?"

"They would not harm him."

"How do you know?"

"Because if I learned that something had happened to him, I think they know I would try to kill all of them if given the opportunity. What we did earlier was proof of our abilities. This is how we are to survive in this land. Just like Father told us."

***

Singletary made his way back to King Phillip's chambers and found he and Stuart were eating. "Ah, Captain Singletary! What of our enormous Moors?" the king asked.

The captain had a bewildered look on his face.

"Singletary?" Stuart said.

"Speak sir!" King Phillip commanded.

"Madness, Your Majesty," Singletary finally replied. "Utter madness, Sire." He asked permission to sit with his hand hovering over a chair.

King Phillip nodded "yes" and the captain sat with his hands covering his face. "The savagery of those men is something I have never seen before," Singletary said. "Pieces of flesh and bone littered the entire cell. It was like we let loose a hundred dogs on those two criminals."

He looked up and noticed the king and prince were eating their dinner. "My apologies, Sire." King Phillip took a large bite from a turkey leg, indicating his hunger was not quelled by Singletary's reporting.

"So, you think those men were going to sell the Moors to Carpenter?" Stuart asked.

"Yes. Considering their abilities are barbaric at best, with proper training they would have been formidable soldiers to fight against on the battlefield," Singletary replied.

"What shall we do with them, Father?" Stuart asked.

"We may need to take the good captain's advice, and give them proper training. Perhaps they could become my personal guard," King Phillip said. "For now, let them be where they are, and tomorrow, take them to the stables to be with their father. Ensure they are properly shackled, as I do not want them to have the opportunity to harm anyone."

"Yes, Your Majesty," Singletary said. He stood and walked out of the king's chambers.

## 24

The next day, five guards came to the Sefu brother's cell. They were shackled and asked to come out of the cell. Once they realized what was being asked of them the brothers walked out of the cell slowly. Apparently, they were not moving fast enough for one of the guards; he delivered a strong blow to Endesha's back with his shield, causing him to stumble to the dirt floor of the dungeon. Amri helped his brother onto his feet, and shot a menacing glare at the guard. "Don't look at me you bloody monster!" the guard said as he punched Amri's face with his armored glove, snapping his head to the right, and sending a spray of blood flying onto the nearby wall. The Sefu warrior turned his head back toward the guard and presented a bloody-toothed smile. The other four guards did not dare strike the Moor.

"I will have my turn to deliver a blow to your face. We will see who has the stronger arm," Amri said in his Sefu language—the demonic bloody smile still on his face. Endesha grabbed his brother's arm and turned him around as the group continued walking down the hallway, up several series of stairs, and through many, many corridors.

Eventually, they were led to the stables and taken to the overhead area where their father was located.

The guards wrapped the Sefu brother's chains around a large wooden beam, giving them enough slack to move in a limited manner within the small space overtop of the stables.

"If you try to hurt any of us, we will kill you and feed you to the dogs you bloody monsters!" yelled a guard, before turning to leave. The four remaining guards continued to watch Amri as they waited their turn to go down to the lower level of the stables. No one wanted to be alone with the Sefu men.

"Father, you are well?" asked Endesha as he hugged Zuberi.

"Yes, my son. I am well," he replied. Zuberi noticed the blood on Amri's face.

"Are you well, Amri?"

"Yes, Father, I am fine."

"Did those men hurt you?" Endesha asked.

"No. They took me here and gave me much food. I slept very well here."

"What is this place? Where they are keeping us, Father?" Amri asked.

"This is where they keep those large beasts that brought us here,"

Endesha stood and looked around at his new surroundings. "This is a long way from our village, Father," he said.

"Yes, Son, this place is where I believe both of your destinies will be fulfilled," said Zuberi.

"I hate the smell of this place." Amri scowled. "I hate that ever since we were taken from the Kuno land, we have had other men telling us what to do. I am growing impatient with all of this."

"There is nothing we can do about it, Brother," Endesha replied. "We are in this place with no allies, no weapons, and no knowledge of the land we are on."

"Endesha, your wisdom reminds me of Coffa. You must have been listening closely to his teachings. It fits you well, Son," Zuberi said with pride.

Amri stood and almost hit his head on the wooden beam of the stable attic. He then stretched his muscles until his joints popped. Frustrated, he went to the edge of the attic's ledge where he could see the armory where the metalsmith was making swords and other weapons. But what was more intriguing to Amri was to his left. From there he could see where the elite soldiers from the Red Guard practiced.

He had never seen fighting like this before, and as he watched, he noticed the soldier's movements with their swords were fluid and powerful. Amri also noticed the different types of weapons available to them: longswords, broadswords, and falchions.

Moments later, Prince Stuart and Singletary entered the practice area. Amri knelt down instinctively, so he would not be detected, but they were not aware, nor did they care if he was gazing upon their actions. "We haven't had a go in a long time, Your Highness," said Singletary.

"Yes, indeed. It has been far too long since we sparred. Fancy a go?" Stuart replied.

"What sword shall we use?"

"Let us use the ones we have on us." Stuart produced his elaborately adorned Arming Sword from its scabbard.

It was over 100 years old and had been given to him by his royal father when he took control of the Red Guard, and all of the Midland Kingdom's Armies, after the defeat of Thomas Carpenter.

The sword had a pearl and iron hilt with a gold cross-guard. It was a magnificent piece of artistic metal craftsmanship of which delivering death was second to its admirable physical beauty.

Captain Singletary walked casually toward the swords mounted on the wall and selected a longsword. As a skilled swordsman, he knew he needed a longer reach to counter the prince's smaller size and equal skill with a blade. "No need in allowing me to have an advantage, Captain. I want you to treat me like any other sparring partner," Stuart said smugly.

"I never intended on treating you any other way." Fitzgerald wasted no time, and delivered the first overhand downward strike. Prince Stuart skillfully parried the strike, and reset his footing to deflect Singletary's quick, but short, diagonal slash.

As the two men were sparring, Amri watched them in amazement—analyzing their every movement with intense scrutiny. The constant clanging of the iron was captivating to all of the Sefu men, but to Amri, it was a way to satisfy his urge for fighting—his lust for war.

He wanted to learn how to fight like the men he was watching. He wanted to fight *better* than the men he was watching. "I like the weapons those men are using down there, Father," Amri said with new-found enthusiasm.

"You will be able to defeat those men with their own weapons in time, Son," Zuberi said.

"I will be the best to ever fight on this land, Father, and I will free us from this place."

"We need to discuss a plan of strategy that will help us survive here," Zuberi said.

"I agree. We must have a plan so Amri does not get us all killed," Endesha said jokingly.

"Let us talk about what we know, and what we do not know," Zuberi said. "We know these men are capable of hurting or killing us at any point, so we cannot show them any signs of aggression. This means we cannot harm any of them, Amri." Amri looked way from his brother and father.

"We should make ourselves as useful to them as possible, and try to appear non-threatening and likeable."

"Sons, I know this goes against all of the things you were taught when we were on our land, but this place is different, and in order to survive we must adapt. Endesha, you must focus on learning their language. You are the most intelligent one of us, and we need you to understand what they want from us. Amri, you must channel your anger, and turn it into focusing it on becoming a formidable fighter on this land. Watch these men fight each other, learn their movements and how they can be defeated. This will help you when the time comes.

"I believe, if we do these things we can survive in this place without constantly wondering if our lives are in jeopardy. Do you boys understand me?" Zuberi asked.

"Yes, Father," Amri and Endesha replied.

"Good. There is some water in a container over there. Use some of it to wash the blood off your face, Amri, and tend to your wounds." Zuberi said. "We are safe here, so you can rest peacefully today." He placed his hands on his son's shoulders.

The Sefu men slept late into the morning and were just waking up when they noticed a small, curly-headed little boy peeking up at them from the wooden staircase. Harold thought the fact that he could not see the Sefu men meant they could not see him either. However, the boy did not consider the Sefu men could easily see his long, curly, brown locks from where they were sitting.

"Look over there. A child is looking at us," Endesha whispered to Zuberi.

"Yes, I see. He is a handsome little one. Maybe he is the son of the chief of this village. Keep your distance boys. We do not want to upset the men that put us here by interacting with this child," Zuberi warned.

Moments later, Stuart Miles could be heard approaching and Harold shot down the stairs fast as a farm mouse. The Sefu men peered down toward the bottom of the stairs, Prince Stuart motioned them to come down. Endesha and Amri complied, and at the bottom of the stairs was a small stack of clothing and some food and water. "Take this to your father and put this on when you are finished," the prince said.

Amri had a look of bewilderment on his face and turned to Endesha for instruction. "I think he wants us to take these things back to Father." Endesha said as he nodded to Prince Stuart, grabbed the food and garb, and turned to go back upstairs.

"Why are these men tending to us so well, Father?" Amri asked skeptically.

"Because they have not decided on what our purpose is," Zuberi replied. "I imagine they think you two are valuable to them somehow. If they had no interest in us, we would still be in that dark place with those other men. But because of what those men from the boat did, and the obvious risk they took in getting us here, I believe we may be able to survive here if we go by their rules," Zuberi warned.

"Or they could just be fattening us up before they eat us," Amri said jokingly as he ripped a chunk of bread away with his teeth.

"I suspect the two of you will be tested very soon. Be prepared to prove yourself," Zuberi warned.

"What kind of test, Father?" asked Endesha.

"A demonstration of your abilities, I would think. I am sure those men told of what Amri did back in the Kuno lands, and they will probably want to see if what they were told he is capable of is true.

"If they are looking for a test, I welcome the opportunity," Amri said.

"Son, do not rush to dig your own grave," Zuberi warned. "If you two fail, all of us will die. Endesha, Amri is used to fighting, but here in this land you will have to let go of anything you may be holding back. You must allow your true self to come through."

"My true self, Father?" Endesha replied.

"What father is trying to say, Endesha, is to let go of your fears. Your true strength is no different than Father's or mine," Amri said.

215

"I am not a warrior like the two of you," Endesha said.

"Yes, you are," Zuberi replied with a chuckle. "You are more like your brother than you may think, my son."

Nodding his head in agreement Amri said, "Father is right, you are much more of a warrior than you think. Father did not see what you and I did to those men from the water. He did not see the delight I saw in your eyes at making those men pay for what they did to us and our mother."

Curious, Zuberi asked Endesha, "What is Amri talking about? Did you enjoy hurting those men from the water?"

"I'm not sure, Father. I was lost within myself. I don't know what I was feeling. I was focused more on hurting them than on what I was feeling," Endesha replied.

"That is exactly what I feel. No different. Do you see now how we are linked?"

"I'm not the one with the mark of the lion—you are, Amri. This was just one time. It won't happen like that again."

"Yes, it will. You are denying what is inside you, Brother. The battle is something you cannot run away from. You have to run *toward* it."

"I will not be consumed by the type of rage you have, Amri. I have seen what it does to you. I have seen how it hurts you, and how you struggle to keep it suppressed here in this place."

"Yes, the rage consumes me, but it may not affect you in the same way. I am asking you to use whatever is inside you to guide your movements. You need to fight with your mind as your first weapon, and a rock in your hand as your second." Amri warned.

"What is your first weapon, Amri?" Zuberi asked curiously.

"*I* am the first weapon. No need for the rock," he replied.

Endesha stood and walked to the other side of the room. "Why do both of you believe I am a warrior?" he asked.

"You forget, Son, Coffa and I were both warriors when we were young like you and Amri," Zuberi said. "You cannot deny what is in your blood.

"You must embrace the fact that you have abilities you have yet to understand, Endesha," Amri said. "I believe that if you are pushed you could be more dangerous than me."

Prince Stuart returned to the stables with several guards. As the group of men made their way up to the attic space Zuberi said, "This may already be the test I spoke of."

"My Father would like to see you again. This time he would like to see what the Carpenter would have had if those men delivered you to them," Stuart said. He pointed toward the stairs with his unsheathed sword.

Prince Stuart did not shackle the Sefu men as they were led down into the practice area adjacent to the stables, and as the two Sefu brothers made their way into the room, they noticed it was filled with many well-dressed individuals. Their jackets had shiny buttons, their shoes were clean, and their hair was neatly coiffed.

The building anticipation in the room made it very warm, which the Sefu men did not mind.

Once everyone was in the room an announcement was made, "Presenting His Royal Majesty King Phillip Miles!" The room clapped a muted applause as King Phillip glided into the space with his heavily adorned crimson and gold robe. He wore a modest golden crown over his silvering hair, and as he walked in a stately stride, he produced a well-rehearsed smile he had delivered more times than he could recall.

"Today is a special day. We are fortunate to witness a gift that was not intended for us to receive, but was in fact intended for Thomas Carpenter.

Two nights ago, we found these Moors shackled in the back of a carriage. Their captors were en route to Tawny, and if they had completed their journey, would have ended up in the hands of Carpenter as human weapons," said King Phillip. "We have been informed, by the now deceased men who brought these Moors into my Midland Kingdom, that they are very dangerous and worthy of the risk taken to transport them.

"We are here today to see if those men were correct in their judgements of the Moors abilities, and if they stand to be impressive, we shall retain them here at Harkstead Castle and use their abilities to the benefit of the Midland Kingdom!" The room broke into loud applause.

The Sefu brothers stood motionless during the king's speech, not understanding the language of the Midlanders, but knowing this man spoke of them. "Prepare yourself, Brother," Amri whispered.

"We will start with the smaller one," King Phillip commanded as the room opened and a circle was formed. Within the circle stood a bearded man significantly smaller than Endesha.

Stuart, using two hands, pushed Endesha into the center of the circle causing him to stumble. He turned around to look behind him and saw Amri towering over everyone. Amri nodded to his brother in approval, and Endesha nodded back in return.

The man raised his fists to a fighting position while Endesha stood still, looking at him. Suddenly, the man threw a right-hand punch to the Sefu man's face, causing Endesha to stumble sideways. Believing the Moor was vulnerable, the pale, bearded fighter struck Endesha again, this time with his left hand. Then another blow from his right fist finally drew blood that cascaded down Endesha's nose. "This Moor is *not* a warrior!" shouted the fighter as the crowd applauded.

Endesha gathered his thoughts as he wiped his face and saw his blood on his fingers. Instead of being enraged, he took notice of his surroundings—he saw the hay they were fighting on. He also noticed the man was barefoot, like he was.

The pale fighter turned toward Endesha to attack again, but before he could step into his next swing, Endesha bent quickly to gather a handful of hay and slung it into the man's face. Then Endesha took both of his legs and pulled them up behind his knees making him fall down onto his back.

Endesha quickly moved on top of the fighter's chest to straddle his upper body while using his knees to restrain his opponent's arms. Lastly, Endesha punched the fighter several times with his right fist, then began to shove large amounts of hay into the man's mouth.

Endesha continued to force the hay into the man's mouth, and the once-pale fighter began to turn bright red.

Just as he was about to lose consciousness, a group of Red Guardsman pulled Endesha off of his opponent and threw him toward his cautiously amused brother, Amri.

"Impressive, Brother. Are you still sure you are *not* a warrior?" Amri said with tremendous pride. The room was filled with quiet murmurs as men tended to Endesha's opponent. They did not applaud until the man was able to vomit out the hay in enough time to breathe the precious air he had been denied.

As the room continued to applaud their approval, King Miles turned to Stuart and whispered, "The use of the hay in this violent display is a sign of intellect. This could be very promising."

"Indeed, Father," Stuart replied.

"Now that we know what the smaller one is capable of, what of the larger one?" King Phillip said loudly. "John Forrester is one of my most celebrated knights of the Red Guard Cavalry, a worthy test for the largest of the Moors, I reckon. Let us see if Sir Forrester can prove this man's abilities are as formidable as the other one." The circle of men opened up to Amri, revealing the large and muscular Forrester—his blue eyes glaring mightily at the Sefu man. His long blond beard and dirty-blond locks were moistened from the temperature in the room, along with Forrester's sweat-filled hatred of any opponent that stood before him.

Amri walked slowly toward him while glancing at the people around the room. They applauded the un-armored Knight of the Red Guard as he raised his muscular arms into the air relishing in the room's uproar.

Amri, like his brother, stood motionless during the theatrics. As the applause died, Sir Forrester ran toward the still-larger Sefu man, who was already estimating the timing of his attack.

Time stood still. Voices turned into muffled tones as Amri's heart began beating violently in his chest, but the warrior in him was at peace. He was alive again; free to do what he enjoyed the most. Free to release what he suppressed the most, the pain he felt from losing all of the things closest to him. Amri's rage grew as he thought of the loss of his home, mother, and the woman he loved.

As Forrester approached Amri in full stride he made the unfortunate error in stopping just short of Amri's reach in order to pull his arm back and deliver a strike to Amri's face with his right fist. This was indeed unfortunate because Amri simultaneously moved his right foot back in order to gather the necessary footing to deliver a crushing downward blow to Sir Forrester's face with his right elbow and forearm. Amri could not contain his emotions within the movement. His muscles were tense with rage and obeyed Amri's wish for maximum damage.

The blow to the Red Guard knight's face left him unconscious but still standing for a fleeting moment before he fell forward onto the hay lined ground. Amri stayed battle-ready until the knight started to convulse violently. Moments afterward, Sir Forrester began to scream and moaned as blood gushed from the left side of his head and within moments his shaking went still.

Amri was breathing calmly as the room was hushed by the demonstration of his immense physical power.

The room snapped back to attention and several gasps could be heard when they realized the knight of the Red Guard was dead.

Shocked at what he had just witnessed, King Phillip said, "It appears that Sir Forrester was unable to provide a suitable challenge for the Moor. We shall be thankful for his years of loyalty to our kingdom, and he will be greatly missed."

He then pointed to Amri and said, "Take him to the dungeons immediately!"

This would be the first time the Harkstead guards had been afraid to follow a direct order from their king. "Restrain, him before you leave unless you want to join Sir Forrester in the afterlife."

Amri was placed in shackles and was gently guided toward the hallway that would lead him down into the dungeons of Harkstead Castle.

As the guests left the gathering, King Phillip told Stuart, "Both of those men are truly special fighters. Imagine what they could do with proper training?"

"Indeed, the larger one is the most formidable fighter I have ever seen," Stuart replied.

"Ensure the larger one is well fed down in the dungeons and his brother as well. Have him returned to his father later on today."

"Yes, Your Majesty." Stuart ordered the guards to escort Endesha back to the stables. He walked slowly as he was still trying to shake off the sting of the blows to his face. Endesha made his way up the stairs leading to the attic above the stables, to find his father, Zuberi, was waiting to receive him. He stood proudly with the assistance of a plank of wood, and his prideful smile was bright as daylight. He welcomed his warrior son with open arms. "My son, you did well. I told you both your tests were coming, and both of you were wonderful."

"Where do you think they took Amri, Father?" Endesha asked.

"I believe they took him back to that terrible place where we were before."

"Do you think he is in danger?"

"No, my son. Amri has proven his worth, and they will not risk hurting him. They will be more afraid of him now than ever before. This is exactly what I told you two was going to happen. Let me look at you."

Zuberi inspected his youngest son's face. "You'll live." Endesha smiled confidently. "Tell me, why did you reach for the yellow grass?" Zuberi asked.

"I remembered an old lesson from Coffa. He once told me to remember what the land gives me because I can use it to survive. So, when I noticed the yellow grass on the ground, I knew I could use it to my advantage. I figured the man would not be able to fight on the slippery grass, and if I could get him off his feet I could defeat him."

"You did very well, Son. I am so proud of you." Zuberi pat Endesha on the back with great pride.

## 25

Deep with the dungeons of Harkstead Castle, Amri Sefu sat on the ground. He was waiting to see if he would finally meet the death he had eluded for all of these years. Violence had never been a concern for Amri. In the back of his mind he always knew his actions would eventually have a severe price to pay, and that debt would be paid with his life.

After the swift defeat of King Phillip's most valuable soldier, Amri figured this was the end of his path and he would be reunited with his mother and dear uncle. However, Amri was proven wrong when he saw the Red Guard assemble in the dungeon hallway for the first time. He noticed this was a significantly different looking group of men than he had seen previously. Their full body armor clanged as they walked toward him as a form of announcement of their presence. The Red Guard knight's faces were covered by helmets adorned with various crimson fabrics and feathers, which complemented their uniformed appearance.

Suddenly, the guards came to attention, and each line turned to face each other within the hallway, creating a path between them. Their coordinated movement signaled someone important was approaching and that someone was Fitzgerald Singletary.

"Captain," said one of the Red Guardsmen as he moved aside to allow Singletary to enter Amri's cell.

He was wearing a suit of armor that was similar to the rest of the men, but shined like nothing Amri had ever seen before. The Sefu warrior did not stand to his feet as Singletary entered the cell.

"You may not understand me, but I do believe you understand war," he said. Water, bread, and a chair were brought into the cell by one of the guards.

Singletary sat in front of Amri with his sheathed sword on the ground to his right. "Drink." As the two men drank the captain continued talking. "I know you do not understand me now, but in time you will learn our language. I believe you are more than what those men who brought you here thought you were." He broke a large piece of freshly baked bread and offered it to Amri. "I see something in you I have never seen before. Your brutality is your greatest asset, but I will show you how to multiply your effectiveness with this."

Singletary lifted his sword off the ground, stood to his feet, and unsheathed his sword. He then motioned Amri to stand as well. "A sword cannot be wielded properly if it is unbalanced," he said. He then placed the sword in his hands horizontally and presented it to Amri. Reluctant, Amri took the sword from the captain, still horizontal, and looked at the fine details on the sword. The hilt featured an elegant knurling which facilitated a secure grip, and the cross-guard was formed with an equally elegant twisting of iron. Amri moved the sword into his right hand—it felt like an extension of his fingers. Without intention, he mistakenly pointed the sword at Singletary, and the Red Guard's armor clanked with intent to rush into the cell. The captain calmly used two fingers to redirect the blade to the side, while signaling the guards to return to formation with his free hand.

Amri turned the sword and twisted it with his wrist. It was light toward the tip, yet heavy in his hand. Singletary noticed the lack of space between the Moors giant hand and the grip.

"You will require a longer hilt, but we have some blades in the armory that you should be able to use. Going forward, you and I will be spending much time together.

I will show you how to wield a sword properly, and in time you will be a great swordsman. For now, you will join your father and brother, and never forget, if you attempt to harm anyone else, your life will most assuredly end."

Amri did not understand what he had been told, but could tell he would not be tested again. He could easily surmise that his actions could be life threatening for the rest of his family.

Amri gave Singletary his sword back, and watched as he placed it into its scabbard and walked out of the cell. The now familiar clank of the Red Guard's armor was heard as the men came to attention as Fitzgerald exited the cell and walked down the hallway. As Fitzgerald proceeded down the hallway, the guards, two at a time, turned and followed behind until there were none left in the hallway.

Moments later, a large man came to Amri's cell. "Let's go, you ugly monster," said Sam. As Amri exited the cell, Sam pushed him in the back. Amri stopped short, and turned toward him. "Keep going if you know what is best for you." He pulled his sword from its scabbard. Amri begrudgingly took the constant pushing from behind as Sam guided him back to the stables.

Endesha was relieved to see his brother was still alive as he saw Amri and Sam approach the stables. "Get up there you bloody mongrel," said Sam as he delivered one last shove to the Sefu's back. Amri leered at the man as he proceeded up the stairs. "*One day, I will kill you with my bare hands, no weapons will be needed,*" Amri said out loud in his Sefu language as he pointed to his escort with his index finger.

Sam walked away grunting to himself as Amri was welcomed by his brother and father. "Son, you did well," Zuberi said.

"It is good to see you alive, Brother," Endesha said.

"It is good to see you both," Amri replied. "Did you see our battles, Father?"

"Yes, I did, and you were who you are," Zuberi replied.

"I was more impressed with Endesha's battle," Amri said as he presented some of the bread he had been given earlier by Singletary.

"Where did you get this from?" Endesha asked.

"The man that talks to us gave it to me," Amri replied. "I think he has found a purpose for us. He allowed me to hold his weapon, and I believe he is going to show me how to use their weapons."

"Of course, they are," Zuberi said. "You are not the only one they will train, Amri. They have found a purpose for both of you, and now you will see how your destines will be fulfilled in this place."

"This time his talk with me was different. He came with many men dressed in the hard, shining shells, like the kind we saw when we first arrived here," Amri said. "They looked like they were his village's warriors, and he was their chief."

"How did you gain his weapon?" Endesha asked.

"He gave it to me."

"What did it feel like?" Zuberi asked.

"I don't know how to describe it, but it felt like it was a part of me, and I want to hold it again."

"You should expect them to begin your training very soon," said Zuberi confidently.

"Do you believe we can survive in this place, Father?" Endesha asked.

"We have no choice but to try. Our goal should be to do whatever it takes to survive here. If we have to kill, then we shall kill. If we are to obey their wishes, then we shall do so.

I need both of you to promise me, whatever happens, you will do these things. Even if something happens to me," said Zuberi.

"If anything happens to you, I will not need to obey anyone," Amri said as he looked over the stable wall, observing the metalsmith working in the distance.

"Amri, you cannot spend your days searching for the death that you believe abandoned you," Zuberi said.

"I don't look for it, Father, but I am not afraid of it either," Amri replied. "I just want to go home, and if I am doomed to be here in this place, then I would rather be carried home by the winds like a feathery seed. At least that way I may have a chance to see our land once again."

"I do not want to die in this land," Endesha said while looking down on the horses below. "Amri, you may be looking to be carried away by the wind on your death, but I see a chance to explore.

I want to know all there is to learn about this place. You seek to destroy this land, and I seek to learn more about it."

"No. I seek to destroy anyone that wishes harm against us, Brother. Nothing more."

"Must you bring strife and sadness too, Amri?" Endesha asked, visibly angry.

"Have you ever thought about how your actions could affect Father?"

"I don't want Father to be hurt, Endesha. I want everything we used to have, I want things to be like they were when we were younger."

"You mean before the lion attack?"

"Yes. Since that terrible day, so many years ago, I have forgotten what it is like to be me. Since then, I have been cursed, and everything, and everyone around me are cursed as well." Amri sat down and looked at the floor.

"Your troubles, Son, are of your own creation. You believe you lost yourself in the mist of that lion attack, but you gained your strength from it. The things you can do in battle were not because of the lion. That power was already inside you. The lion gave you a shell, like the tortoises by our old watering hole." Zuberi looked deeply into his eldest son's eyes. "We may not be free in this place, but you are the freest of the three of us, Amri."

"I do not understand, Father," Amri replied.

"The lion attack gave you the freedom to fight without fear. That is one of the greatest assets a warrior can have. A fighter that is not afraid can be a leader of men, or a killer of many men. Take this time to find your peace, Amri. Make the connection with your inner-self, so you can learn how to channel your fury into pure, intelligent thoughts. It will make you far more effective as a fighter," Zuberi said sternly. He took a big bite of the bread in his hand before turning to address his younger son.

"Endesha, you may not believe your calling is to be a warrior, but in this land, that is what you are.

Your childlike stubbornness is not useful anymore. You, like your brother, must adapt and grow. You must also look within your inner-self to learn how to take advantage of your natural ability to fight. If you do not, Endesha, you will be no different than Armi in making things unsafe for us in this land."

"Father is right. You have to accept *who* you are and quit running away from *what* you are," said Amri.

Endesha stood and started pacing from one end of the attic to the next, finally coming to a stop to sit next to his father.

"I know what you are trying to tell me. I also know Amri and I have to do what these men want us to do, but I don't like it. I realize now that we are not free in this place. We were better off on the waters," said Endesha.

"Brother, we shall do as Father says and work together to keep ourselves safe. But know this, Endesha, if anything happens to our father, you and I will have nothing left to live for other than each other. When that time comes, you will have to make a decision," Amri said as he sat down next to his brother and father.

"What kind of decision is that?" Endesha asked.

"To join me in eliminating everyone here, or run away without me," Amri said as he stared at the weapons in the adjacent training room below.

## 26

Prince Stuart hastened down the castle corridor. He had been summoned to his father's throne room, and as he hurried there, he came upon Fitzgerald Singletary. "His Majesty sent for you as well?" asked Stuart.

"Yes, it sounds as if it is important," Singletary replied.

The two entered King Phillip Miles' chambers to find him sitting on his throne waiting for them. It was a fine and majestic chair made from some of the finest wood in England, and carved by one of the best craftsmen in the Midland Kingdom. King Phillip loved to sit in it and look down on the people four steps below. The throne room was a grand place with extremely high ceilings, smooth stone floors, and intricate stone walls that echoed the king's voice as he spoke.

"Men, come forward," said King Phillip.

"Yes, Your Majesty," the two men replied in tandem.

"I summoned you here because I have word that Carpenter is gathering another army," said King Phillip.

"We have defeated him before, Father, and we shall do it again," Stuart said.

"Do not be over confident, my son. According to our informants his new cavalry alone will be three times as large as his first one.

The Carpenter has enlisted the services of a former soldier of ours, Peter Harris of Derron," King Phillip said while gritting his teeth.

Singletary looked to Stuart with a puzzled look on his face. "Lord Harris? Why does that name sound familiar?" he asked.

"He was the leader of the Red Guard before I took control," Stuart replied.

"Indeed, and he had aspirations to do more than that," King Phillip said.

"What do you mean, Father?"

"When you were much younger, Son, Lord Harris demanded that I give him control of the city of Derron as a gift from one family member to another," King Phillip replied.

"Family?" Stuart said.

"Yes. He is in fact my younger cousin, and his thirst for wealth and power forced me to banish him from Harkstead Castle many years ago. Now he has joined ranks with Carpenter. We may all be in great danger, but I have an idea," King Phillip said as he straightened his back to look directly at the two men below him. "The Moors in the stables are something I have never seen before. Their size and abilities are far more formidable than any Red Guard soldier. If we could find a way to tame them, I believe they would be an unstoppable fighting duo," King Phillip said.

"How would we go about taming them? The larger one seems to only be tolerant of us because of their elder father, Your Majesty," said Singletary.

"I do not know how to tame them. I do know they will comply if they believe we might harm their father," King Phillip replied.

"Please allow me to ensure I am understanding of what you are requesting of us. You would like us to train the two Moors in the stables in formal swordsmanship?" asked Stuart.

"Yes," replied King Phillip.

"You would also aspire to have these men fight with our infantry in battle against Carpenter?" Stuart asked cautiously.

"No. I do not want them to fight with our infantry. I want them to remain here at Harkstead Castle as a means of protection for Prince Harold and myself," King Phillip said.

"You would like them to be your personal guards, Sire?" Singletary asked.

"Indeed. Such men shall be a menacing sight standing to my side in this room. I want all that come before me to marvel at, what I have decided to call, my 'Dark Warriors,'" King Phillip said with aristocratic pride. "Singletary, you are one of the finest swordsmen in the Midland Kingdom. See to it those men are taught all that you know. I want them to be as skilled with a blade as they are imposing to look at."

"Yes, Your Majesty," Singletary replied.

"Stuart, see that they are well fed. I want those men to be as strong as we know they are. Their slight appearance may be due to their long travels from wherever those men found them," King Phillip said.

"I will see to it that they are well-fed, Sire," Stuart replied.

"You may now leave. And remember, we must be prepared for anything going forward. Carpenter must not be underestimated," King Phillip warned.

"Yes, Sire," they replied. The two men left King Phillip as he gazed at the crimson and gold tapestries bearing his family's crest on the walls of the chamber.

Later that day the Sefu men were startled to see a large group of Harkstead servants arrive at the bottom of their attic stairway. Within moments, the servants had lined the stairs and began passing food up to the Sefu men.

"Look at all of the food they are bringing us!" Endesha said with joyous hunger.

"Are they giving us one last meal before disposing of us?" Amri quipped.

"No, my sons, your purpose has been decided, and you two will have to become the warriors they believe you will be," Zuberi said as he joined Endesha in the excitement of seeing so much food being given to them.

The servants left the Sefu men with more food than they had ever seen in their lives. They did not know where to start. They finally decided to try some of the wine, but it was too bitter. They recognized some berries that were on a small platter. "I know these will taste good," Endesha said as he filled his mouth with a small handful. His eyes rolled back in his head with pleasure, and his smile was so big he could barely contain the half-chewed berries in his mouth.

"I guess those *do* taste good." Amri laughed as he placed a few berries in his mouth.

The Sefu men enjoyed the various fruits from their new land. Apples, blueberries, and sweet plums, were things that did not grow in their native Africa.

The sweetness of the fruits was only challenged in popularity by the soft texture and wonderful smells from the basket of freshly baked breads. Amri was about to join his father in trying a piece of bread when he noticed a rather large piece of meat on another tray—a whole roasted turkey. Amri tore a leg off and bit into it with fury, the flavor was delightful to him. This meal made him think of the feasts they used to have back at his village, and for a brief moment, Amri felt sadness. "We have not eaten like this since we were back home," he said.

"You are right. It has been a long time, Brother," Endesha said.

"We should be truly grateful for what the land has given us. You two should prepare yourselves. I sense this meal comes with expectations," Zuberi warned.

"What do you mean, Father?" Endesha asked.

"Clearly, these people want you two to be as healthy as possible," Zuberi replied.

"Before they kill us," said Amri.

"If that is the case, maybe I should have some more meat," Endesha said jokingly. The Sefu men shared a small laugh.

## 27

The next morning, Prince Stuart and Singletary arrived at the Sefu men's attic. The brothers did not know what was in store for them, but felt certain it was related to the warning their father had given them the day before. "You two come with us," Stuart commanded. The Sefu brothers did not move, they did not understand what they were being told.

"Your Highness, they do not speak our language." Singletary gently reminded Stuart.

"Oh yes. I forgot, thank you."

The two men motioned with their sheathed swords to follow them down the stairs. Zuberi looked at his sons, and said, "You will find out what they want from you today. Do your best to please them."

"We will, Father," Amri replied.

The two brothers were escorted to the armory adjacent to the stables, and visible to Zuberi from his perch in the attic. Stuart gave the brothers practice swords made of wood, and said, "This is called a waster, you will use them to practice so you do not lop each other's arms off." The two brothers looked at the wasters, then at each other with childlike bewilderment. Sensing their first failure in instruction, Singletary said, "Your Highness, maybe we should show them, then let them mimic our movements?"

"Agreed," Stuart replied. Singletary unsheathed his sword, and Endesha flinched in unnecessary fear.

"Why did you move, little boy?" Amri snipped under his breath.

"I don't know," Endesha replied.

Singletary and Stuart were standing face to face with their swords drawn. "The secret to being an excellent swordsman is understanding your footing," Singletary said as he pointed to his feet. His stance was wide with enough spacing to keep his upper torso in a straight line. The Sefu men would need to learn that this was the posture needed to block and return sword strikes. The prince and captain began to simulate a sword fight. Their movements were slowed to show the precision of their movements. Amri and Endesha watched them with great concentration.

After a few minutes, Stuart and Singletary sheathed their swords and walked over to the armory shelves. Each took a waster and stood face to face with the Sefu brothers. They took their first positions and waited for the Sefu brothers to do the same. They could tell the brothers had indeed been paying attention to what they were shown as the two Moors shadowed their stance. Singletary noticed Amri's posture was incorrect and used his waster to straighten his back and adjust the angle of his sword's "ready" position.

"All right, large one, I want you to block my strike," said Singletary as he tapped his waster against Amri's. He then used the upper portion of his sword to hit the side of Amri's knee on his lead leg. Amri did not block Singletary's strike. He hit Amri in the same place with more force, and it was still left unblocked. With the connection of the second strike, something rose up within Amri, a familiar feeling came over him.

Without thought, he blocked Singletary's next strike, and even countered, with impressive speed, a strike to the captain's shoulder.

The surprising sting from Amri's strike made Singletary smile, and he said to Stuart, "I think these Moors will do just fine."

Over the next several days, the Sefu brothers became more familiar with the teachings of their captive instructors. Both sets of men worked diligently to share their knowledge while respecting each other's ability to kill one another if needed.

Amri enjoyed the lessons Singletary was teaching him. Singletary thought he was giving the Moors the basic skills to perform the task of being King Phillip's personal guard. Amri and Endesha Sefu had no intention for their skills to be remotely "basic" in any form. Both brothers began to practice their offensive and defensive strikes in the evening under the watchful eyes of their father. They practiced their craft religiously, often late into the cold English evening.

"Good," said Zuberi with a pleased look on his face. "You two are fighting like the men that are training you. Endesha, you must use your mind to keep Amri from using his strength against you! Amri do not let your anger alter your technique. The two of you have different strengths and weaknesses. The idea is to fight using your strengths while not allowing your enemy to discover your weaknesses."

"Father, how can we *not* allow our enemies to discover our weaknesses?" Endesha asked.

Amri shook his head, and sat down on the other side of the room. Zuberi hobbled over to his youngest son, kissed him on the forehead and said to him softly, "You must kill your enemy before he discovers your weakness."

"Father is correct. In battle, you do not have time to show any skills you are lacking," Amri said. "You have to be so good with your abilities, your enemy does not have time to react to your actions. This is why we have to do our best to learn the fighting style those men are teaching us."

"A word of caution, my sons," Zuberi chimed in. "You must not let your trainers know your skills are more advanced than theirs."

"If they know our abilities are better than theirs, they may try to kill us for fear they would not be able to stop us. Which is exactly what I am hoping will happen," said Amri.

"No. You will suppress showing your trainers your abilities unless absolutely necessary. Let them believe you do not understand their commands and are learning slowly," Zuberi said.

"What have you been doing while we have been training?" Endesha asked.

"I found some long wood and carved myself a walking stick. While you two are sleeping after your training, I go see the man that is shaping fire. I was not sure if he would allow me to watch him, but he did not seem to mind me looking over his shoulder," Zuberi said while leaning on his finely carved walking stick.

"That man is not shaping fire, he is in charge of creating the weapons in this place," Amri said.

"I am aware of that, Amri. My plan is to learn how to make these people's weapons, so I can create weapons for the two of you when possible."

"Is that all that you have been doing, Father?" Amri asked.

"No. I have also been tending to the animals below. I figure the men do not restrict my movements because of my age. They do not see me as a threat to them," Zuberi replied.

"Have you been outside of this area since we were brought here?" Endesha asked curiously.

"I have not. I believe we are not meant to be seen. We know they want us to live and learn how to fight with their weapons, and they are teaching you two themselves. The question we need to find out is; why?" Zuberi said. "There is also something I want to warn you both of, as well."

"What is that, Father?" Amri asked.

"There is a little one that likes to watch us from a distance," Zuberi replied. "I believe it is a little boy."

"A child? I have not seen a child," Endesha said.

"Yes, you have Desha, he had blue eyes, and curly brown hair. Right, Father?" Amri asked. "I have seen him many times since they came to us with food the first time."

"I did not see him that day," Endesha said.

"I see everything," Amri said.

"Then you must understand, Amri, the child is dangerous to us. If anything happened to the young one while around us, they would hold us to blame, and we would all perish," Zuberi said with a serious tone. "We must ensure that the child is not around us."

"Father, that may not be possible. If this place is the child's home we cannot control where that child goes," Endesha said.

"I understand, but for now, you are to avoid that young boy. Do you understand me?" Zuberi demanded.

"Yes, Father," both sons replied.

The following morning was sunny. Beams of sunlight shone brightly through the small cracks of the old Harkstead Castle stables. There was not much activity below as the riders had not yet left for their daily activities, and the horses were calm and quiet.

The Sefu men were asleep in their attic above the stables. When a faint noise, not loud enough to wake any of the Sefu men but Amri, was heard from below. Instinctively, he opened one eye to scan the area. The sound seemed to be coming from the stairs, and it was getting closer. Amri focused his eye on the stairs in front of him. The sound continued to get closer... closer, and Amri's breathing ceased. Now with both eyes open, he tensed his muscles, preparing to respond to an attack. But when he saw the sight of brown, curly hair over the top of the stairs, Amri's breath returned to him. It was the nine-year-old Prince Harold, and he was supremely curious about the guests in his father's stable attic.

Amri had slammed his eyes shut as the boy made his way into the room, and continued to lie as if asleep as he watched—through slivered eyes—young Harold discover a piece of fruit, and quietly eat it while observing his father's dark-skinned guests sleep above his favorite pet horse. Harold noticed Endesha's wide, pronounced nose. It was considerably larger than his, and he decided he wanted to get a closer look. He crawled on his hands and knees toward where Endesha was laying, gathered up the courage to extend his index finger, and finally touched his nose. Endesha's eyes shot open, and he recoiled in fear.

"Ah! He screamed as he scrambled backward away from Harold, pinning his body up against the wall. Harold recoiled as well, but he did not seem to be afraid of Endesha. Amri was full of laughter saying, "You almost jumped over the wall to the animals below."

"This is the boy I was telling you two about last night," Zuberi said as he tried to suppress his amusement.

"What do we do now?" Amri asked.

"Nothing," Zuberi replied. "Maybe he will go back to his parents after he is finished playing with us? We should try to tell someone he is here with us." He looked below to see if anyone was obviously searching for the boy.

Harold did not know what to make of his knew dark-skinned friends. They did not look like any men he had ever seen before. Their skin was dark like leather, and their eyes were the same shade of brown. The older one had soft-looking, very gray hair, the largest one had a bountiful amount of long black hair, and the smaller one had no hair at all which peaked Harold's curiosity. Endesha had a condition that prevented him from growing hair. His uncle Coffa had a similar condition as well.

Harold summoned his bravery, went back to where the fruit was, picked up and apple, and offered it to Endesha. "Apple," the boy said. Endesha did not respond. Harold extended his hand further and repeated, "Apple."

Endesha quickly figured out what the child was attempting to do, and replied, "*ah-pull.*"

Harold nodded and repeated once more, "Apple." He put the fruit in Endesha's hand.

"*ah-pull*," Endesha said again as he took the fruit from the young prince.

"Ap-ple." Harold bit into his fruit.

"Apple." Endesha took a bite from the fruit given to him by his new royal friend.

Amri sat up and started to shake his head in disgust saying, "Father told you not to interact with that little boy last night, and the first thing you do this morning is interact with the little boy. Yet, you think I am the one that is eager to die."

"What are you two saying?" Harold asked. "You guys make funny sounds with your mouths."

"You see that, Endesha? Do you know what that is? Death," said Amri as he smiled at his father.

"I have to go now. I will be back soon," Harold told the Sefu men. He waved his hand to gesture "good-bye" and the Sefu men mimicked his movements in return. Harold quickly ran down the stairs, around his pet horse, and out of the stables.

"You seemed to have made a friend, my son," Zuberi said.

"I thought you did not want us to be around the child?" Endesha asked with a confused look on his face.

"I listened to both of you last night, and you were correct in saying we cannot control where he goes. We can only hope that if we keep him safe, we will in turn remain safe too!" Zuberi said.

## 28

It had been months since Harold's first visit, and he had been visiting the Sefu men more frequently. During his visits, he had been helping the Sefu men learn how to speak English, and to his credit, was a good little teacher. Harold and Endesha even found they enjoyed each other's company. Endesha especially liked having the child around because it meant he wasn't the youngest anymore. Amri did not want to be bothered by Harold, and did not entertain thoughts of engaging the young prince in any way other than to learn his language.

One day, Prince Stuart stopped by the attic space after a training session. "Have you seen my little brother?" he asked the Sefu men. "Of course, you do not understand me." He motioned with his hand to reflect the height of a small child, and repeated his question, "Have you seen Harold?" They shook their heads to indicate no knowledge of the young boy's whereabouts. "If you see him, bring him to me inside." Stuart looked to Endesha—who, in turn, looked surprised that Stuart was directing his words toward him. "Harold says you are his friends, and *you* are his best friend." He poked a finger at Endesha. Stuart continued on to say, "Well, if you see him bring, him inside to the king's chambers." He then turned and left the stables.

An hour or so later, the young prince arrived at the stables covered in dirt and filth, and did not say a word as he climbed the stairs to the attic. Endesha saw the young prince, and looked to his father, who smiled and said, "You have your orders."

Amri joined in his father's amusement and said, "Good luck with that."

Endesha turned back to look at the filthy young boy, and told him in English, "Inside. I have to take you to father."

"Your. You forgot to say 'your' father," Harold replied.

"I have to take you to *your* father," Endesha said again with purpose.

As the two walked through the castle corridors, many people stared at the large, brown-skinned man being led by the young prince. Endesha could not tell if the people staring at them were looking at him, or—quite possibly—the dirtiest child in the Midland Kingdom.

When the duo arrived at the king's chambers, Harold did not want to knock, and stood motionless in front of the door. Endesha remembered it was customary to pound your closed fist against the door, but he did not remember how, so he punched the door with his closed fist as if he was fighting a man. "That is not how you knock on the door!" Harold said loudly.

King Phillip heard the intense bang on the door from Endesha's misunderstood door-knocking technique, and as he opened it, did not notice Endesha standing next to Harold, but said, "My word. What happened to you, dear child?"

"Father, I took my horse for a ride, and he threw me off," Harold explained.

"You got that dirty from one fall?" Phillip asked.

"He seemed startled, Father, and would not let me remount him. I had to walk him all the way back here."

"Who were you riding with?" his father asked.

"I went out by myself."

"Harold, you know you are forbidden to go outside the castle walls. Especially by yourself." He was obviously restraining his anger, when Phillip finally noticed Endesha standing near the door. "Did you bring Harold here?"

"Stuart said bring here," Endesha said with fading confidence in his speaking ability.

"Thank you. You may return to the stables now." Phillip dismissed him.

"No, Father can he stay? His name is E-dasha," Harold said.

"En-Desha." Endesha corrected the young prince.

"Endesha," the boy repeated.

Endesha nodded in approval.

"I am teaching Endesha, his brother, and father our language, Father," Harold said with much pride.

"Are you? You seem to be doing a good job, my son," said King Phillip. The king noticed the way Harold and Endesha interacted, and even though it was curious to him, it pleased him to see his young son take charge and show the initial spark of leadership he would need to properly rule the Midland Kingdom one day.

"Have the guards take you to your quarters, so the maidens can clean you properly. We will discuss your indiscretions of today, tomorrow. See to it both of you eat, and then you shall rest," said King Phillip as Stuart arrived in the room.

Stuart looked at his filthy, tattered young brother, and started to say something to him, but seeing the frustration on the king's face, decided to let the young prince and his large brown friend continue exiting the room.

After they left, Stuart said, "What happened to him?"

"He went riding without any protection. You do realize what could have happened to him if he was recognized, or worse, kidnapped by someone associated with the Carpenter."

"Yes, Sire, my apologies. I spoke with one of attending maidens, and she said he had been in his bed one moment, and gone the next. She thought he snuck out of the castle around midday."

"The Moor, Endesha, said you told him to bring Harold to me."

"Yes, Sire."

"Maybe we need to keep Endesha with Harold. He would be a suitable guard for the boy, and they seem to like being around each other." King Phillip sat down, and took a large swallow of wine from his perfectly polished brass goblet.

"I agree, Your Majesty. Harold needs a companion we can trust to be both friend and protector."

"Then make it so. Allow—what was his name again...? Oh, Endesha, to be in the castle with Harold as needed." King Phillip shook his head in disgust as he recalled the way Harold had looked.

*** 

Once Harold was clean, and the two of them had eaten the dinner prepared for them, Harold looked at Endesha from his lavishly adorned bed, and said, "I mustn't leave the castle by myself. I know Father is not happy with me."

"Not smart," Endesha said.

"Will you come back here tomorrow, Endesha?"

"Father says so, yes. You rest," he said gently as he stood to his feet and smiled at the young prince before leaving the room.

"Goodnight!" Harold said to Endesha as he left. Overwhelmed by his use of so many new words, Endesha surrendered to his lack of confidence and waved goodbye awkwardly before leaving the room.

He returned to the stables to find Amri and his father curious to hear what happened with Harold inside Harkstead Castle. "Did you take him to his father?" Zuberi asked.

"Yes, I did," Endesha replied while producing several items from the private meal he had with Harold. As Zuberi and Amri sampled some of the delicious cakes and pies, Amri took a break from eating to ask, "Was his father upset with him?"

"I think so. The boy had left the castle alone."

"How did you get this food?" Zuberi asked.

"After a woman cleaned him, we were fed before he was to rest."

"Did you go to places inside we have not seen before?" Amri asked.

"It was different than the parts we were taken to. The young boy took me through the main hallways, and there were many people looking at us."

"Were they looking at you?" Zuberi asked.

"I'm not sure. Probably."

"Sounds like you have an opportunity to teach instead of being the one that is taught," Zuberi said.

"What do you mean, Father?"

"It is your turn to be for him what Coffa was for you," Zuberi said smiling.

"I am not a teacher."

"But you could be to him what Uncle Coffa was to us, Desha." Amri agreed with his father.

"Maybe this is your destiny, my son. Look at you. You are eating the finest food, and walking freely without being told what to do. You have created your value to these people. This is a good thing." He looked at his sons with great pride.

"If he is to be Coffa to the young boy, then what does that make me? A caged animal?" asked Amri.

"Your purpose has yet to be defined for these people, my son. You and I both know you are considered more of a threat than your brother and I," Zuberi said.

"No matter. I am enjoying my lessons and training. I feel alive when I have those weapons in my hands," Amri replied.

"You are becoming very good, Amri, I must agree. Maybe you could be their Sefu supreme warrior, or something," Endesha said with laughter.

"Whatever it is they are training me for, I am looking forward to it. I need to smell blood, so my mind stops reminding me of how Nsia smelled," Amri said as he looked to the ground.

## 29

Almost three years had passed, and there had been many changes at Harkstead Castle. King Phillip Miles had been keeping a close eye on the Carpenter's rising Army yet he had not attacked any major Midland cities or smaller villages within the kingdom in years. Endesha and Harold had become very close, especially now that he was approaching his twelfth birthday.

The Sefu men had not been allowed to leave the castle since their arrival almost three years ago. They made the best of it by learning the language of the Midland people and had made improvements to their attic space, including a place for Zuberi to carve and create his own artifacts.

The Red Guard was becoming older and new recruits were not meeting Prince Stuart's high standards, so change was in order. King Phillip was unhappy with his current cavalry, and was pacing from one chamber wall to the other, seething with anger. His flowing crimson and gold robe billowed majestically behind him as he changed directions. The King had never noticed he paced when angry, but everyone around him knew it as a clear indicator of a sour temperament and to avoid his sight. "What of the Red, my son?" he finally spoke.

"The Red Guard is sufficient in size, Your Majesty, but I am concerned they are not as sprite as they once were," Stuart replied.

"Was it not yours and Captain Singletary's responsibility to ensure the Red Guard lived up to their reputation as the Midland Kingdom's deadliest fighting cavalry?"

"Yes, Your Majesty, but the elder members of the Red are becoming too old to fight. The many years of inactivity from the Carpenter may also be cause for their declining performance. We have no other foes," Stuart replied.

"Maybe it is time to test their abilities—see which of them are still truly worthy of fighting under Harkstead Castle banners."

"What do you have in mind, Father?"

"Gather the Red, and march them to the fields near Thornton at night. There they will fight my "Dark Warrior" to prove they are worthy of being called elite."

"Sire, you want them to fight Amri to the death?"

"Who is Amri?"

"Amri is the one you refer to as your "Dark Warrior," Your Majesty."

"How do you know these things, my child?"

"He told me, Sire. They can speak our language now."

"Very well, then tell Amri he is to not kill any of the Red Guardsmen, but only test their abilities."

"Shall I tell the members of the Red not to harm Amri?"

"No. If Amri is what we think he is, they shall not be able to harm him."

The next evening, Prince Stuart arrived at the stables and made his way up to the top of the attic stairs.

The Sefu men were relaxing when Prince Stuart approached. "I am here to take you on a mission," Stuart said to Amri.

"Am I allowed to ask what kind of mission?" Amri replied.

"When you address me, you end your sentence with, Your Highness." Amri looked at the prince with a blank expression on his face. "Come with me now," said Stuart as he went back down the stairs.

"I will see you soon," he said to his father and brother.

"Be safe, Son," Zuberi replied.

Amri gave Endesha a slight stare; it was a non-verbal communication between the two brothers that meant Amri felt he would be fine, and not to worry, so Endesha held his peace.

At the bottom of the stairs was the familiar face of Sam. The same man Amri threatened to kill with his bare hands years ago. "Tonight, we get to see how good you really are!" Sam said. The foul stench of wine and rotten food stuck within his maw wafted when he spoke. Amri did not respond.

Prince Stuart mounted his prized white purebred Spanish stallion, and joined by his Chief of Command, Captain Fitzgerald Singletary, riding an equally majestic black horse.

Amri was carried to Thornton on the back of a Flemish, which was ideal for a man of Amri's massive size. This was the first time he had been allowed to go beyond the gates of Harkstead Castle, and breathe air that was not carrying the stench of horse manure and hay.

As they rode, Amri looked up to the night sky, and once again, he could see the stars.

It had been so long since he had seen them, and on this particular night, the sky was as clear as it had been when he lay on the beach at night with his dear Nsia. A sudden gust of wind—so strong it moved the horses off course for a moment—made Amri shut his eyes and murmur, "Thank you mother." The wind reminded him of her love and safety on the voyage to the English land he now called home, and he knew she was still with him.

Upon arriving at the fields of Thornton, Amri saw a large group of men standing on the field. Some of them wore armor and some did not. Stuart dismounted his steed, walked toward the group and said, "Tonight we will see if some of you are truly worthy of wearing the colors of the Royal Red Guard. I fought alongside many of you when we won the battle of Aveston. Tonight, will be a test of your mettle. Tonight, we will see if you still live up to what is expected of a member of the Red Guard. The most feared cavalry in all of the Midland Kingdom!" The men cheered.

"Most of you have heard of the king's dark warriors, but many of you may not have seen one of them before now. This is Amri, and as you can see, he is like no man that has ever walked English soil. Ownership of him and his brother was intended for the Carpenter, and his enormous size and power were to be used against us as a secret weapon to spill our blood. On this eve, Amri will challenge you and your skills, and through this, you will prove if you are worthy enough to remain as one of the true elite warriors of the Midland Kingdom. Who shall be first to fight him?"

"I will fight this wretched Moor," Sam said as he walked forward through the large crowd of men.

"Very well, Sam, you will be the first to prove your place and rank within our cavalry," Stuart said.

Sam was clothed in chainmail and some light armoring—Amri was clothed in something similar to what a farmer would wear: thin, and ill-fitted to his large body.

The fields of Thornton were not exactly suitable for fighting. The land was soft from many days of English rains, and the grass was high where the horses had not grazed. Amri stood motionless in the middle of a circle of men. Several wooden torches lit the area, and Amri's darkened muscles could be seen in detail as the men stepped back several paces to give the fighters room to see each other before they began.

Even without the armor that Sam had, Amri's formidable presence was undeniable. His long black dreadlocks covered the scars on the right side of his face, and his sinister smile confused many of the Red Guard soldiers who thought he should have been scared.

When Singletary tossed Amri the sword he would be fighting with, Amri caught it with the pommel facing up and blade down; he deftly spun the sword in his hand to bring the blade up. A sign of true swordsmanship and something Captain Singletary had not trained Amri to do.

It was time for Sam to prove he belonged with the Red Guard. His anger was at its highest as he walked toward Amri, his two-handed broadsword held in the prone position.

As Sam approached, Amri noticed the fires on the torches stood still as if even the wind did not want to miss any detail of what was to come. He took a defensive position as Sam swung violently, striking Amri's sword with a crossing slash. Amri easily blocked it, and the following slash to his opposite side.

With every blow given, Sam grunted like a mad animal. His eyes were filled with anger, and his long blond hair whipped behind his neck with every strike he made. Amri had yet to counter any of Sam's offensive blows. It almost seemed as if Amri was not paying attention, and this observation became undeniable as Amri dropped his guard after a series of blocked strikes allowing Sam to land a punch to his face with his off hand. This brought Amri into focus, and as Sam turned his back to Amri in delight of being the first person to physically touch the king's dark warrior, Amri came into his altered self.

"*My turn*," Amri said to himself as he twirled the sword within his right hand and adjusted his footing. Sam turned back, took his position, and lunged at Amri with a straight forward strike. Amri blocked it, parried to the right, and countered with a downward slash.

Sam, almost unable to block Amri's blow, stumbled backward as he tried to quell the power of Amri's strike. Embarrassed and in full rage, Sam foolishly raised his two-handed broadsword above his head in preparation of a mighty downward drive.

Amri wisely noticed the error and kicked one of Sam's knees, forcing him off balance and causing him to lower his sword to his side. This left Sam's right side unguarded and Amri struck him in the face with his left hand. As Amri threw the punch he knew he wanted Sam to feel his power, but he knew he mustn't kill him. He used only enough power to hurt Sam and possibly embarrass him a bit as well. Time seemed to stand still as Amri's left handed punch made Sam's head snap to the left in an unnaturally fast way.

Globs of spittle, along with blood and teeth, released themselves from Sam's mouth as Amri's darkened fist traveled across the landscape of Sam's bearded jowl.

A hush came across the crowd of men as Sam stumbled, then dropped to one of his knees. He tried to use the downturned blade of his sword as a means to assist him in standing upright, but could not maintain his balance. The match was over; Amri was victorious, yet one could not tell by looking at him—the "Dark Warrior" remained ready.

As men helped Sam away from the fighting area, Amri did not show any pleasure in his triumph. He did not think he could not fight all fifty members of the elite cavalry, but knew he wasn't being given any other option than to do so.

One by one, each member of the Red Guard Cavalry took their opportunity to fight the king's mighty "Dark Warrior," and none of them was successful. As Amri tired, some came close by landing skilled strikes with their swords against him; others could not withstand the awesome physical strength the Sefu man possessed.

Frustrated and annoyed, many of the Red Guard suggested they should gang up to kill Amri with the logic that, "He could not defeat us all at once." Prince Stuart reminded them, the King's wishes were for Amri to fight individual members of the Red Cavalry, and his purpose was to test their abilities, not be killed by their blades.

It was late in the evening when Singletary suggested, "Maybe we should end this challenge. The men are weary, and Amri looks to be in no condition to go any further."

"Indeed, we shall stop here," Stuart replied.

Stuart approached the visibly tired Amri and said loudly, "Let every man here know his place within the Red is not guaranteed. Amri has shown us all how much we have to learn.

Not only from the pain he has inflicted on us, but deaths from our enemies he has prevented here by exposing our weaknesses. We shall return to Harkstead Castle and take what we have learned here to train mightily. We must earn our right to wear our King's colors with pride and with great skill." Stuart raised his sword high above his head.

The soldier's cheered despite their Sefu delivered wounds giving them much pain and discomfort. Amri kept to himself as the men gathered their belongings and began mounting their horses. Singletary walked up to Amri and said, "You did well today, Amri, and you managed to not kill anyone."

"If I had, would you have stopped them from trying to kill me?" Amri asked.

It took a moment before Singletary responded, but when he finally did, he avoided Amri's question, and instead said, "The men got a chance to see they were lacking skills which is a problem you do not seem to have, Amri." The captain took back Amri's sword, and inspected it and cleaned it with a cloth before putting it back in its scabbard. "It appears you have been doing some practicing on your own. There were several instances in which you performed skills I did not teach you."

"I learn quickly."

"I believe you are holding back on your true abilities. I would advise you to not seek an opportunity to use them because that would not favor well for the rest of your family."

Amri looked down at Singletary with suppressed anger as he mounted his Flemish and followed the captain back to Harkstead Castle.

When the men returned, the stablemen took their horses. Endesha and Zuberi were waiting in a shadowy corner of the stable to see if Amri was one of the riders. For a moment, they were fearful the riders killed him, but to their relief, Amri was one of the last riders to re-enter the castle walls. He was visibly hurt with many bruises and blood covering his dark skin, but he was alive, and Zuberi was relieved when he said to Amri, "You did well, my son."

Endesha was able to get Amri up the stairs to the attic. "I told you they would not touch me," Amri said to Endesha in the Sefu language.

"It looks like they tried their best to not touch you," Endesha replied.

"Hold your tongue, Amri, and rest," Zuberi commanded.

Within moments, he was in a deep slumber. Endesha and his father gathered water and rags in preparation to clean Amri's wounds. Zuberi lovingly cleaned Amri's bloodied body, and much to his surprise, found the blood was not his. "Look Desha the blood on Amri is not his, it is from the defeated," Zuberi said.

"Maybe Amri has finally become what he did not want to be," Endesha said.

"What is that?"

"A monster."

Amri slept through the night, the morning, and finally awoke at midday. The sun's rays were not warm and inviting to Amri.

It seemed like his body was waiting for him to wake so he could feel the pain he could not feel while sleeping. "Is it morning yet?" he asked.

"Morning has long past, my son," Zuberi replied.

"How do you feel, Amri?" Endesha asked.

"I've had better days," he replied.

"What did they do to you last night?" Zuberi asked.

"They had me go against the members of a special fighting group that is supposed to be the best in the land."

"Were they any good?" Endesha asked.

"Not really. They were better than I expected, but I was holding back. Father was right about not showing them my true abilities."

"They now know you have skills that could be superior to theirs. You must be careful, Amri," Zuberi said.

"I understand, Father. I will remain diligent in keeping my skills veiled." Endesha brought Amri some food. He sat up and began to eat it very slowly. "There is an enemy of these men outside of this place called the Carpenter. The men that call themselves the Red Guard said he is building a large army and they must prepare for an attack at any moment. My job last night was to show the men what they were lacking in battle," said Amri.

"It sounds like they are not prepared for combat if you were holding back your abilities from them," Zuberi said.

"Indeed. I do not believe these men could stop an attack from this Carpenter person."

"I am glad you were able to defend yourself without killing anyone," Endesha said as he looked at his father. "Amri, we are never going home. You know this and *I* do not want to die in this place."

"*Hark-stead*, is the name of this place, Endesha," said Amri.

"Harkstead Castle, not our home, but it is where we live," Endesha said.

"If this is not our home, then are we really living?" Amri replied.

"What do you mean, my son?" Zuberi asked.

"Father, we were chased out of our own village to live with another tribe, only to be banished away. Then it got worse; we were brought to this place on a boat, sold as human weapons, then forced to be a fighter and caretaker for a little boy. Is this living to you, Father?" Amri asked with despair in his eyes.

Zuberi was shocked to see his warrior son so troubled. He wanted to tell him things were going to be all right, but he could not. He did not know what the future would bring, but he knew his time on earth was coming to an end. He worried that without his presence in his son's lives they may lose their self-control and ultimately perish as well.

Zuberi took a deep breath and with great sadness in his heart said, "Amri, we did have all of those terrible things happen to us, but you must understand they were for a reason. Your life could have ended years ago with that lion, but you survived then just as you have survived to this point. I know you miss our home, your mother, Coffa, and Nsia, but know that Endesha

261

needs you, and *you* need him. Family is the only tie to our homeland that we have in this *Hark-stead* place.

All the two of you have is each other, so you must work as hard as you can to survive for one another. I will not be here with you boys forever, and it is my wish that you two have long lives here in this place."

"Father, do not say such things. You will be with us for many more years," Endesha said with confidence.

"One day, you two will have children of your own, and you will tell them all of the stories of our homeland. You will teach them our Sefu language, and they will be great warriors just like you both are. Enough of this talk. Amri, you need to eat more. Endesha will help you walk afterwards."

"Yes, Father," Amri and Endesha replied together.

Many hours later, Amri was starting to feel better. He had spent much of the day resting, and that rest was helping his body repair itself. The consistent availability of food helped as well. The ease of access to sustenance over the last few years had also provided Amri and Endesha with physically imposing bodies.

Their darkened skin, huge muscles, and tall stature had made them the subject of many whispers within Harkstead Castle.

Amri was especially daunting with long black dreadlocks covering his scarred face. Many of the young maidens in Harkstead Castle had taken interest in visiting the stables, hoping to get a glimpse of the "Dark Warriors" that were rumored to be kept within. King Phillip had forbidden any female to be in the stables in an attempt to keep the owners of curious gazes from becoming vessels for Sefu passion.

Stuart arrived at the stables with young Harold just as the sun started to set. "Hello, Endesha," the young prince said.

"Hello, Harold," he replied.

"We came here to tell you our father, King Phillip Miles, is requesting your presence in the throne room tomorrow evening," Stuart said.

"What is this about?" Amri asked suspiciously.

"You will find out when it is time. If you are worried it will be like last night, I assure you now, it will not. Your efforts were appreciated, and I believe my father will not have you performing that function again. He has different plans."

Amri and Endesha looked to each other after Stuart's last statement.

"Can Endesha come with me to my room?" Harold asked Stuart.

"No, Harold, let Endesha and his father tend to Amri. You will see them tomorrow."

As Stuart turned to go down the stairs, Harold waved goodbye to Endesha and the other Sefu men.

His innocence and sincerity reminded the Sefu men that life was indeed worth living knowing that at least one person did not believe them to be the monsters others saw them as.

## 30

The next day, the Sefu brothers found themselves standing before King Phillip Miles, all of his top advisors, and personal servants in his majestic throne room. He was looking especially regal with his golden crown sitting perfectly atop his head as each graying hair seemed to be turned up or down with purpose.

Prince Stuart and Fitzgerald Singletary escorted the Sefu brothers; both wore formal garments adorned with the crimson and gold colors of Harkstead Castle. Neither of the Sefu men seemed to be impressed with the king's intentional display of regality, but this formal event was not for the benefit of the Sefu brothers. The intention of this display was to inform everyone within Harkstead Castle of a very important declaration as to who his "Dark Warriors" were and their new purpose to the crown.

"Before me stand two Moors that many of you have never seen before. They come from a place very far from here. A place we will never go, nor would we ever want to visit. These Moors look like something from our most terrible dreams, and that is exactly what they are—demons and monsters— which is why they are here before you. Amri and Endesha are now my personal guards, and shall stand here beside me. Carpenter may have his army but he does not have two "Dark Warriors" at his side," King Phillip proclaimed. He then motioned to Captain Singletary and told him, "See to it that Amri and Endesha are given clothing worthy of my excellence."

"Yes, Your Majesty," he replied.

Endesha did not know what to think of the information they had been told. Amri was emotionless.

In the back of his mind, he did not care what was being asked of him, he only wanted to know when he could return to the stables. Unfortunately, that was no longer going to be possible for the Sefu brothers.

"Stuart, I want you and Singletary to escort these men to their quarters," said King Phillip.

"Yes, Your Majesty," Stuart replied. "Guards!" Eight heavily armored guards with their swords drawn approached Amri and Endesha from behind. "This way gentlemen."

It was at that point, Amri and Endesha realized what their father had been preparing them for. At that precise moment, the two Sefu brothers knew their lives would never be the same, and their father had the foresight to see this before it had actually happened.

As the Sefu brothers walked up the series of stairs to the main levels of Harkstead Castle, they could not help but notice the many fine paintings of former kings of the Midland Kingdom the sun revealed as it shone into the hallways. Where there were no paintings, the walls were adorned with tapestries and fine artifacts that gave Harkstead Castle the same sense of extravagance as its king.

Moments later, the Sefu brothers arrived at their new quarters. It was a small room at the end of a long hallway, a great distance away from the maidens and caretakers, but close enough to the king's personal quarters that, if summoned, the brothers could be at his side within minutes. This newly created role would be easy for a member of the royal family to understand, but explaining it to the Moors proved to be difficult for Stuart and Singletary.

"Gentlemen this is your new home," Stuart said with pride.

"What about our father? We want to be with him," Endesha replied.

"You will no longer be with your father. He shall remain in the stables, but the king requests you remain here," said Singletary.

As Amri was looking around at the details of their room, he said, "You will not allow us to see our father, or we can see him freely?"

"You shall see him when you accompany the king or myself on a mission," Stuart replied. "You are to serve as His Majesty's personal guards. When the king leaves the castle, or if he summons you, you are to be at his side to protect him. Endesha, you have another task as well."

"What would that be?" Endesha asked angrily.

"You are to continue being a companion to Harold."

"What is a *com-pan-yun?*" Endesha asked.

"As before, Harold will be in your care, and you will protect him with your life along with providing for him as needed."

"What if we do not want to do the things you are telling us?" Amri asked.

"Guards!" Stuart yelled, and the eight armored guards promptly entered the Sefu men's room and lined the walls. Stuart turned to look at Amri and said, "If you refuse to follow the king's directions then you and your brother shall perish. After your father, of course."

"How do we know you have not killed him already?" Amri asked.

"I assure you, I have not done anything to him, but you are in no position to question me regarding your father," Stuart replied.

"You will need more soldiers in this room if you did harm our father… Your Highness," Endesha replied.

Both Sefu brothers looked at Stuart, then turned their collective gaze to the eight soldiers in their room. Audible clangs were heard as the armored soldiers shifted their weight uncomfortably. The tension in the room had risen, and the men knew the Sefu brothers were prepared to die if provoked. "I will leave you now. Endesha, you are to join Harold in his quarters in the morning," said Stuart.

"Very well, Your Highness," Endesha replied begrudgingly.

"Good. Enjoy your new surroundings." Stuart left with his armored guards and Singletary following behind.

"Once again, Father was right. This was going to happen to us whether we wanted it to or not," said Endesha.

"I hate this place," Amri said as he looked around the room. He noticed the bed, and the linen on it; he also noticed how much nicer it was compared to the stables.

Endesha noticed Amri looking around, and said, "These people think this space is supposed to shame us."

"They don't know how nice this is compared to where we have lived before," Amri said, feeling some happiness from this ordeal.

The two Sefu brothers shared a brief laugh together before their attention turned back to thoughts of their father. "We will see Father again, right Amri?" Endesha asked.

"When we leave the castle to be with the king, we may see him in the stables."

"True, Brother. We don't have many options do we?"

"We *have* options, they are just limited."

"Fight back, and be killed?"

"Exactly. The other option is to do what they are asking us to do, and survive like Father told us to."

"You are starting to sound like Father now, Amri."

"His words are heavy on my heart, and I cannot allow my actions to affect your life in a negative way. Like Father said, we are family, and we have to work together to survive this place.

I will tell you, Brother, if something happens to Father, and if I have to, I will rid this place of every pale-skinned person that stands against me," Amri said with a stern tone in his voice. "You must be prepared to fight without me at your side."

"Now you are really starting to sound like Father. Stop saying such things."

"Do you care for the little one, Harold?"

"I do enjoy spending time with him. Being with him reminds me of our days in the wild with Coffa."

"Regardless of how these men feel about us, teach the little one our ways. Maybe he will grow up to see us as men just like him."

"Maybe."

***

Back in the Harkstead Castle stables the sun was returning to the horizon, and Zuberi worried that his sons had not yet returned.

At first, he believed something was wrong and they were in danger, but something within his spirit told him they were fine. Giving into that feeling brought Zuberi much peace, and so, using his walking stick, he decided to go down to feed the horses. This was something Zuberi had enjoyed doing over the years. Being with the animals reminded him of the Sefu village with its vast wildlife, his beloved Faraha, and his dear brother, Coffa.

Sometimes, after everyone on the castle grounds had gone to sleep, or if the stables were empty, Zuberi would slip out back door, drag an old barrel against the stable wall, and sit down. Often, he looked to the sky hoping to see the same stars he had seen when he was a little boy. This evening was different; his heart was weary for the love of his life, and on this night, he found the same star he used to gaze upon with his beloved wife. It was the very same star Coffa had shown him when he was a young boy.

So much had changed since the first time he had laid eyes on that star, and there was a great absence in the heart of the old Sefu man. Zuberi's sons were grown men now, and there was nothing on English land that appealed to this old man from Africa.

Zuberi knew he had to begin preparing for his reunion with Faraha. As he looked to the sky he said softly, "I have to do something for our children before we can be together again my love."

The next day, Zuberi started collecting any spare metal he could find and hiding it under piles of old hay and manure. His hands were not as skilled at carving as they used to be, but his talent for working with his hands was enhanced after training with the metalsmith adjacent to the stables. For months Zuberi had been working on a sword for Amri—a sword that was unlike any sword ever made at Harkstead Castle.

Zuberi intended the sword to be a tangible record of the Sefu family's journey with intricate carvings and details that chronicled their passage from their village to this new land.

One evening, the metalsmith returned to finish an item he had been commissioned to create and caught Zuberi attempting to forge his sword in the remaining embers from the nearly extinguished fire.

Scared of what the consequences of his actions would be, Zuberi stood still, looking at his feet. The metalsmith looked at the unrefined edges of Zuberi's sword, and was impressed with the Sefu man's craftsmanship. He took the sword from Zuberi to have a closer look at the blade, and holding it with both of hands, noticed its raw balance, and large length. The size of the weapon gave the metalsmith no doubt that Zuberi was making a blade for Amri.

"This is a bloody nice blade, old man. Let us make it the best ever," the metalsmith said with a smile.

Relieved, Zuberi knew he had just gained an ally, and was pleased he would be able to give Amri the sword he believed he would need.

The Sefu boys had not been back to the stables in several days, but Zuberi had been busy working with the metalsmith, so their absence had been bearable for the elder Sefu man. The sword he was making for Amri would be more than a record of the Sefu family's journey; it would become the only creation the two equally talented craftsmen ever produced together. The metalsmith's hands would no longer obey his mind, so he would instruct the elder Sefu man through each step. For days Zuberi banged on the massive blade, and although Zuberi had great hand strength, his eyes were weak.

The metalsmith had great vision with weakening hands, so both men assisted each other. Together they worked for months on the most beautiful, but deadly, work of art the Midland Kingdom would ever see.

***

As the months went by, the Sefu brothers would occasionally get short glimpses of their father when they went out with Harold or Prince Stuart. The sight of his boys provided Zuberi with the energy he needed to complete the last major task of his life—a suit of armor for his massive warrior son. Zuberi worried the king would never give Amri the protection he would need in battle, so, to ensure Amri would be safe, the old Sefu man worked tirelessly to armor his "Black Lion." However, time was running out for Zuberi, and his sons, even from afar, could see their father weakening.

After many months away, the Sefu brothers were finally allowed a visit their father. "Endesha look at you; you are almost as big as Amri," said Zuberi.

"No, Father, I'm not as big as Amri. He is just fat," Endesha said, even though he had added considerable muscle mass over the last few months.

"It is good to see you, Father. Are you still tending to the animals?" Amri asked.

"Yes, my son. I try to get to them as much as I can, but my body does not move with my thoughts anymore," Zuberi replied with a smile. "I am so happy to see the two of you. I told you that your destinies were tied to this place and look at you both now. You are looking well, you have more food than you have ever had before, and most importantly, you are *still* together. I am so proud of you both." Zuberi beamed with great pride. "What do you both do inside the castle?"

"I am a caretaker for the little one, and Amri is constantly with the king, or Prince Stuart," Endesha replied.

"With the king?" Zuberi asked.

"Yes, Father. Endesha and I are the king's personal guards, and one of us is with him at all times within the castle," Amri replied.

"I am sure you two can handle those responsibilities."

"We can, Father, but we worry about you here in the stables by yourself," Amri replied.

"You shouldn't, my sons. I am well here. I feel your abilities will be tested by this Carpenter person. You should prepare for the challenge ahead of you. I believe your destinies are tied to this man."

The Sefu men enjoyed their time together not knowing this would be one of the last times they would enjoy with their father.

They shared many laughs that afternoon. Jokes were told about Amri's awkwardness around Nsia and Endesha's childhood fears from the old village, and although the visit was pleasant, both brothers could see something about their father was different.

His light seemed dimmer, and it was unsettling to the massive brown-skinned men. The brothers noticed the animals below were restless; the horses were noisier than they had ever been, and even though the Sefu men tried to console them, they refused to settle down. It seemed to the Sefu brothers like the animals knew Zuberi was fading, and both brothers believed the animals were correct.

## 31

A knock was heard on the outside of the Sefu brother's door. Amri opened the door to find Singletary on the other side. "We must leave at once. Come with me," said the captain.

"I will see you soon, Brother," Amri said to Endesha in their Sefu language.

As Singletary and Amri walked down the corridor, the captain said, "There have been reports of the Carpenter's soldiers seen north of here in Hainsbridge."

"All right," Amri replied as they hastened toward the stables to meet up with several Red Guard Cavalrymen preparing to ride out. As they mounted their horses, Amri could see his father looking down on him from the attic. Zuberi smiled and gave his son a slight wave as the group quickly departed for Hainsbridge.

After half a day's ride at full gallop, the group of men arrived in Hainsbridge. There were no signs of Carpenter's men, yet something was not right. The streets were absent of people, and there was stillness in the air. Many of the families from Hainesbridge had left after Carpenter's first attack years earlier which had left only a hundred or so people in the small village.

A crash was heard in the distance, and the men quickly produced their swords from their scabbards.

At that point, Singletary noticed Amri was unarmed, and as he shook his head in displeasure at his lack of arming the Sefu warrior, he reached into a long sack draped on the side of his horse and produced a simple longsword for the Moor.

The group of men from Harkstead Castle were only a baker's dozen including Amri. "Search the buildings," Singletary said, pointing one group of men in one direction and the rest in another. Amri followed behind Singletary as the men moved through the small village slowly. There were many abandoned buildings and small homes. Some had not been repaired since the first attack, and the ashes from the fires inside remained unmoved. Singletary said, "I do not like the way this looks. Fall back and regroup, then we shall go further into the village."

Moments later, sounds of men yelling was heard on the opposite side of Hainsbridge. Singletary's group figured it was their men and turned around to head back to them. As they rode toward the source of the noise they saw their fellow countrymen being ambushed by a group of Carpenter's cavalrymen.

As Amri rode his Flemish down the hill, he noticed two riders swinging wildly from their mounts at his fellow Harkstead soldiers, and targeted them as he joined the fight. The loud clanging of metal embracing metal could be heard at an ear-piercing level in the heart of the village.

A few Harkstead soldiers were cut down as they tried to fight off the group of Carpenter's men led by a man named George Davis. Davis was in the middle of the fight when he saw Amri ride past him toward the two riders. As Amri approached the riders, he saw a war hammer on the ground. He dismounted his Flemish, placed his sword tip in the ground, and picked up the war hammer.

The first rider was swinging his sword downward at the Harkstead fighters, and as Amri approached from behind, he used the hammer's sharp hook to grab the rider's armor and pull him to the ground. The rider's body hit the earth, and Amri felt the vibration from the impact in his feet. Before the rider could recover from the fall, Amri disarmed the man by knocking the sword out of his hand with the hammer's shaft, and promptly delivered a crushing punch to his face.

Suddenly, Amri became aware of someone standing over him, and with a confirming glance upward, he quickly rolled on the ground to his right. The enemy soldier missed hitting him with his downward slash, and instead, hit his own rider in the head. Amri jumped to his feet as his opponent was hindered by his weapon's blade being stuck in the rider's skull. Amri reset his footing just in time to block his opponent's strike with the shaft of his war hammer.

He knew his weapon did not have a reach that could counter the sword's strike, but could see the sword that Singletary gave him was only four paces behind him. Amri adeptly blocked three of his opponent's slashing blows before parrying to the left and retrieving the sword from the ground.

He flipped the sword to its upright position and took an offensive stance with both hands on his weapon. He felt alive, his heart was racing, and he wanted to take all of his aggression out on the unfortunate person in front of him. Amri's back was facing a building, and knew he could use his surroundings to his advantage, so he formulated a plan as the enemy soldier lunged at him with a piercing strike.

He easily blocked it and countered with a series of strikes and slashes delivered in an attempt to turn the enemy's back toward the building.

Within moments, his plan worked, and the enemy was fighting his way toward the building. Amri gave the enemy fighter a mighty kick to chest, knocking him against the old stonework.

In a panic, the Carpenter's soldier powerfully drew his sword over his head to deliver a downward strike, but instead, lodged it between the stonework of the wall at his back. His hand slipped from the hilt as he tried to dislodge it, and Amri wasted no time in delivering his sword into the man's mid-section. He forced the blade deep into the man's body until he could feel stone at the tip of his sword.

Amri quickly checked his surroundings to see if he was in any immediate danger. With confirmation of his safety, he reached up to dislodge the sword from between the stones, and withdrew his own from the soldier's body. Amri watched the man briefly; he was still trying to breathe as blood purged itself from his body. Seeing enough, Amri began to walk away, but quickly changed his mind. He turned back to the soldier, now slumped on the ground, and using both blades decapitated him with a devastating scissor slash.

Lord Davis could see his job in Hainsbridge was complete, but before ordering his men to retreat, he had a message to deliver to Singletary. "Tell your king that Carpenter is ready to take what belongs to him," he said as he was lifted by one of his remaining riders and carried out of the village square. The rest of Carpenter's men ran to mount their horses on the other side of the village.

"Shall we give chase, Captain?" asked one of the Harkstead fighters.

"No. We have to find the villagers first before we lose the sun. Gather the dead, and have all able men come with me," Singletary commanded. He saw Amri running in his direction with a second sword in hand, a man dead on the ground, and a man without a head behind him. Choosing to ignore what he saw Amri do in his first battle against the Carpenter's soldiers, Singletary told his men, "Go into every home and building, and find the villagers."

It was not long before Singletary heard a call for him from up the hill. "Captain! There are some people in here," said one of his men.

He rode up the hill, dismounted, and entered a room in one of the buildings filled with around twenty people. "Where is everyone else?" he asked the group.

"There are more people in a building a few paces up the hill. The rest of our village were in the fields for the harvest," said a female villager.

"How far are the fields from here?" Singletary asked.

"They are a short ride to the east," she replied.

"Make haste. The sun will be setting soon," he commanded.

The men rode quickly to the fields, and within minutes discovered the missing Hainsbridge farmers slaughtered by Lord Davis' men. The sight was too much for some of the Harkstead soldiers—the bodies of women, children, and men lying on the ground did not sicken Amri. He walked slowly through the fields looking upon the death beneath his feet.

Their baskets were still full of vegetables and fruits when Lord Davis and his men attacked them earlier in the day.

Singletary and his men rode back to Hainsbridge to inform the villagers of what happened.

After several hours, the dead had been collected, and the captain dispatched a rider back to Harkstead Castle. Fearing Lord Davis' return and the darkness of night already present, Singletary decided it would be best for his men to stay the night in Hainsbridge.

Later on that evening, in the old village inn, the men sat talking and drinking ale while Amri sat on the floor in a corner of the room. One by one, they left to find sleep until only Amri, Singletary and two other men remained.

After a while their attention turned to Amri who had been sitting on the floor, silent and motionless, for the majority of the evening.

"Hey you bloody Moor! Aren't you going to say anything?" said the man sitting farthest away, his crossed legs propped on the tabletop.

Amri did not break his stare from the floor. Again, the drunken man yelled at him, "You are one ugly big Moor. You are not one of us. We should kill you and send your burnt body to the Carpenter so he can see what his men will have waiting for them if they attack us again!"

The other man sitting in front of the fireplace, dragging his boot along the ax blade half-stuck in a piece of wood, started to laugh in agreement with his drunken mate.

Amri turned his head to look directly into the threatening man's eyes, and said, "Follow-through with your desires, and your deaths will come faster than your drink can find your stomachs."

Singletary could tell Amri was of sound mind, and the rest of them had clearly had too much ale in a very short amount of time.

"Gentlemen, let us not make a foolish mistake given our saddened emotional state and inebriation, for Amri would most assuredly kill us all," said the captain. With his back to Amri, he had not noticed the Sefu man was already on his feet with sword in hand, twirling the handle, and waiting for an excuse for bloodshed.

Amri was speaking the truth when he said the men's deaths would have come before their drinks found their stomachs. In fact, in his mind, their deaths were already orchestrated to perfection. Amri's first move would be to drive his right hand down on the end of the table causing Singletary to spill ale all over his face, and the man with the foul mouth would fall backward from the table. With his chair so close to the window behind him, he would stay tipped against it. Secondly, Amri would shove the man sitting in front of the fireplace backward to the ground, cracking his skull, then, taking a log from the fireplace, would throw it at Singletary, thus setting him on fire. The last of the four fluid movements, would see him take the ax from the piece of wood, and throw it at the foulmouthed man as his chair returned to its normal position after its tilt into the window seconds earlier. The ax would hit the man with such force, the only thing keeping him from falling backward through the window would be his knees catching the bottom of the table.

A foolish mistake it would have been indeed because as Amri stood, the men prepared to reach for their weapons.

Singletary could see the purpose in Amri's eyes, and sobering quickly, acted to avoid their deaths being moments away. "Do not reach for your weapons," said the captain.

"This Moor is nothing but a slave, and you allow him quarter with us?" said the man at the end of the table.

"He should be outside with the horses," said the man in front of the fireplace.

Amri had heard enough, and said, "I am a slave to no one. I killed your enemies with my blade today, and for that, I will never be *your* slave."

He gave Singletary the look so many victims of his rage had seen before. With that glance, Singletary knew he could not control Amri, but Hainsbridge was not the place to confront the armed Sefu warrior.

"Men, we shall calm our tongues and tend to our rest. We ride for Harkstead Castle at first light," Singletary said as he looked across the table to the men in front of him. Amri sat down on the floor again, this time facing his targets with his sword in hand. There would be no rest for him that night.

Singletary and his men left Hainsbridge early the next morning. No one spoke about what happened the night prior. Amri worried he may have put his family in jeopardy, but believed in his mind he was just in protecting himself against his drunken captive allies.

As the men rode briskly, Amri heard Singletary yell across to another rider, "Our rider did not return yesterday with word from the king." Something was wrong, and Amri could feel it in his spirit.

The weather was cold as the men continued their ride back to Harkstead Castle. As they crested a hill on the path, one of the riders commanded the group to stop immediately. "Ahead, My Lord," said the rider.

"I see," Singletary replied.

"Looks like the Carpenter's army, My Lord," said the rider.

"Get off your horses, men," he commanded quietly. After looking more closely, Singletary could see the dark-blue and yellow colors of Thomas Carpenter's uniforms. A massive group of men—between 500 to 1,000 men stood in the fields just outside of Harkstead Castle.

The small Red Guard contingency would not be able to return to the castle through the main gates. There was a secret way into Harkstead that few men knew, and Singletary was one of them. "Back on your horses, men, and follow me. We will head south and double back to the castle," he commanded quietly.

As the group of men mounted their horses and turned around, Amri gave the battalion of enemy fighters one last gaze. He wondered what type of fight they were going to bring to him.

Hours later, the men finally approached the forest just south of Harkstead Castle. It had been a very long time since there had been any need to enter the castle from this side, but Singletary took no time in locating the path. As they rode, he scanned the forest looking for the secret markings etched in the trees that would lead them to the entrance. "There's the first marker," he said, pointing ahead of them, and prompting his horse to a canter.

The men came before a massive wooden door with the royal seal of the Miles family set in iron across the middle. "How do we get inside?" asked one of the riders.

"You would think this is the door, but it is not," said Singletary as he dismounted his horse.

He walked several paces to the right of the door, and moved some overgrown vines out of the way to reveal another door. "Amri, we will need your help to open this."

Amri walked to the heavy wooden door and pulled mightily. The old wood creaked and bowed in protest of him forcing his power on the old lumber. Finally creaking open, a mighty gust of wind was felt as the air rushed from corridor beyond the old door open. "Inside men. We shall leave our horses here," Singletary commanded.

Once inside, the men followed the captain, amazed by the displays of weapons, silken tapestries, and fine artwork that lined the walls of the stale-aired secret corridor.

The men walked with purpose—which didn't afford Amri any opportunity to appreciate the weapons and armor on display—finally arriving at the base of an upward spiraling staircase.

They climbed until they came to another massive wooden door. The captain turned the handle, and yanked, but the door did not budge. Mumbling to himself, he turned the handle slightly more and yanked again. The door opened, and they exited into the dungeons. From there, they ascended out of the belly of the castle, and within moments, were discovered by a member of the king's council.

"Captain, how did you get here? Carpenter's army is right—"

"I know. We saw them on the way here from Hainsbridge and came to the castle from the southern entrance," Singletary said as he walked toward the king's throne room.

He then looked at Amri, and said, "Make your way to your quarters, gather your brother, and meet us in the throne room. Do you understand?" Amri nodded in agreement. Singletary turned and went to the left as Amri stood in the hallway alone.

For a brief moment, he thought he might be able to gather his brother and father and attempt to flee the castle while everyone was distracted by the sudden appearance of Carpenter's army. Shaking his head in disapproval, Amri continued on to his quarters where Endesha was patiently waiting for his older brother to return.

## 32

Endesha was glad to see his older brother walk back into their room. "You look like you were in a fight brother," he said to Amri.

"I was. We were ambushed by that Carpenter person they spoke of in the past. Get yourself together. They want us to be with the king, we are to go there now," said Amri.

When the Sefu brothers opened the door to leave, there were guards and maidens standing outside. The women had a large pile of bronze-colored armor with them, and rushed inside the Sefu men's room with the guards following behind. The women worked at a desperate pace getting the armor on the massive African men. One smaller woman had to stand on a stool to assist Amri with his armor. The maidens were about to place bascinets on the Sefu men's heads when a guard said, "The king says their faces are to be shown."

The Sefu men were led by the guards into the king's throne room where the energy was at a frantic pace. The room was alive with chatter regarding the news of the Carpenter's army just outside the castle borders.

"Take your place beside the king, and do not allow anyone to draw close to him. Not one step," said the palace guard. The Sefu men took their place next to the regally attired king as the room continued discussing what the Carpenter's intentions were and strategy on how to defeat his army.

Prince Stuart entered the room and spoke directly to his father, "Your Majesty, the Carpenter's battalion is confirmed to be over 750 men. It includes archers, cavalry, and many infantries."

"I suppose he believes he can take Harkstead Castle with this new army of his," King Phillip said with great concern in his voice.

Suddenly, a young squire burst into the throne room. "Carpenter himself is at the castle gates!" he said. The room grew quiet and all eyes turned to the king for his response.

"Let him in," Phillip said with contempt in his voice.

As Harkstead Castle's portcullis rose, Carpenter's confidence rose as well. Donned in a long, flowing, dark-blue cape and ornate black battle armor, Carpenter crossed the castles threshold with arrogant confidence. Flanked by two of his commanding officers, one being George Davis, the trio of men rode their horses through the village to the royal house within the castle walls. He was met by royal guards, and escorted into King Phillip Miles' throne room for the first time. The Harkstead guards escorting the Carpenter and his men were still on high alert when the king waved to them, signaling them to gather their peace.

Thomas Carpenter looked around the room and could not help himself when he said, "Such a fitting palace for a man of my royal stature." Leaving his officers behind, he continued walking down the main isle of the throne room toward King Phillip and his Sefu bodyguards. "It is unfortunate that I will have to take down all of this ghastly crimson and gold."

"You will do no such thing," said King Phillip angrily.

"Ah, the king has spoken."

"Why are you here Carpenter, and what are your intentions with your battalion camped outside of my walls?"

"Intention? My intention, *Your* Majesty, should be easy for you to deduce at this point. I am here to tell you I am willing to accept your surrender and for you to give me Harkstead Castle and the rest of the Midland Kingdom." Thomas noticed some dirt on his armored boot and wiped it off on the ornate rug he was standing on. "You have the audacity to march yourself into my castle and demand my kingdom while surrounded by all of my soldiers? Are you mad?"

"I prefer the term "ambitiously prudent," not mad. Besides, if I do not return to my men, they have standing orders to attack in due course, so that is why you are going to let me leave this place without injury." He paced confidently in front of the Midland King.

Carpenter then turned his attention to the large, armored, dark-skinned men flanking the king. "What type of monsters are these men?" he asked with great curiosity. "They look quite ferocious, and I believe this one is the one you spoke of, Lord Davis?" He looked over his shoulder at Davis for confirmation while pointing at Amri. "I will spare their lives, and they can be at my side. No need to join you in the dungeons below. There are dungeons here, are there not?"

"Enough! You know very well there are having been housed in them yourself, thief. I've had enough of your madness! If you are seeking a battle with me then you shall have one, Carpenter. Be aware, my army outnumbers yours, and you will never penetrate our castle walls," King Phillip said.

"Ah, penetrate, yes. That is something I do enjoy," Carpenter said as he gazed at the maidens in the room. "But I have no intention of challenging your dear castle walls. My plan is for your men to come to me."

"Why would I give away such a strategic advantage of fighting behind the walls of Harkstead Castle?" asked King Phillip.

"Well, uh, Your Majesty, you will have no other choice but to come to my location because I will be cutting off all routes in and out of Harkstead Castle, thus turning this palace into your own personal coffin." The room gasped as Carpenter chuckled to himself with prideful pleasure. "Nothing will come in or out of Harkstead Castle, and I will attack anything en route, as well. Thus, choking you from within. Isn't it genius?" Carpenter asked with a devilish smile on his face. "Oh, and I would like to inform you that I know about your little secret."

"What secret?"

Carpenter proceeded to take one step toward the king in an attempt to whisper the secret into his ear when he noticed a lock of black hair on the ground. It was his. He returned his gaze to the king to find his nose was millimeters from the two Sefu brother's blades—still in their downward facing position—until the Carpenter took an unsettled step backward. "Indeed, Lord Davis, the king's Moors are very skilled as you mentioned. Keep the hair. I will retrieve it from one of these maidens when I return to claim my crown."

"Your presence is no longer desired here. You must leave now," King Phillip commanded.

"I agree. It is time for me to leave you all. Besides, seeing you sit there with your face as crimson as your robe just drives me into a state of boredom.

Consider this your warning. If you do not send a rider with word of your surrender, I will attack anything inbound or outbound from this castle. Good evening." He gazed lustily at one of the nearby maidens as he began stepping backward toward the exit. Carpenter then changed his focus to the king before finally turning on his heel, his long flowing cape twirled with the same arrogant spirit and billowed behind as he stalked from the room.

After Carpenter's departure, the room became alive with chatter. Many people talked about what the impact of his plan would be on the people within Harkstead Castle. There were many things for King Phillip to consider.

Without the ability to leave the castle, Carpenter could attack the cities and villages within the Midland Kingdom without concern for a military response from the king's armies. With a blockade, the amount of food coming into the castle walls would stop, and eventually the Harksteadian people would suffer from starvation. Feeling overwhelmed, King Phillip commanded everyone but his son and his closest advisors to leave his throne room.

"How many soldiers do we have within the castle walls right now?" asked the king.

"We have just over 800, Your Majesty," replied one advisor.

"How is this possible? My army is well over 1,100 men!"

"Yes, Your Majesty, but some of those men are out in the kingdom protecting villages and collecting taxes," Singletary said.

"What are our options?"

"Father, we can try to wait Carpenter out, and see if he will become impatient with his blockade," Stuart replied.

"That will not happen, my son, he is committed to his plan. You can see that in his eyes."

"There will be much blood shed as word cannot be sent to tell the people to avoid routes to the castle," Singletary said.

"I will not allow him to slay the innocent, or walk into this room again and claim my kingdom," King Phillip said defiantly. The king sat quietly as his advisors muttered to each other, discussing strategy. Finally, the king made his decision and stood to address the room. "We shall not sit still as Carpenter attempts to choke us from the outside. We shall offer no him no surrender. In fact, we will give him the fight he is looking to have.

"We know he does not want to damage the castle, so he will remain standing his ground outside of the walls. This will be to our advantage; his army will be fully exposed to our archers from the upper battlements. Once his initial lines are reduced we will send out cavalry and infantry to defeat Carpenter or at least push him back," said King Phillip. "Stuart!"

"Yes, Father," Stuart replied.

"Assemble our forces and every able-bodied man within these walls to take arms. Activate the Red Guard, and have them take protective positions to defend the palace if our walls are breached."

"Yes, Your Majesty," Singletary and the advisors replied.

The king sat down with great concern on his face, and as the room emptied, only he and the Sefu men remained. He had temporarily forgotten they were standing next to him when he said to himself, "I will not let you have Harkstead, Thomas Carpenter. I'd rather die than allow that to happen."

## 33

The Midland Kingdom Army had assembled overnight, and were standing at attention in the bitterly cold morning air as they waited to receive their weapons. Squires scrambled to arm the Harkstead fighters with steel swords so frigid the cold bit through their gloved hands.

All of the horses had been removed from the stables, and Zuberi had spent the night preparing them and handing them off to the cavalrymen. When all of the horses had been matched to their accompanying rider, the Sefu elder slowly walked the lines of soldiers to get a closer look at their adorned armor and armaments. Although he did not understand what the men were saying, he knew a battle was upon them.

Prince Stuart arrived wearing his highly polished battle armor with crimson adornments. Fitzgerald Singletary was close by, and as usual, donning his own slightly less ornate set of armor. Prince Stuart climbed to the top of a platform to deliver, what he believed to be, a speech of a lifetime. "Men, we gather here today with one purpose—defeat the Carpenter's army and rid our kingdom of him for good!" Stuart paused as the men cheered. "I know his numbers make it seem like he cannot be beaten, but I am here to tell you he will be defeated on this day because we are ready to fight him to the end!

"Remember this, his army consists of a group of thieves, mercenaries, and vagabonds purchased and dressed to make you believe they are trained fighters."

"The Carpenter would like for you to believe we are outnumbered and at a disadvantage, but we are not. We have the training and we have the will to defeat anyone who dares challenge us. This is our land, our castle, and for centuries we have successfully defended them.

Today, we shall have the same result as the warriors who fought for this castle in the past. Victory!" Stuart yelled to his mighty group of cheering fighters.

Inside his chambers King Phillip was pacing the floor nervously when he heard a knock at the door. Without prompting from the king, the doors swung open, and Prince Stuart made his way into the room. "Father, the men are ready and await your command to start the battle." The king closed his eyes momentarily and took a deep breath. "I give the command to begin. May the Lord help our men today."

"Yes, Your Majesty," Stuart replied and turned to leave.

"Stuart!" the king yelled hastily to his son.

"Yes, Father?"

"Command without emotion, and lead without fear, my son." He kissed Stuart on his forehead softly.

"I will, Father." Stuart knelt before his father then rose and left the room.

Amri and Endesha were standing in the corner as the two men were talking. Neither of the Sefu brothers had an opportunity to sleep or talk to each other since the previous night.

"The two of you can leave me now," the king said to them. "I will call for you if you are needed."

As Amri and Endesha walked out of the king's chambers to return to their quarters, they could see the Carpenter's army through the window in the long hallway that led to their room.

"This is not going end well, Brother," Endesha said to Amri in their Sefu language.

"I don't care. It's not our fight," Amri replied. "We must eat and rest. That is all I care about right now."

"If they start the war today, what will we do?"

"Nothing. Our orders are to protect the king, and that is what we are going to do, at least for now."

"For now?" Endesha repeated, confused.

"If something happens to our father, I cannot promise I will not turn on these men. You have to be prepared to defend yourself without me," Amri replied. "I seek the same freedom the winds have, and I do not have it here in this place. We shall let these men kill each other, and in the end, we will walk out of this place, free to live and exist as we please."

"But what if they challenge us?"

"Then we shall kill them all."

Back in the stables, Zuberi decided it would be best for him to return to the attic prior to the battle starting. As he started to climb the stairs he had ascended and descended several times before, his breath escaped him. Every single stair proved to be a challenge for the Sefu man. Zuberi reached for the railing as his chest began to tighten with increasing intensity. Initially, the elder Sefu man became fearful, knowing he was losing his life.

However, as the moments went by, a calming sense of gratitude overcame the old man as he reminded himself his lost love was waiting for him in the afterlife. As his limbs became harder to move, Zuberi lay on the staircase where he took his last breath without injury.

The metalsmith discovered Zuberi's body after he returned from delivering the armaments to the Harkstead fighters. He was deeply saddened by the loss of his talented old friend.

As a last act of respect, the he carried Zuberi's body back to the attic and laid him gently on his bed. He then draped Zuberi with a fine, white sheet. The metalsmith said a quiet prayer to himself, then voiced out loud, "I will give him what you wanted him to have."

*

"Listen to them cheer inside their castle walls," said Carpenter smugly as he carved a small arrowhead out of wood with his dagger. "They actually believe they can will this battle, Lord Davis."

"They may be thinking this is a mercenary army like before," said Davis.

"But this is not a mere mercenary force. That is where they will make their second fatal mistake."

"What was the first, Your Majesty?"

"They did not kill me when they had the chance."

*

Stuart returned to the castle courtyard with news of the king's decision to commence the battle. "What of the men, Captain Singletary?" Stuart asked.

"All of the men are in their positions, and we await your orders, Your Highness," Singletary replied.

"Fine. Have the archers take their marks, and wait upon my orders to fire," Stuart commanded.

"Yes, My Lord."

The bitter cold made it difficult for the Red Guard archers to hold their arrows steady. As they scanned the near horizon, they could see their targets easily within range.

"Ready!" commanded Singletary.

With mighty precision, the arms of the Red Guard archers moved in concert with each other.

"Aim!"

Each archer focused on one individual target, their arrows nocked, muscles tense, and their breathing slowed—some not breathing at all to ensure a more accurate shot.

Stuart was on top of the battlements near the archers when Singletary commanded, "Fire!" Suddenly, a flood of Harkstead arrows rained upon Carpenter's men with deadly accuracy.

*

From his vantage point at the most distant portion of the large cavalry, Carpenter said, "Looks like I will become King of the Midlands today. Order the men to hold their positions and wait for them to exhaust their supply of arrows."

"Your Majesty, many men will perish if we do that," said one advisor.

"That is why we gave them shields, you fool. Ensure they are used!" Carpenter barked in reply.

"Yes, Your Majesty." The advisor scurried away.

The Red Guard archers pummeled Carpenter's Army relentlessly with a rainfall of arrows. Unfortunately, Carpenter was correct: the impact of the Harksteadian arrows was hardly effective against his soldiers' shields and the Red Guard's supply of arrows was dwindling quickly.

"Advance the infantry twenty paces forward," ordered Carpenter. "Maybe this will entice the turtle to leave its shell." Watching the opposition struggle, he and his leaders began to laugh.

*

"Carpenter's men are advancing, Your Highness!" Singletary yelled down to Stuart from the battlements.

"Tell the archers to hold their arrows," Stuart commanded.

"They have no arrows to hold!" he replied.

"Come down from your perch immediately!"

Once Singletary was back on the ground level, he met briefly with Stuart to discuss their next move. Several things were at play. Carpenter's men were advancing, and the aerial strike was not as effective in eliminating large numbers of the enemy army as Singletary and Stuart had hoped. The two Midland leaders knew they could not allow Carpenter's men to advance too close to the castle because if they did, the Red Guard would not be able to keep them from charging the castle gate.

This knowledge led Stuart to make a tough decision. "We have to send a group of fighters out while holding a strong position in front of the gate."

"What if they try to advance while our men are rushing to their positions?" Singletary asked.

"They will not risk advancing too many of their fighters at one time," Stuart assured him. "We have the advantage with our numbers to prevent them from attempting that. However, if we take too many losses, they will be able to advance on our castle with little resistance." Turning to his troops, Stuart commanded, "Raise the portcullis, and open the doors! Remember, men: try to go as deep into their ranks as you can. We must try to push them back as much as possible!"

Slowly, the thick iron portcullis was hoisted up and locked into position. The heavy wood-and-iron doors were opened from the inside as the Harkstead cavalrymen galloped out of the castle, followed by a chorus of yelling Midland fighters.

*

"Ah! Here they come, screaming like savages," Carpenter said.

Hundreds of Harkstead fighters rushed into the hardened steel blades and shields of Carpenter's men. The fighting began at a frenzied pace. Men swung their swords wildly at anyone they did not recognize as their own. Harkstead cavalrymen pummeled their opponents with weighted and spiked maces.

Many of the first men to make it to Carpenter's front line were impaled by the pikes that were raised just as they approached. The long and pointed poles were quite effective in slowing down the advance of Stuart's soldiers.

*

After several hours of fighting, the Midland contingent had to reconvene at the entrance to Harkstead Castle.

"Your Highness, we have taken many casualties," one fighter reported.

"Shall we send another wave, Your Highness?" asked Singletary.

"Yes," Stuart conceded, "but send the men with poleaxes and sparths to assist with removing those pikes. They must use their blades to fight and cut them down, so our men can advance without being impaled."

Once the men were given the proper weaponry, they were sent back onto the battlefield, but getting past the pikes was difficult. To cut the pikes down, the Midland fighters had to remove the impaled bodies of their countrymen, which was time-consuming and left them exposed to the barrage of arrows Carpenter's men fired toward them.

*

"More arrows! More bloody arrows!" Carpenter commanded. "I will have my victory today!"

"The Midlanders are trying to cut their way through the pikes," said Davis. "They are not prepared for this battle, nor are they prepared for my battle plan."

"You mean my ideas for your plan. My brilliance is tantalizing. I cannot wait for this to be over, so I can look Phillip in his old, red face and order his head to be cut off!" said Carpenter gleefully. "Do you think he will fight with his men?"

"No, Your Majesty, he will not fight with his men, but he will not run away, either. That is the type of man he is."

"Well, you should know. You were once a member of his Red Guard."

"We must continue pressuring them to send more men out to the battle."

"Advance the infantry again!" Carpenter ordered.

*

The bitter cold of the day gave way to the freezing night, and the fighting did not slow as the sun's rays retreated into the horizon. The bodies of many fallen Midland soldiers lined the grounds leading toward Harkstead Castle. Wave after wave of Midland soldiers were sent out, and few returned. The earth began to soften with the moisture of the bloodshed on the battlefield.

"We are not making any progress fighting this way, Your Highness," Singletary said. "We are amassing too many casualties fighting a large force without our own formation and ranks."

"How many men do you believe we have lost?" Stuart asked.

"I have been told the number is around four hundred, Your Highness, but there is no way to know with certainty," Singletary replied.

"Sound the horn to signal our men to fall back. We will regroup and join together in formation."

"What of the Red Guard, Your Highness?"

"The Red is our last defense and best used in melee with hand weapons."

"We do not have enough soldiers to fill the ranks."

"Give the archers swords, and that will help fill in the ranks"

Singletary offered to lead the group out, and after a long pause, Stuart shook his friend's hand, and said, "Thank you for fighting with me. I shall see you on the battlefield or in the afterlife, good friend."

Fitzgerald led the newly formed Harkstead contingent—armored cavalrymen with spears and foot soldiers carrying double-edged axes and spiked flails—out toward the blood-soaked battlefield.

*

The resulting casualties of Carpenter's army were surprising, and Carpenter was not pleased with the Midlanders' change in strategy.

"Why did you allow them to form their ranks?" Carpenter bellowed. He was red in the face, and spittle flew from his mouth with every word. "They are going to push us back from our position!"

"They will not, Your Majesty. They do not have enough men." Davis said. "They have one more push in them before their ranks will be depleted."

"What do you suggest?"

"Order the archers to fall back, and send more of our heavily armed soldiers ahead of the armored ranks."

"Make the order."

*

Under the cover of night, most of the horrific fighting occurred. Heavy broadswords and axes produced more blood and limbs lost than the fighting during the daylight hours.

The sounds of men fighting could be heard far beyond the castle walls. The Sefu brothers would have heard it in their room, but they were asleep after the long day in service of the king.

A knock was heard at the Sefu brothers' door, but it went unanswered. Another series of knocks sounded quickly. Amri, stirred from his slumber, opened the door and was told by a king's maiden that he was needed in the king's chambers.

Inside the chambers, King Phillip was standing at his window, looking out into the darkness; listening to the constant clanging of metal and screams of pain from the men below. He saw Amri from the corner of his eye and said, "Go down to the castle gate and get word from my son on the status of my armies."

"Very well," Amri replied. Ordinarily, the king would never allow anyone to talk to him in such a manner, but Phillip's mind was tending to more pressing matters, like how to keep his only biological son safe from Carpenter. He knew if Harold was killed, there would be no true heir to the throne, and the Midlands would be lost.

As Amri made his way down to the castle gate, he could see the men who were injured earlier in the day.

The scene at the gate was frantic. Amri saw Stuart plotting strategy with his advisors, but he did not bother approaching him. Instead, he decided to continue walking. This was the freedom he spoke of earlier with his brother.

Amri walked under the portcullis and beyond the castle walls. He could see the men fighting in the distance, he could smell the blood in the air, and could hear the moaning of the injured men laying on the ground in front of him. Amri thought about how easy it would be for him to slip away from the castle, and the fighting, and take the opportunity to explore this new land on his own. But he could not. Thoughts of his father and brother flooded his mind. Amri knew he had to do as he was told to protect his family. Reluctantly, he turned around and ran back toward Harkstead Castle.

He found Stuart Miles and said, "Your father sent me to get a status on the battle."

"Status? Tell him we are taking great losses, and he needs to be prepared to leave the castle if we cannot hold Carpenter's men off," Stuart said.

"I will tell him what you said," he replied.

Amri was walking toward the entrance to the palace when a voice called for him, "Amri! Over here!" It was the metalsmith. "I am sorry but you must come with me. Your father…" he said.

Amri's heart began to beat violently. "What happened? Is he alright? Please take me to him!" he said.

The metalsmith escorted Amri through the courtyard to the stables, and as they approached he ran past the metalsmith.

He went into the stables, ran along the hallway that separated the horse stalls, and up the stairs to the attic. As Amri's feet touched the top of the stairs he saw the sheet covering his father's body, and in despair he fell to his hands and knees.

He wept with such sorrow his massive body could not gather the strength needed to stand and walk, so as he sobbed, he crawled to his bedside.

The metalsmith heard Amri's wails of sadness as he lifted the sheet to reveal his father's lifeless body. Distraught, he fell onto his back; his long black dreadlocks could not absorb the tears falling from the corners of his eyes and covering his ears. The pain of losing his father was too much for Amri.

Thoughts of all he had lost rushed through his mind: Coffa, Nsia, his mother, and now his father were all gone. In back of his mind he hoped it was all a bad dream and when he woke, his father would be sitting up working on some project with Endesha by his side. Amri cried himself to sleep that night, and, unfortunately, when the morning came, his father was just as he was hours before. The sun was suppressed by the clouds, and Amri could only think of his beloved father as he sat on the floor next to his bed.

All the tears Amri had were shed, and the emotions had produced an unwelcome headache. He felt a vast emptiness in his heart, and for a brief moment, he felt jealous of the fact that he had to live in this new world where men were fighting each other to the death just outside the castle walls. Suddenly, Amri remembered that there was a war occurring outside.

He then also remembered Endesha was still back in their room and did not know about their father's passing. He gathered himself and proceeded to leave the attic.

He did not want the image of his father lying motionless to be in his mind, so he refused to look behind him before he went down the stairs.

As Amri made his way back to the palace entrance he saw a large group of people gathered around a fallen soldier.

He proceeded in the direction to get a closer look, and as he drew closer, he saw it was Prince Stuart.

During the overnight hours both Fitzgerald Singletary and Prince Stuart joined the battle hoping one of them would be successful in pushing Carpenter's men back from their position. The morale of the remaining men was broken. Many of the Harkstead fighters were too injured to go back into battle. Singletary's reduced cavalry proved to be more efficient when fighting in formal military formation, but the losses were too much.

Amri could hear men still fighting in the distance, but he did not care. He needed to inform his brother about their father's passing. He quietly retreated to the shadows of the palace walls, and slipped into a side entrance he had learned about from Harold. Once inside, he quickly ascended the stairs and found a guard waiting outside his and Endesha's bedroom. "The King will have a word with you," said the guard.

"I have no words for him," Amri replied.

"My orders are to escort you to him immediately."

"Then you shall be a failure in following those orders. I must talk to my brother now."

The guard drew his sword from its scabbard and said, "I am warning you, you will go to the king as ordered!"

Within seconds, Amri had hold of the soldier's sword-hand wrist and drove his right elbow into the guard's throat causing him to drop his sword.

As the guard was gasping for breath with both hands on his neck, Amri picked up the sword and drove it so hard into his head, the guard's body remained upright after his legs went limp. Suddenly, Endesha opened the door, "Amri what are you doing?"

"Father…" Amri said.

"What about Father? Oh no! No!" screamed Endesha.

The Sefu brothers shared a brief embrace before they were interrupted by King Phillip. His face was saddened, and his body did not swell with the confidence it once had. "I was told about your father's passing, and I want you both to know it was not by my word that he died. I also lost someone close to me last night, my son, Stuart. I have no right to ask anything of the two of you, but I know that you, Endesha, are someone that Harold feels safe with, and I am not sure we will be able to hold off our enemy from taking our castle, and the kingdom with it. Please, Endesha, take Harold away from here. He is the true heir to the Midland Kingdom and must be kept safe," King Phillip said. "You do not have to do it for me, but would you do it for the child?"

"I will," Endesha replied.

The broken king looked to Amri, and was not given the same empathy as his brother offered. "I owe you no such duty. The only reason you are alive is because I believe your death is coming by your enemy's hand," Amri said.

"I have nothing to offer you, Amri. I deserve whatever happens to me, but know this—you are the most powerful warrior this land has ever seen. Even though my people do not deserve your protection, your brother needs your help so he can get Harold out of this castle. I deserve your vengeance for the way you and your family have been treated, but I offer you the chance to be what you are obviously destined to be—a warrior," said King Phillip as he reached into his robe, pulled out a small bag of gold, and offered it to the Sefu brothers.

Amri took the small, but heavy bag from the king and tied it to his belt.

"Endesha, Harold has relatives to the north that he can take you to once you leave the castle from the entrance below the dungeons. You came in that way before, correct?" Phillip asked.

"Yes, I've been there before," he replied.

"Please hurry."

"I will."

The two Sefu brothers looked at each other and shared a tight embrace. "Know who you are little brother," Amri said.

"I do. Be careful, Amri," Endesha replied. Amri did not respond, instead he hugged his brother one last time before Endesha hurried away to Harold's chambers.

## 34

Amri stood in the hallway and watched as Endesha hastened away to retrieve young Prince Harold. He then looked down at his feet and noticed the pool of blood from the dead guard was slowly traveling into their quarters. King Phillip, unsure of what the hulking Moor was thinking or feeling, knew Amri could easily kill him, said, "I have been informed by the metalsmith that your father left something for you. If you want to know what it is, he will show you where to find it.

"You should not worry about Harold," Amri said. "My brother is a greater warrior than me. That is what I love about him." He gave the king a menacing stare.

Amri made his way to the metalsmith's shop, and walked around the back to the small room where he was sleeping. The door was too narrow for Amri to walk through, so he knocked gently on the already opened door. "Oh, there you are. Did you have words with the king?" asked the metalsmith.

"Yes. He said you have something for me from my father."

"Oh yes, let me show you." He rose from his bed, and headed to the corner of his workshop. The small man reached into a large wooden chest and produced a long item wrapped in fabric. "This meant everything to your father. He risked his life making this for you. I caught him sneaking in to use my tools after I'd left for the day. We finished it together just days ago."

Amri unwrapped the fabric, and inside was the most beautiful sword he had ever seen. It was perfect in size and length, but it was something else that caught his eye; etched into the sword's blade were words in the Sefu language,

*"The person that holds this sword is protected from evil by the creator of the land that evil travels on."*

Amri also noticed his family's journey was pictured with meticulous detail. On the other side of the blade, Zuberi etched the story of how Amri defeated the lion. Toward the bottom of the cross-guard he saw his father had named the sword *"The Lion's Heart."*

As he continued to examine the blade, Amri discovered even more significance. He found his family's history forged in hard steel, and the edges of the sword's cross-guard were made to look like up-turned lion's fangs. The grip of the sword was inlaid with what Amri thought were teeth, and as he ran a hand along them, the metalsmith said, "Those belonged to you and your brother. Your father had kept them since you were young. Including them on your sword was my gift to your father," said the metalsmith. "From one father to another father. That was my favorite part."

"What is your name, sir?"

"My name is Joseph Cannon."

"Thank you for this. It means everything to me."

"You are very welcome, young man, but there is one more thing you have not noticed."

"What is that?"

"Look at the pommel of the sword, the bottom part." Amri raised the sword in front of him and saw a piece of fabric hanging from the bottom with a bead at the end. "That is your mother's hair and some of the fabric from her dress," Joseph said.

Astonished, Amri quickly smelled the fabric. Instantly, he knew it was his mother's hair and dress. He began to cry softly to himself for a brief moment.

"Rise to your feet young man," Joseph said. "Every sword must be balanced and true. How does it feel in your hand?"

Amri spun the sword in his hand and took a few practice slashes. "It feels like it is a part of me," he replied.

"Good. I took the liberty of creating a scabbard that I believe your father would approve of." Joseph presented it to Amri. It had the face of a lion carved onto both sides. "Keep your sword inside this scabbard. It is made strong and can be used in a fight along with your sword, if needed."

"Thank you so much for all that you have done for my father and me," Amri said with great appreciation.

"My people believe all is lost out there on the battlefield, but I believe you can help our people, and save many lives. But you cannot fight without a suit of armor, and after watching you practice all of these years, I had to create a different type of suit for you."

"You made me a suit of armor?"

"Yes. It is my finest work, and the last suit of armor I will ever make. My hands cannot stand the abuse anymore." Joseph reached down, moved aside a floorboard to reveal a hidden compartment, and asked Amri to lift a large crate from within. "Open it," said Joseph. Amri did so, and inside, he found a bascinet. "Put it on." Amri carefully lowered it down over his head. "To your left is the water pot I use to cool my steel, look at yourself in the reflection."

Amri was startled to see the dark, bronzed face of a lion with long fangs covering each of his cheeks in the reflection. "Your father spoke of people calling you the Black Lion where you came from. I thought it was appropriate for you to look as such. With all of that hair hanging out of the bascinet, you look like a lion too. Let me help you with the rest of the suit."

Piece by piece, Joseph helped Amri don the rest of the armor, and although the metalsmith's water pot was not big enough for the Sefu man to see his armored reflection, Amri knew it was stunning. "What do you think?" Joseph asked.

"I love it," Amri replied.

"I know you rely on your speed, so that is why your armament is minimal in the joints. I concentrated the majority of the metal on your chest and back. Your legs are also covered, but I believe you will not allow anyone to get that close to you. The chainmail is a special weave I made for you. It is light but strong and should give you the freedom of movement you need," Joseph said while adjusting the fit to Amri's massive body. "Put your bascinet back on." Amri did as instructed. "Now, nod your chin down quickly." His faceplate fell down over his face with a clank. "You are now ready to fight. Oh, but I forgot one last thing. You cannot fight without the colors of the Midlands." Joseph tied the crimson colors of the Red Guard around Amri's waist with the sword and scabbard attached to it. "Your father spoke of your greatness, and I have done all I can to help you achieve your destiny. You are the last hope for my people. Please help us defeat our enemy." Joseph ran his fingers along the lion's head he had stamped into Amri's chest plate. "Be the Black Lion for us," Joseph said.

Amri gently hugged Joseph Cannon and told him, "I will do what I enjoy doing the most."

"And what would that be, Amri?"

"Inflicting pain."

Amri left Joseph's shop and walked toward the staging area. The men were still strategizing when they saw Amri walking toward the castle gates. To them, he looked like an armored demon from their worst nightmares.

Sam had been wounded earlier in the battle, yet his hatred for Amri did not stop him from hobbling over to him. "How dare you wear the colors of the Red Guard!" he spat. Before he could say another word, Amri punched Sam so hard his head slammed back to rest between his shoulder blades, and there it remained.

"I told you I would kill you," Amri said to himself, then continued to walk out beyond the castle walls.

The battlefield was cluttered with the corpses of fallen warriors. Amri continued his slow walk from the castle, and with every step he thought about the events that had brought him to this point. He looked to the sword hanging from his hip and felt sadness for his father. It was then Amri realized he was no longer in the castle, and his spirit came alive. He was no longer in a cell, and was not running away from his enemies—he was walking toward them.

This time, no one was telling him what he should not do or how he had to suppress his will to fight. In this place, this battlefield, Amri realized he already had his freedom.

He had gained it as soon as he put Joseph Cannon's armor on, and no human on earth could take that away from him.

As Amri continued his slow walk toward the battle in front of him, he could see men fighting against each other. One of Carpenter's cavalrymen spotted Amri in his dark, bronzed armor and commanded his horse to a fast gallop in hope of intercepting him as he approached the battlefront.

Amri could see the rider coming in his direction, immediately assessed his surroundings, and was quick to notice a very large iron mallet on the ground. The rider approached, lowering his long spear as he intended to slaughter Amri in stride.

As Amri Sefu watched the horseman hurtle toward him, he broke the long stride he had maintained since leaving Harkstead Castle, spun counter clockwise, and just as the rider's spear missed his right shoulder, he clubbed the horse squarely in the chest with the iron mallet. The wooden handle shattered into pieces, and fell away from Amri's hand.

The beast cried out in pain as the force of the blow caused it to flip over itself in the air, crushing the rider beneath it. The horse laid on the ground writhing in pain before finally taking its last breath. The animal's cry and the ensuing clatter had been heard over the din of the battle, and Carpenter's soldiers had turned their attention to the giant armored man.

Having lost his bascinet in the scuffle, Amri bent to pick it up, and placed it back over his dreadlocked mane. A quick nod brought the Black

Lion's faceplate down, and Amri turned to face the incoming assault. "*More*," he said to himself.

The air was calm on the battlefield, but through his bascinet, Amri thought he heard bugs flying around him. Suddenly, he heard something whiz past his ear, then another.

He turned to his right to find group of young, and obviously frightened, archers shooting arrows at him. As Amri started to turn toward their direction, he immediately dropped onto his back to avoid an arrow flying toward his face.

Infuriated, he gathered himself off the ground quickly and moved as fast as he could toward the group of young archers, and in fear and haste, the inexperienced archers could not nock their arrows quick enough before the armored warrior dove into the group. Grabbing one of the arrows, he shoved it into the nearest archer's eye, then used the archer's body to shield himself as he picked up a bow and loosed arrows at the archers who had scattered when he ran at them.

From a distance, Thomas Carpenter saw the large man in dark armor throwing archers about, and said, "What the bloody hell is that?"

"I don't know, Your Majesty, but he is very big," Davis replied.

Amri noticed a pair of throwing axes holstered to the chest of a dead soldier.

Grabbing one, he threw it laterally across his chest, cleaving an archer just below the throat. As soon as he had let the ax fly, a Carpenter soldier grabbed Amri by the shoulder. He began to turn toward his attacker, but from the corner of his eye, Amri saw an archer rip the ax from his cleaved enemy, and launch it back at him. He parried to his right and spun the man gripping his shoulder around in time for the ax to strike his enemy in the chest.

Ripping the ax from the soldier's chest, Amri threw it with precision back at the young archer, killing him instantly.

He was feeling more alive than he had ever felt before. His eyes were wide and his heart was calm. *It is a beautiful day to die*, Amri thought. As he turned to move on to his next skirmish, a blow to his chest slid his feet backward through into the blood-soaked ground. A very large enemy soldier, wielding a two-handed broadsword, then followed with a kick to the midsection. Armi reached for Lion's Heart, and as he held it in his hands, time stood still for a moment. Amri noticed the ground swell under the weight of his enemy's feet, his sword was too large and heavy to swing quickly, and he was out of breath from the kick he had just dealt. The enemy soldier raised his mighty two-handed broadsword into the air, preparing to bring it downward for slashing blow when Amri drove the Lion's Heart into the man's foot.

The man screamed in pain, but it did not last long; Amri pulled out the two stilettos strapped to his back and drove them up under the man's bascinet. The incredible force behind Amri's knives raised the man's body off the ground—with the exception of the foot still pinned to the earth by the Lion's Heart. The insatiable Sefu warrior looked deep into his enemy's eyes as he drove the knives still deeper into his flesh.

The Carpenter's soldiers did not know what to make of the massive, dark, armored man who donned the colors of the Midland Kingdom's elite fighting force.

Amri threw the body of the enemy soldier down and retrieved Lion's Heart from the ground. A horn sounded in the distance; he turned to see the remaining Red Guards' hurtling toward him.

They had been inspired by Amri's fighting, and raced to the frontline on horseback and foot.

A massive sword fight began with Amri taking the lead. The Lion's Heart was indeed the best sword Joseph Cannon and Zuberi Sefu ever made; its balance and weighting was perfect in his hand, and he killed dozens of the Carpenter's soldiers in a blind rage. To the enemy soldiers, Amri moved too fast for a man of his size, and to Amri, Carpenter's men moved as if they were made of stone and mortar. He killed as swiftly as the wind blew, and true to his title of *"Black Lion,"* his roar was carried across the battlefield by the same winds that had been following him throughout his life.

\*\*\*

"I can't believe this is happening! You said your plan would work!" Carpenter bellowed. Before Davis could respond he was knocked off of his horse by a broad ax to the chest. Carpenter looked down at Davis, then in the direction the ax had come from to see Amri in the distance, empty handed.

Amri drew Lion's Heart from its sheath, and Carpenter yelled, "Enough of this foolishness! Order the cavalry to rush the castle, and kill that man!"

Word of the order spread quickly within Carpenter's ranks, and every soldier that was not fighting Amri or the Red Guard charged the Harkstead Castle gate.

Deep inside the palace, Endesha and Harold were preparing to leave the castle by means of the secret path below the dungeons. "Why are we leaving, Endesha?" Harold asked.

"So you can be safe, little one," Endesha replied.

"They are rushing the courtyard!" said a handmaiden near a window.

"We must go now!" Endesha said as he placed Harold on his back like Coffa used to do with him. "Hold on tight!"

He took a torch from the wall and ran as fast as he could down the hall and several flights of stairs, all while trying to remember the locations of the doors that led to the dark, stale, secret exit. "Almost there!" Endesha said.

Before long, they found the hall that would lead them to the door of their escape route, and away from Carpenter's men. Endesha lowered Harold back to the ground, and said, "Hold my hand." As the two approached the large door, Endesha suddenly stopped walking when he heard men outside it. He could not tell who it was, but knew very few people were privy to the location of the door.

Unfortunately for Harold and Endesha, Davis, as a former member of the Red Guard, knew of it and had given the location to the Carpenter's men. The men on the other side had a ram and started driving it into the door. Endesha knew he did not have much time before the old wood would give way, and he and his ward would be killed. He had to think fast. He picked up Harold and placed him around the corner at the beginning of the hallway. "I need you to stay here: don't move, cover your eyes, and begin counting. By the time you reach one hundred, I will be back for you," Endesha said.

"Okay," Harold replied.

Harold started to count, "One, two, three…" As he did, Endesha scanned the area looking for things he could use to fight with. He saw some long tapestries, pulled them down, tore pieces off, and wrapped them around his forearms.

Moving farther down the hallway he found some old swords and shields hanging on the wall, and grabbing them down, placed them strategically in various places along the hallway. Lastly, he came across a small, unlocked door. Upon opening it, he found some bottles of wine. It looked as if it was from the king's special collection. Endesha uncorked a bottle, drank some, and thought to himself, *Know who you are.*

He placed the torch near the end of the hallway and poured the rest of the wine onto the tapestries he had pulled from the walls. He heard a loud crack as the wood started to give way, and Endesha knew he was in for the fight of his life. Using the items he had collected, he made a small torch, and as the men burst through the door, he threw it into the tapestries lining the entrance and set them on fire.

As Harold continued to count, "22, 23, 24, 25…"

Time seemed to stand still for a moment as Endesha did not understand why the Carpenter's men seemed to be moving so slow. To the Carpenter's men Endesha was the fastest man they have ever battled when he engaged them with a sword in each hand. Some of the men were on fire as they rushed into the hallway, others pushed their way into the hall and were met by Endesha—moving in swift precision with his swords. It was like nothing Endesha had ever experienced before, fighting was like dancing to him.

The Carpenter's men saw death before they could see who was wielding the blade that cut them down.

As Endesha gave ground, he retreated to the shield had driven into the ground earlier and used it to block the blows from the enemy fighters.

He had prevented further retreat as he knew in the back of his mind that Harold was in the distance unprotected.

After killing more men, Endesha fought his way backwards toward his large torch. One of the Carpenter's men attempted a strike that Endesha had to dive to the ground to avoid. With two men left, he knelt on one knee, grabbed the torch, and rose to his feet. Inhaling deeply, he blew the wine he had kept in his mouth the entire time into the flames, setting the men's shirts on fire. Endesha quickly killed the two men and collapsed in exhaustion.

"95, 96, 97, 98, 99, and 100," Harold finished counting just as Endesha appeared from around the corner. Bloodied by several cuts and bruises, but very much alive, Endesha picked Harold up and held him close to his body, so he would not see the dead soldiers on the ground.

After they made it outside, Endesha took a few well-earned breaths, and asked Harold, "How do we get to your father's place in the north?"

\*\*\*

The horn signaled the remaining Red Guard soldiers to retreat back to Harkstead Castle. Amri was preparing to run back toward the castle when he saw one of Carpenter's riders approaching from behind. He reached up and pulled the enemy soldier's scabbard as the horse rode past, causing the rider to crash into the blood-soaked earth. He mounted the steed, rushed back to the Harkstead gate, and quickly dismounted to continue engaging the enemy.

"Lower the gate!" Amri bellowed.

The Red Guard and diminished Midland Cavalry tried to prevent the Carpenter's soldiers from entering Harkstead before all of the Midland fighters were inside the battlement.

All except for Amri who was still fighting when he heard the portcullis' massive locks release.

Just as the gate began to crash down to the ground, he stopped fighting, and walked into the courtyard as the portcullis narrowly missed him from above.

Amri continued to walk as he gathered his breath and noticed the Midland fighters defending Harkstead tirelessly. He gripped the Lion's Heart in his hand and dispatched the few fighters that crossed his path. He made his way back to Joseph's workshop. "Come with me, we do not have much time."

"The Carpenter's soldiers have breached the battlement?"

"Yes, and if we lose the courtyard you will perish, we must go now."

"Where are we going to go?"

"I need to find someone. But first, I need to take my father from this place and give him a proper Sefu burial."

"I will hold your bascinet."

"Thank you."

Amri moved as quickly as his armored body could to retrieve his late father. He found fresh cloth to wrap his father's body, and placed him over his shoulder. Amri would have been gentler with his father's body if he had more time, but he and Joseph had to leave before the enemy made their way into the royal house.

He remembered the secret entrance, and as he and Joseph made their way through the royal house, they found King Phillip standing by a window overlooking the courtyard. "Did my brother make it out safely?" Amri asked.

"I'm not sure, but I forgot to give him this royal decree naming Harold as the heir to the throne of the Midland Kingdom. Please take this with you."

Amri took the decree along with the bottle of wine he saw sitting on the floor next to the doomed king. After drinking his fill of royal wine, the duo began heading down the hallway that led to their escape when King Phillip shouted after them, "Are you two heading to the north to join Endesha and Harold?" Amri turned back to look at the king, then looked to Joseph before returning his gaze upon King Phillip, and replied, "No. We are heading south to Brixham to find a man named Burton. He is going to help me keep a promise."